the
vanishing
game

the
vanishing
game

KATE KAE MYERS

BLOOMSBURY

NEW YORK BERLIN LONDON SYDNEY

First published in the United States of America in February 2012
by Bloomsbury Books for Young Readers
www.bloomsburyteens.com

For information about permission to reproduce selections from this book, write to
Permissions, Bloomsbury BFYR, 175 Fifth Avenue, New York, New York 10010

Library of Congress Cataloging-in-Publication Data
Myers, Kate Kae.
The vanishing game / by Kate Kae Myers. — 1st U.S. ed.
            p.   cm.
Summary: Seventeen-year-old Jocelyn follows clues apparently from her
dead twin, Jack, in and around Seale House, the terrifying foster home where
they once lived, and with help from childhood friend Noah she begins to uncover the
truth about Jack's death and the company that employed him and Noah.
ISBN 978-1-59990-694-2 (hardcover)
[1. Supernatural—Fiction.   2. Brothers and sisters—Fiction.
3. Twins—Fiction.   4. Foster home care—Fiction.   5. Death—Fiction.
6. Mental illness—Fiction.]   I. Title.
PZ7.M9872Van 2012   [Fic]—dc23   2011017508

Book design by Regina Roff
Typeset by Westchester Book Composition
Printed in the U.S.A. by Quad/Graphics, Fairfield, Pennsylvania
2 4 6 8 10 9 7 5 3

All papers used by Bloomsbury Publishing, Inc., are natural, recyclable products
made from wood grown in well-managed forests. The manufacturing processes
conform to the environmental regulations of the country of origin.

To my family

the
vanishing
game

how it starts

Life is a series of shallow breaths. And in any breath, everything can change.

Breathe in.

Eating the last of the cereal with my brother, Jack. Running away from home.

Breathe out.

Joking around while we washed dishes. Firing a gun.

Breathe in.

Taking boring notes in history. Getting pulled out of class by the school counselor. Hearing the news about my brother.

Breathe out.

All in a shallow breath.

✦ ✦ ✦

The high school parking lot of Troy Tech filled with kids hurrying to their cars. They were eager to beat each other onto the street but desperate to get ahead of the buses. Since it was the Friday before spring break, the general feeling was of being paroled from prison. Lucky for me I'd gotten out of the counselor's office a couple of minutes early, which meant there were only three cars ahead of my beat-up little Civic. I inched forward, wanting my freedom like everyone else. Maybe wanting it more.

My cell phone hummed and I checked the text. It was from Brooke, wanting to know if I was going on the camping trip. Six of us roasting hot dogs and marshmallows. Telling ghost stories. Trying to make each other laugh. Could I ever laugh again? I didn't think so.

If Jack were still alive, we'd both be going. But three weeks ago my twin brother was in a fatal car accident. Since then, everywhere I went the pain of losing him went with me. It wore me like a backpack, slapping a rhythm of heartache against my soul with each step.

I didn't really want to go camping, but the thought of hanging around all week with my foster family depressed me. Even worse, I knew the memories of Jack's presence in the house would cause a constant grieving whisper.

The car ahead of me turned onto the street and I slid through the stop sign after it. Ten minutes later I pulled into the driveway of the large two-story house where my brother and I had lived for the last three years. Going through the door, I heard the sounds of a cooking show on TV and little kids wrestling with the family dog. It smelled like oatmeal brownies. Jack's favorite.

"That you, Jocelyn?" my foster mom called from the kitchen.

Before I could answer, Marilyn peeked around the corner, an oven mitt on one hand and a spatula in the other. She blew at her bangs to get them out of her eyes. "Did you decide if you're going camping?"

"Yeah. I think I will."

"Good." A timer beeped, drawing her back into the kitchen. She called to me over her shoulder. "Hey, a letter came for you. It's in your room."

I opened the hall closet, grabbed a sleeping bag, and headed upstairs. Going into my room, I dropped the bag on the floor. My mind was on the camping trip; what to pack, what to wear, what to avoid talking about. I noticed the letter. Probably more college stuff, I thought.

Picking it up, I stared at it, my lips parting in a silent gasp. A tremor passed through me: the aftershock following an earthquake.

It was from Jack.

One

MARATHON

Staying in the shadows of buildings whenever possible, I ran along the sidewalk. The soles of my shoes slapped the wet concrete and beat out a desperate chant: *get to him* . . . *get to him* . . . as car engines droned in the distance. I wove my way down side streets and across open walkways, out of breath by the time I turned onto Arsenal Street, which connected with Watertown's public square. Caught in the muted circular halos of the streetlights were swirling spirals of rain. They reminded me of Van Gogh's *Starry Night*, my brother Jack's favorite painting. At any other time I would've appreciated the abstract beauty, but just then all I could think was, *it's way too bright out here.*

Rain soaked me to the skin. Blinking through a blur of watery mascara, I stepped up the pace. A bank sign displayed the time: 10:07 p.m. I was three hours away from the safety of home, and more afraid than I'd been since leaving this upstate New York town nearly five years ago. Even as the rain plastered my T-shirt to my body and stung my face, my mind was somewhere else. The white noise of fear blocked out any pain.

Two cars were coming down the road, their low beams like penetrating flashlights. I stepped back into the shadows, my heart hammering and lungs aching. After they drove by, I bolted across the wide street. Entering the public square, I ran past the Lady Spray fountain, its water hissing under the rain. I skirted the large brick buildings that faced the central plaza and felt less vulnerable in their deep shadows. A few seconds later I darted down an alley, then crossed the deserted parking lot of a bank. Only two more blocks! As I ran, one desperate question kept circling through my head: will he still be there?

Noah Collier was a guy of habits, and because of those habits I knew there was a chance I'd find him. A minute later I rounded a corner and caught sight of my goal: a poorly lit parking lot. My eyes tore around the lot and relief surged through me when I saw his black Jeep Cherokee.

I studied the gray-stone building. He was still inside, sparring at his martial arts dojo, but there was no way I could simply walk in and try to find him. Instead, I'd have to wait. How long, though? I couldn't just stand around and be a target for whoever had been following me. I hurried to his car and pushed aside the wet strings of hair that hung in my face. I grabbed the door handle. It was locked. Then I thought about last night when I'd been spying on him.

He'd hauled several boxes out of the back end of the Jeep. Going to the rear, I opened the hatchback.

I shoved away a case of bottled water and climbed in. It wasn't easy—at nearly six feet, I was tall for a girl. I curled up on the floor and shut the door, then lay in the dark, trying to catch my breath and listening to the rain pummeling the roof. Maybe this was better anyway, since he probably wouldn't like finding me in his passenger seat.

Although it was a relief to be out of the rain, the sense that someone was following me brought more anxiety as I realized what a vulnerable position I was in. Crammed beneath the hatch with no weapon and hardly able to move, I couldn't defend myself. I strained my ears for the sound of approaching feet through the downpour. If I'd been tailed, then whoever was out there would be here in the next few seconds. My adrenaline surged again, and I seriously considered peeking out the window. I didn't, though, and after a couple of minutes it seemed possible that I'd gotten away.

Now that I was lying still my body started to cool off. It didn't take long to get chilled, and I found myself wishing Noah would get here soon. Of course what I'd do then wasn't exactly clear, since he might not give me much time to explain. Shivering, I tried to get comfortable. While I waited, my thoughts were a dazed blur. How had this happened?

During the entire day that I spent spying on Noah, I hadn't planned on actually talking to him. But less than an hour ago my car had been stolen from the parking lot of an Internet café. Inside it was nearly everything I'd brought with me when I traveled from my foster parents' house in Troy, including my money, clothes, cell phone, and netbook. Now all I had left in my pockets were a couple forms of ID, the key to my missing car, and the envelope that had made me decide to come here in the first place.

Even more unnerving, instinct said someone was following me. Instinct, it seemed, was honing its blade on my nerves, warning me that whoever had taken my car wasn't going to let it end there. Asking Noah for help was the only plan I could think of, since going to the local police was not an option.

The sound of a lock springing open startled me, and I caught my breath. Was he finally here? The driver's door opened and a harsh white light glared from overhead. I squinted and scrunched lower. What now? I already knew Noah was a guy who wouldn't react calmly to my hiding in his car, no matter what I had to say. Jumping up from the back of his Jeep when he didn't expect it might get me a fist in the face, or worse. I decided to keep still.

He climbed in and slammed the door, extinguishing the dome light. The engine started and a song I didn't recognize pounded from the radio. The Jeep pulled out of its parking space and moved from the lot into the street. We accelerated. Shadows began to glide in and out of the windows like dark, filmy bats. If I'd been uncomfortable in the cramped back end before, once we got moving the jostling made it even worse. The luggage area of a Jeep wasn't exactly meant for passengers, and I needed to move because pins and needles were starting in my feet. I didn't dare rise high enough for him to catch sight of the top of my head, so I carefully tried to readjust my position. As we turned a few sharp corners I had to brace myself. It was also stinking cold in the back, and if he happened to be running the heater up front, none of the warm air was reaching me.

The drive lasted about ten minutes, but it seemed a whole lot longer. Hiding in the back of a car belonging to a guy I hadn't talked to in nearly five years was way outside my comfort zone. Would he even recognize me? I'd changed a lot. As I listened to the rain, the radio, and the swish of windshield wipers, I tried to think of what to say when we came face-to-face.

"Hi, Noah. Believe it or not it's me, Jocelyn Harte, and I think we really need to talk. I know it's been a while, and we didn't part on the best of terms, since you told me if you ever saw me again you'd kill me, but we were only kids back then and you didn't really mean it, did you?"

Sure. That would work.

We left the center of Watertown and drove along Woodard Hill Road, which ran beside the Black River. I should have felt relieved, knowing I was safe from my pursuer, but I didn't. Instead, I worried about how alone I was. No, not alone. Worse. Dependent on a guy who had no idea I was hiding in the back of his car.

In time the Jeep slowed and swung left, and after a few more minutes we turned onto a driveway and came to a slow stop. I heard the garage door slide up; then we pulled forward. The droning rain suddenly stopped, and the inside of the car was lit by the glaring overhead bulb. The garage door closed behind us. Noah turned off the engine and the radio fell silent. I kept very still, lying low and pressing against the back of the seat. I analyzed each noise.

The driver's door opened. Noah got out and slammed it shut. I heard his feet crunching on gritty concrete and my ears strained for every sound. I knew it would be much smarter for me to wait until he was inside before approaching him. I wouldn't dare knock on the door leading from the garage into his half of the duplex, but I could slip outside, go around to the front, and ring the bell.

He walked away from the Jeep. I heard a door open and close. For a few seconds I breathed a little easier, though my heart was still pounding. I crawled to my knees and peered out the window. I was alone. The hatchback couldn't be opened from the inside, so I climbed over the backseat and got out. I scanned the garage and saw two doors. One led inside, the other to the backyard. That was where I needed to go, but I'd have to be quiet so he didn't hear me. I knew from spying on him that the other half of the duplex was empty. At least there wouldn't be the problem of avoiding nosy neighbors.

I'd taken only a few steps when the soft sound of grit crunching on cement startled me. Spinning around, I saw

Noah's large frame half a second before he slammed into me, knocking me back against his Jeep. The jolt sent a crack of pain up my neck and I cried out. He squelched the sound by wrapping his hands around my throat. I struggled against him, but he had the arms of an orangutan. I couldn't reach him with my blows and he easily avoided my kicks. Fighting him didn't work, so I desperately tried to explain, but his hands gripped harder until only a few grunts and gasps escaped me as my body fought for air. He had me. There was nothing I could do.

Frantic, I dug my fingers into his hands, but with no result. I couldn't think of anything else to do but offer him the name that might set me free. I looked into his angry face and began to repeat two important words over and over again. No sound came out, and I probably looked like a grounded fish with its mouth flopping open and closed, but I kept trying. I repeatedly mouthed the two words as clearly as I could, looking up at him with wild eyes.

Why didn't he get it? I was inches from his face! Couldn't the idiot read lips? Blood was now pounding in my ears like some roaring surf, and my face felt swollen and hot. A dim haze began to cross my eyes. He was going to kill me!

I dropped my hands and stopped struggling, staring up at him in one last effort before unconsciousness settled in. I begged him with my eyes, but it didn't work. Pleading for help was something I'd never been good at. Besides, it was hard to come across as helpless when I was pushing six feet and staring into the eyes of a guy who barely had two inches on me.

The iron grip around my throat eased just enough for me to pull in a couple of breaths. His face moved closer to mine. "You have two seconds to explain."

I opened my lips to speak, horrified when no sound made its way out of my windpipe. His fingers began to tighten again. I salvaged every last bit of strength I had and croaked, "Third freak!"

Noah dropped his hands like I was made of hot coals. He stepped back and stared. Several expressions crossed his face: astonishment, doubt, and then anger. I didn't pay much attention, though, because my body was too busy gulping in air with delirious greed. My limbs were trembling, and I felt myself start to slide down the side of the Jeep. He leaped forward to catch me, but I swung my fist up with all the strength I could find. It contacted him quite hard in a rather sensitive area and he doubled over, landing on his knees with a groan.

We sat that way for a while, my back against the tire and my rear on the cold concrete floor and him slumped nearby. We stared at each other, but neither of us said a word.

two

THE ENVELOPE

I was grateful for the heat coming from the gas fireplace as I sat on the raised hearth, drying my hair with a small towel. Except for one dim lamp, the flames gave off the only light. Shadows hovered in the corners of the room and bumped their heads on the ceiling.

Glancing around, I saw that Noah's half of this older duplex had worn carpet, walls in need of paint, and windows with cheap aluminum casings. A shabby bookcase was against one wall, crammed with paperbacks, and the furniture looked a bit beat up. Despite all that, everything was orderly.

From what my brother, Jack, had told me, I knew that Noah used to share this place with a roommate until the guy moved in with a girlfriend. Noah got stuck with the lease but had enough money to get by.

Jack and Noah had been best friends since we were

kids. They were a couple of computer geniuses who ended up making a security program together. It was bought out by a company that also hired them as part-time programmers.

Thinking about Jack caused an uproar of emotions inside me. For three weeks now I'd lived with the grief of losing him, and it was like having my heart crushed beneath a heavy stone. Until the envelope came.

"So what the hell happened to you?" Noah asked from the corner of the couch.

"Please don't swear."

"Still a prude, huh?" When I didn't answer he added, "Hell is technically a place, not a swear word."

It was an old debate. I sat in silence, my neck still throbbing from the brutal squeeze he'd given it. My voice was now throaty in a semi-sexy way that bothered me. I didn't look at Noah but felt his eyes drilling a hole through me.

"Okay, so what the *heck* happened to you?"

I ran my fingers through my soaked hair. "It's been a rough day."

"That's not what I mean, Jocey," he said, calling me by my childhood nickname. "You don't look anything like you did. What's with all the makeup and blond hair?"

"I grew up! What'd you think? That I'd stay a dorky kid forever?" My eyes flitted to the nighttime windows that were weepy with rain. "Close the curtains, will you?"

Noah paused a few seconds before giving in. He jerked

the drapes shut and sat back down. "I wouldn't have even believed it was you if it wasn't for those two little moles on your neck. They look like a vampire bite. I used to sit and stare at them, you know, and fantasize about biting you there."

A memory came to mind—the first time Jack and I saw Noah. It was in the boys' bedroom at our new foster home, Seale House. He was kneeling beside a black garbage bag cut open into a large rectangle. Using clear packing tape, he'd been meticulously pleating it into a cape. All these years later, sitting by his fireplace, I couldn't remember how long his Dracula phase had lasted. Eventually it was replaced by the Darth Vader–Luke Skywalker combo, and later by a black ninja.

My fingers fluttered up to my neck. "I never knew that."

He smiled, though it wasn't a pleasant let's-renew-our-friendship sort of grin. If anything, it made me uneasy. I tossed aside the towel I'd been drying my hair with. The heat from the fire was comforting since my clothes were still damp.

"I'm surprised you came back here. You hate this town."

"I didn't plan to. But then, after the accident . . ." My voice trailed off and I couldn't finish. I listened to the quiet murmur of the rain.

"Jocelyn, I'm sorry about Jack. Really sorry."

A painful lump tightened my throat. I nodded, biting my lower lip.

"When Jack and I were chatting online," Noah added, "he told me that a year after you two left Watertown, you ended up in foster care again. And that's where you've stayed."

"The Habertons are good people, and their home is nothing like Seale House. They're a large Catholic family and we live in Troy, just outside Albany. Brent is a doctor at the hospital there. Marilyn is the mom, and she's great. They both are."

"You call them by their first names?"

"Yes. They suggested it, since we were so much older than their other kids. They've done a lot for us. Even got me and Jack into a private tech school, so he could be a programmer and I could focus on digital art. I took classes in the morning and did an internship in the afternoon. My hours were completed two weeks ago, though. I'm back to a regular school schedule now."

"Were you doing graphic design?"

I nodded. "Jack did the same kind of internship, but of course he was programming for ISI."

"He told me a little about your high school and your foster parents. So do they know you're here?"

"No. It's spring break. I was going camping with friends but decided to cancel and drive up here instead."

"So why'd you come back to Watertown, Jocelyn? And why'd you do a crazy thing like hide in the back of my car?"

His voice sounded wary, and silence hung between us

again. Unsure about telling him my reasons, instead I said, "Are you still mad about what happened the night I left Seale House? I was just a kid, you know." He looked away and I stood. "This was a mistake."

"Sit down. We're not done yet."

I hesitated, studying him with apprehension. He added, "Why are you so jumpy? I'm not going to hurt you."

Unexpected tears welled in my eyes, blurring my vision the way the rain had done earlier. It both horrified and humiliated me, and I turned into the shadows to hide. He got up from the couch and came over, standing next to me. I didn't look at him but felt his nearness the way I felt the heat from the fire.

"You never cry." His voice sounded unnerved.

"I'm not crying," I lied. He was right, though. I'd never been a crybaby. But three weeks ago when I got the news that Jack was dead, I'd been heartbroken. Then yesterday, when I'd found that envelope, hope had soared like a sparrow winging its way to the sun. Going from such despair to that teetering height had left me dizzy. It also threw me into a panic. I was desperate to get to Jack and find out what had happened to him. I drove up to Watertown and started spying on Noah, believing my brother would come to the one guy he'd always trusted. But when he didn't show up, my world felt like it was sinking into a chasm. That was why it didn't take much for the tears to start coming.

Noah caught my jaw in his fingers and turned my face

to him. I saw his lean features swimming through the wet blur and jerked away, which freed a tear to spill down my cheek. I brushed it off. He put his hand on my shoulder and pushed me down onto the hearth. This time he sat next to me.

"You don't need to worry. A lot has happened since those days, and I'm not that boy anymore."

"That's what I'm afraid of."

"What do you mean?"

"Once upon a time there was a boy called *Freak* who became my hero."

He shook his head. "Don't, Jocey."

"I remember my first night in Seale House. Hazel Frey put Jack and me down in the cellar. We were so afraid. Jack usually tried to tell me everything was going to work out. But he was quiet. Miserable, like me. You're right, I don't cry, but that night I did."

"Kids were always terrified of the cellar."

"It wasn't just about being scared. It was more about hope being squashed like a spider under a shoe. Seale House seemed so big and impressive. For the first time in a long time there was a little bit of hope. But when Hazel locked us in the cellar, we knew what she was going to be like."

✦ ✦ ✦

The large house had grown quiet. Jack and I were sitting together in the dark when we heard the lock turn. The door at the top of the stairs opened and a little light came through. Then a boy we'd seen before came creeping down the steps in a Dracula cape. He had a flashlight.

"Here," he said in a low voice, handing us paper plates filled with cold roast beef and dinner rolls.

He told us his name was Noah, and then he showed us a large cardboard box. Opening the flaps he said, "You can use what's in here."

The anxiety inside me eased a little as he pulled out blankets, pillows, and a flashlight. Tossing this last to Jack he added, "Don't leave it on all night. If the batteries run down I have to sneak new ones from the junk drawer. She'll notice if we go through them too fast."

Digging out a short stack of graphic novels from the box, he handed them to me and I smiled. "Thanks, Noah."

"Just be sure everyone's gone to bed before you use this stuff. Because if Hazel finds out, she'll go ballistic."

✦ ✦ ✦

"I can still see you sitting on the bottom step, explaining how we needed to wait until Hazel got zoned out on her marijuana. After that we could open the box. While we ate, you sat and talked with us, do you remember?"

"It was a long time ago."

"It seems like yesterday to me." I shifted a few inches away from Noah to look at him. "You asked if I was a boy or a girl, and I was embarrassed." A couple of days before coming to Seale House, my mother had cut off my hair, the only thing that showed I was a girl since I looked so much like a tall, awkward boy. "I was okay with your question, though, since you were being kind. I remember sitting on a pillow while you told us all about vampires."

Noah blew out a sigh. "I'm tired. Does this have a point?"

"I want to know what's wrong with Seale House."

"Other than it's half burned down now?"

"Exactly." I rolled my head once to relieve the tension in my neck. "How did that happen?"

"I don't know. Someone probably lit a match."

"Whoever burned it down must've really hated the place. Guess I can't blame them, because there was something wrong with Seale House. Something scary. Maybe it had a poltergeist."

"Poltergeist?"

"Ghost, kid-eater . . . whatever you want to call it."

Noah studied me like I was nuts. The flames etched his face with flickering tattoos. "That was all pretend. Just little kids making up stories."

"Sure. I've been telling myself that for years, trying to escape from a place that doesn't want to let go."

"That's crazy! Why are you pulling up all this junk from the past?"

"Believe me, Noah, meeting you again was the last thing I planned to do. But I got in some trouble tonight and didn't know where else to go."

"What happened?"

"My car was stolen, with almost everything I had still inside it, including my phone and money." I didn't add that I was also sure someone had been following me. "So can you just help me for now, until I figure out what to do? Then I'll get out of your life and you can pretend this unhappy evening never happened."

"Fine. But first tell me the real reason you came back to Watertown."

This was the Noah I remembered, never willing to let anything go. I took in a deep breath and then slowly exhaled. "I'm looking for Jack."

Noah's expression grew withdrawn. "Jack's dead."

"If you say so."

"What's that supposed to mean?"

I shrugged. "I got a newspaper clipping in the mail about the fire at Seale House. It came in a Jason December envelope."

"That's not possible!"

I dug the damp, folded envelope out of my pocket and handed it to him. There was the name printed in block letters on the top left corner. It felt as if we were once again two kids handed a riddle.

✦ ✦ ✦

It was a humid July morning. Noah and I were sitting in our hiding place high up in the branches of the giant pine. No one could see us. Weeding the flower beds was done, and we didn't need to start making lunch for the younger kids until noon. That meant we had one golden hour to decipher the clues. Jack had vanished but left a note challenging us to a game.

"If you are reading this," I read aloud as Noah peered over my shoulder, "then it means you're close to finding me. This clue leads to the final piece of the puzzle. There are pages where it is hidden, but it is not in a book. It is in plain sight, but do not take your time or it will be torn away. You must find me soon. —Jason December."

A warm wind swayed the branches and stirred the scent of pitchy pine as Noah and I sat there, struggling to understand the clues. It wasn't until we analyzed the name "Jason December" that Noah finally figured it out.

*"Got it!" He pulled a stubby pencil from his pocket and wrote on the back of the letter. **J**(uly) **A**(ugust) **S**(eptember) **O**(ctober) **N**(ovember) **December**. "It's the last six months of the year."*

"That's right!" I gaped at Noah with newfound respect. "You're as smart as Jack."

"Smarter."

I didn't argue as we scurried down the tree and headed back to Seale House. We now knew that the last clue would be taped behind the calendar in the kitchen. It was a glorious moment.

After that, every treasure hunt Jack sent us on and every message from him came with the code name Jason December. It was our secret and only the three of us knew what it meant.

✦ ✦ ✦

Noah, who had been studying the printing on the envelope, finally looked up at me. "Why are you smiling?"

My mouth fell sober. "Just remembering the first Jason December letter."

I started to cry for real this time, no longer caring what Noah thought of me. I didn't look at him, but I sensed from his stiff posture that he was uncomfortable.

"I think he's still alive, Noah." I shoved down the sob until my voice was steadier. "And I know that if he's in trouble he'll come to you. You're his best friend."

I didn't confess that I'd been spying on him, hoping Jack would show up.

"He's not still alive." Noah's voice was quiet. "He couldn't be."

"It's because of you Jack ended up working for ISI and pushing himself so hard. And maybe it's because of them he got in trouble. What if something happened to really upset him or make him want to disappear?"

Noah just looked at me, shaking his head. His unwillingness to accept my theories caused my sense of purpose to falter, since he knew my brother better than anyone except me. I thought of the many times Jack had stayed up late chatting online with Noah, renewing a friendship that meant everything to him.

It had started more than a year ago, when Jack reconnected with Noah through a social network. After catching up on the past, they began gaming and instant messaging each other. Avid programmers, they worked on coding together, including making a security program that could latch on to invading hackers, tracking and identifying them.

This was a big accomplishment and got some serious attention in several programming clans. Then one day they were approached by a company named Internet Security, Inc.

✦ ✦ ✦

Impatient, I checked the time on the dashboard of my Civic. I didn't want us to be late for first period again, or we'd lose lunch privileges and get stuck on campus. Ready to honk the horn, I was relieved when Jack ran through the front door and practically dove inside the car.

"I told you to hurry!" My voice was cross as he slammed the door. Pulling away from the curb and stepping on it, I added, "Ms. Biddway is going to shoot lasers out her eyes if I'm late to class again."

"Forget her. Guess what I just got?" He didn't wait for my answer. "An e-mail from ISI. Do you remember how they asked Noah to program for them? Now they want me too."

"How are you going to find time for that?"

"Easy. The e-mail said they'll contact the school to see if I can start an internship with them at the new semester."

"No way!"

"Since my grades are good, I'm sure the principal will let me. And you won't believe how much they're offering to pay."

✦ ✦ ✦

Working for ISI had made both Jack and Noah pretty good money for guys their age, a payoff they'd been happy to get. It had also tied up a lot of Jack's time, so there'd been a price.

My thoughts came back to the present, and I studied Noah's uncertain expression as he examined the creased newspaper clipping that had been inside the envelope. There was a photo of Seale House dated the day before Jack's accident and a caption beneath. I'd practically memorized it.

Police say a historic home on Keyes Avenue was partially destroyed when fire broke out early this morning. The house was currently unoccupied and in foreclosure. Cause of the blaze is being viewed as suspicious by fire officials, and an investigation will follow.

Flipping it over, Noah looked on the reverse side but saw no note. "Honestly, I don't know what to make of this." He stuffed the clipping back in the envelope and handed it to me.

"Spend the night if you want." He pointed at a door down the hall. "That's a second bedroom. The laundry closet is next to it, so feel free to use the dryer for your clothes. And some T-shirts are in the dresser."

He stood and headed away from me. Over his shoulder he added, "In the meantime, try to get your head together."

I didn't bother to thank him. Now I realized Noah didn't believe me. Did he think what I'd shown him was a hoax? For a few seconds my confidence that my brother was still alive wavered like a candle flame in a cold draft. But then I mentally sheltered that hope, unwilling to let Noah's faithless logic extinguish it. Besides, there was one thing I now knew for sure, and it was a bit of information I was very glad to have: Noah hadn't been the one to send me the envelope from Jason December. Since only Noah, Jack, and I knew about that code name, no one else could have sent it. My brother was alive and somewhere in Watertown, because the postmark showed it was sent from here.

Why Jack had faked his death and sent me this clue was baffling. And yet I knew he wouldn't have let me suffer like I'd done these last weeks without a reason. Once I found him, he'd tell me everything.

three

WATERTOWN

I woke from a dreamless sleep to see muted morning light, and peered at the clock on the nightstand. It was nearly eleven and another overcast day. Lying there relaxed, my mind turned again to my brother. My twin, Jackson Harte, and I were the only children of our mother, Melody. Insisting we'd nearly killed her during childbirth, she'd immediately demanded that the doctor tie her tubes.

Jack and I were both tall and looked a lot alike, except my eyes were blue and his were brown. Coming from a fine-boned, five-foot-three mother, we could only guess about our father. We never knew him and Melody wouldn't talk about him. More than once Jack and I made up stories, always assuming he was tall. During one of our ongoing games of make-believe, we decided he played center for an NBA team.

✦ ✦ ✦

"Which one do you think he could be?" I asked as we watched the playoffs on TV. I was ten and kept studying the brief glimpses of faces the cameras showed, hoping to find an obvious resemblance to the man who might have contributed to our DNA.

"Narrow it down," Jack replied. "It's none of the Hispanic guys. At least not for you because of your blue eyes. My dad might be, though."

"Hey, brainiac, did you forget we're twins?"

"That doesn't matter."

"Of course it does!"

"Not if Mom had sex with two different guys on the same day." He laughed at my expression. "It can happen, sis. I read about it in the newspaper."

I glanced away to hide my expression. A few minutes later I left the front room and went into our tiny, shabby bedroom. Outside the window dry pellets of snow, hard as salt crystals, hit the panes.

"Hey," Jack said, coming into the room. "Five minutes ago you said she probably slept with the whole basketball team, remember?"

"It's not that." I turned away from the brittle snow to look at him. "What if it's true and we're only half brother and sister?" The idea that Jack and I might not share 100 percent of our DNA was devastating.

He shook his head. "We didn't get our brains from Melody, right? She couldn't finish a word search to save her life. That had to come from our dad."

I smiled and nodded in agreement because I desperately wanted to believe that was true. He came over and threw his arm around my shoulders. "Guess what? I have a puzzle for you. Think you can figure out the clues?"

"Of course."

"It's not going to be easy. No hints this time."

"I didn't need any last time."

+ + +

The memory made me smile to myself and then fight back tears. Jack was the only family member I'd ever loved or cared about. He protected my sanity, the same way I protected his. In the whirlwind childhood of Melody's neglect and her boyfriends' brutality, we gave each other the mutual nurturing an only child would never have had. There wasn't any sibling rivalry between us. Sometimes there were teasing words, but nothing ever meant to cut.

My brother's sudden death had left a huge hole in my life. My grief was intense. Visits with my therapist didn't help, even though he kept assuring me healing took time. What saved me was getting the unexpected envelope from Jason December. I just needed to keep going and figure out where Jack was.

I climbed out of bed and winced because my neck was sore from Noah's chokehold last night. Going into the bathroom, I saw my clothes had been laundered and were neatly folded on top of the hamper. Had Noah washed and dried them out of kindness, or because he didn't like the idea of a pile of soggy stuff left on his bathroom floor? I figured it was the second reason. On top was a new toothbrush, comb, and an envelope with my name on it; cash was inside. Though I should have felt grateful, it left an unpleasant taste in my mouth. Maybe Noah gave me the money to make sure I got out of his house and didn't bother him again.

After showering, I wiped the foggy mirror and examined my face. For a second or two as I stood there, I caught a glimpse of the young girl I once was as she hid just behind my reflection. Like a ghostly hologram, Jocey faded in and out, her image overlaid by my slimmed-down face and recent ice-blond highlights. During the last few years I'd spent a lot of time trying to make her vanish, though coming back to Watertown was bound to resurrect her. Once again I was that preteen girl with dishwater hair, a flat chest, and a defensive expression. I'd been so gangly, awkward, and such a late bloomer that I was sometimes still surprised by what I now saw in the mirror.

I grabbed the blow-dryer, working on my hair. It was long and shiny. At age twelve I deeply hated having short hair and made a silent promise to myself that someday it would be long. I never let anyone butcher it again.

Turning off the blow-dryer and refocusing my eyes on the mirror, the old Jocey's image finally faded away. Now, at almost eighteen, I admitted there'd been a plus to my unattractive looks back then. Considering all the men that drifted in and out of Melody's life, if I'd been pretty like my mother I'd likely have gone through much worse stuff than I had. But because all they saw was a tall, scrawny kid that could've passed for a boy, they left me alone. The best of them ignored both me and Jack; the worst had a cruel streak we avoided by becoming invisible.

I smoothed my hair and wished for some clips to pull it back. It would have also been nice to have some lipstick and eye shadow, but even at my worst I was so much prettier than my younger self had ever been.

After dressing, I left the bathroom and walked through Noah's house. I realized he was gone and shoved down hurt feelings. He'd probably skipped out to avoid seeing me. Going into the kitchen, I raided the pantry and ate a bagel. Then I called a taxi, which took twenty minutes to show up. I locked the front door behind me. It had been a mistake to come to Noah for help. My car was still missing, along with everything I needed to get back home, but if I could just find Jack it would be okay. My brother and I had always taken care of each other. Even if he was in trouble, the two of us would work it out together.

I had the driver drop me off in the middle of Watertown and spent the afternoon visiting places where Jack and I had gone as kids. This included a couple of computer and game stores, our favorite fast food places, and the Flower Memorial Library that I'd once loved. I didn't learn anything new, but it helped me feel less anxious, as if I were getting closer. Eventually I ended up at an Internet café and paid to check my e-mail for anything from Jack. I was soon disappointed. After that I searched the web for an hour, checking out his favorite forums. No sign of him.

There was nothing left but to take the loathsome next step. I started the long walk to Keyes Avenue. It was time to face the one place I'd been avoiding.

Nearing twilight, I wandered down familiar streets leading into the older neighborhood. To the west the troubled sky was an odd shade of brownish purple. It reminded me of a growing bruise. Opposite, in the east, distant rain clouds hung like layered scarves of dark gray. A new storm might be coming to town, though whether it would bring another downpour like last night, I couldn't be sure.

As if drawn by a magnet, my feet led me back to Seale House. Standing on the sidewalk across the street, I studied the oversize house that dominated the neighborhood. It had steps going up to massive double doors, and a front of pink stone that turned terra-cotta in the lowering light. Shadows deepened on the porch, dimming the glass panels in the doors and obscuring the windows. For a second there seemed to be a silvery movement behind one darkened pane. I told myself it was just the reflection of a passing cloud.

The house that had once looked so beautiful on the outside was nearly ruined, charred black on the east side. I couldn't help but stare at it with a thrill of miserable pleasure like the one I felt two years ago after learning that Melody, my vicious mother, had finally partied herself to death.

I squeezed my eyes shut for a few seconds, wanting to block it out. Yet even with my eyes closed the house stayed, seared onto my retinas as if it had the power to give off UV rays. Once again I was twelve years old.

✦ ✦ ✦

We moved up the pebbled cement walkway. A sound like a contented sigh escaped me as I looked at the grand house in front of us. I heard Jack's teasing voice just low enough for the social worker to miss his words. "You're in love."

I didn't bother to tear my gaze away from the large porch and pink stone that shimmered pale in the direct afternoon rays.

"So are you," I whispered back, knowing what he was thinking because I could hear it in his voice. We were both hopeful that foster care wouldn't be so bad after all. In fact, maybe it was going to be great.

He shrugged, turning playful. "Think we've died and gone to heaven?"

We reached the porch steps before I could answer.

✦   ✦   ✦

My eyes slowly opened. After all these years I finally formed an answer and murmured it out loud. "No, Jack. We died and went to hell."

The light was fading fast. I reminded myself that the only thing worse than going in Seale House would be going inside when it was dark. No amount of desperation could make me enter it after the sun went down, so I started across the street. Mentally routing the quickest path, I told myself, "Just get in, see if you can find something, and get out." It wasn't like I had to stick around.

There were only two times that any of the foster kids ever used the double doors fronting Seale House: when they came there to live and when they left for good. Veering to the right, along the side of the house that wasn't charred, I passed oleander bushes and prickly holly plants guaranteed to discourage kids from climbing out the windows. I looked up at the panes of old glass that blindly reflected my image. My racing imagination made it seem as if they were eyes watching me through cataracts. I glanced away and noticed the grass was longer than I'd ever seen it. There were also weeds in the flower beds, something that had never been allowed during my time here. I slipped through the space between the worn wooden fence and the house—a tight squeeze since I was no longer twelve.

Near the back corner of the house was the small side door that we kids had used so many times. I put my hand on the knob, half expecting some sort of electric jolt but there was nothing except the feel of cold metal. It was locked, of course. I closed my eyes for a couple of seconds, remembering how Jack had done it: *twist the knob to the far left, lift it up, and jiggle it a few times.* The hinges were loose, which allowed just enough movement to slide the lock out of its slot. It popped free and the door slid open without a sound. This was worse on my nerves than if it had made a loud creak. Jack and Noah had kept the insides of those hinges well oiled so we could sneak out and Hazel Frey wouldn't hear us. But who had kept it smoothly working in the years since the foster home had been closed?

I entered the small coat room and then crept up two steps and through an open archway into the kitchen. It was dim in the house but not dark, so I could still see. There was a long worktable in the center of the room, different from the one Hazel Frey had owned. Shards of crockery and glass were strewn across the floor as if someone had gone on a dish-hating rampage. Chairs were upended; one lay in splinters, and the ancient gray linoleum was warped and water stained.

The smell of greasy smoke covered everything. I asked myself how Seale House had allowed this, remembering the few times some of the little boys had tried to light the curtains on fire. The flames would immediately go out, as if the house was extinguishing the fire. Little Dixon had called it a magic trick. Just thinking about it gave me the creeps.

I hurried across the kitchen, ignoring the crunch of broken glass beneath my shoes. The dining room still had the same sideboard, table, and benches from years ago, but the mirror now had a large spiderweb crack in its center. The smell of smoke grew stronger, and it tickled my throat in an unpleasant way. Turning, I was startled by shadows.

For just a second it seemed I saw my old roommate, Angry Beth. She was crouching down, holding one of the knives she'd stolen from the cutlery drawer. Her close-set eyes shimmered in the dark as her wavy red hair seemed to fade into the wallpaper. My heart raced at the memory, even though I knew that's all it was. Angry Beth became a shadow again, but I could still feel her malice. She was so full of hate. Not really for me, unless I got in the way, but for everyone.

My body was so tense by then that I could hardly force

myself to keep moving. My ears strained for the sound of her harsh whisper, even as I reminded myself that Beth couldn't be here now. Certainly she'd grown up and moved on, the same way I had. My heart thudded like crazy anyway. Not far to go.

A few steps more and I faltered, frozen by the sound of a voice speaking low. It came from another room. Unlike Beth's ghost from the past, this person was real.

four

THE CELLAR

One voice became two, the pitch and drop of garbled conversation entwining with the sigh of the wind. I turned in the direction of the sound and saw a flickering light. Flashlights? Then I realized nothing cast that kind of yellow glow except open flames. Had someone come to Seale House planning on finishing its destruction? My first instinct was to volunteer my help until I remembered that people who were up to no good, as Hazel Frey would have said, were seldom friendly. So I stayed in the darkest part of the shadows and moved quietly, just the way I'd learned to do during my months spent here.

✦ ✦ ✦

"Like a mouse," Jack cautioned.

"Right . . . a six-foot mouse," I whispered in reply.

He grinned. "You're not six feet tall."

"Not yet."

+ + +

The memory of my brother's playful voice made my heart hurt, but I told myself to focus. I moved forward and peeked around the corner. The large front room was opposite the entryway's double doors and had been the nicest place in the house. Reserved for visiting guests and social workers, the only time children were allowed in was when we dusted the furniture or politely brought lemonade or tea to Hazel Frey's visitors. Now, though, the once-lovely room had a blackened east wall, ruined furniture, and some strange visitors.

There were five kids a little bit younger than I was. They were dressed in black tees that advertised bands or had slogans I couldn't quite read. They wore tight, low-crotched jeans, chains, and piercings galore. Their hair was either dyed black or bleached white, and they wore eyeliner a mummified Egyptian would be proud of. At first glance I thought they were all boys, but watching them from the shadows it looked like a couple might be girls. Luckily for me, they were mesmerized by a small fire. Its light distorted their features and seemed to make tribal images leap across the walls.

The windows were covered with a heavy coating of soot, making it dark inside, and lace curtains hung in melted clumps. A soft wind drifted through the burned section of roof and stirred the flames, causing cinders to spiral upward. What would Hazel Frey think, seeing this? Five years ago, she wouldn't have even let these kids through her front door. And yet here they were, making a campfire in the living room. I guessed they were from the neighborhood, content to sit in a burned-out house and have their anarchist ritual. A couple of them joked with each other in slangy murmurs, while the others stared at the flames with fascination and sipped from dark bottles. I quietly stepped back. Instinct said to take off and come again tomorrow after they were gone, but I was afraid that once I left Seale House I might not find the nerve to return. I turned away. Next stop, the cellar.

I went back to the kitchen and tried not to think too much about where I was going. Across from the staircase that led to the second floor and next to the bathroom was a closed door. I reached for the knob and felt my adrenaline spike, since what lay below was scarier to me than the fire starters in the other room. Going down in the cellar was the most unnerving task I could take on, but my desire for the truth forced me to keep going. Opening the door slowly so it didn't squeak, I slipped into the dark. My heart started doing an unpleasant little tap dance.

As much as I didn't want to go down the steps, it was the only option left. I knew that if Jack had left me a message somewhere inside Seale House, the cellar was where he would put it. At first I had assumed the newspaper clipping about the fire was just my brother's way of letting me know what happened. And that he was telling me to find Noah. Now, though, I figured the clue was more direct than that. He'd probably meant for me to come here all along, and instead I'd been overthinking it, the way I usually did.

I left the door open a crack, too scared to close it all the way, and stared down into the inky black well. Snatching the keys to my missing car from my pocket, I fumbled until I found the tiny LED on the chain. I pressed the button and a small, circular blue light relieved the darkness, showing the rough board steps just below me but nothing else. Still, it was surprising how that tiny bit of light helped ease my dread as I moved forward.

Halfway down a new idea came to me. Could Jack possibly be so frightened that he was hiding in this cellar? I couldn't image such a thing, but anxiety spurred me on.

"Jack?" I called in a loud whisper. "You down here?"

There was no answer.

"Jack?" I tried again.

✦ ✦ ✦

"Why do you have to hide it here?"

"I hate it when you whine," my brother said, though there was nothing hateful in his tone. If anything, he sounded cheerful.

"Stop acting so tough. I know you're as scared of the cellar as I am."

"You're wrong, sis. I love this place. So many good memories of our first days here, you know? Besides, this is the perfect hidey-hole. Who's gonna come down here and snoop around? Even Beth is spooked by the cellar."

✦ ✦ ✦

Jack didn't answer, and I felt really dumb. Of course my brother wasn't hiding down here! Was I crazy? Cold, dank

39

air rose up to greet me. I would have shivered if I hadn't already been sweating. It wasn't until I reached the final step that I noticed I'd been clenching my teeth and breathing through my nose. The tiny LED didn't dispel the deep gloom as it glanced off stacked boxes and old furniture. A sheet-wrapped Christmas tree made me gasp when the light first hit it. Beyond those things, I knew, was the massive oil furnace that glowed hot during winter but lay like a hibernating ogre in the warmer months. Around the corner and farther back was the darkest spot the children were most afraid of, a wall of moist black dirt next to the cement foundation. That's what gave the cellar its earthy smell of decay. I grimaced. It had been years, and yet the odor was both familiar and sickening.

Seven-year-old Dixon had been more terrified of the cellar than anyone, screaming us all awake because he had nightmares about it. According to Noah, Dixon was sure the dead bodies of disobedient kids were buried in that moldy earth. Outwardly we all scoffed at such an idea; secretly, we half believed it.

I peered into the farthest shadows and shone my tiny light around. It confirmed that Jack wasn't down here. In a way that was a relief. Even though I was anxious to find him, it would have been horrible if his situation was so desperate that he was forced to hide in this cellar. I just needed to see if he'd left a message for me in his secret hiding place.

I circled around the wooden steps, ready to slip beneath. My plan was thwarted by several boxes stacked under the stairs. Holding the light between my teeth, I grabbed one and dragged it away as the car keys jiggled against my chin. The box was heavy, probably filled with books or something stupid like bricks. I grunted and slid it away, hoping the sound of cardboard scraping across cement didn't carry to the floor above. The blue light flitted like crazy as I worked to free the space under the stairs.

I climbed beneath, crouched down, and focused the light on the bottom step. It was the only one that was a solid wood box; the others above my head were nothing but boards. Staring at it, I realized that I'd forgotten to get a screwdriver. Prying the facing off would be nearly impossible, but I had to try anyway. I detached the LED and held it in my mouth as my fingers used one of the keys. It was awkward to reach under the steps, but I worked the key back and forth, trying to slide it between the boards. I was making a little progress when I heard something. I stopped to listen.

Feet stomped across the upper floor and someone screamed or laughed; I wasn't sure which. There were angry voices followed by a crash, as if someone had smashed another kitchen chair. The cellar door suddenly jerked open, and I clicked off my light. Instinct told me that being found by those edgy kids wouldn't be a good thing, but I didn't want to stay in an uncomfortable crouch under the stairs either. Especially not in the pitch black. The only light I could see was a little flicker, and I worried that the fire was spreading. Maybe the kids carried torches made from furniture legs.

They were silent now, and yet I doubted they were gone. Were they standing at the top of the stairs, looking down into the darkness the way I'd done ten minutes ago? Were they daring each other to enter the cellar in some sort of creepy game, or did they suspect I was here? I didn't move as my eyes focused on the slight flicker of shadowy grays from above.

Waiting, waiting . . . but who was up on the stairs? Despite the cold concrete sucking the warmth out of my body, my underarms were drenched and my face felt hot. Was it just my imagination trying to send me deeper off the high-dive of fear, or was someone up there actually waiting for me to move? I was making little breathy sounds, so I clamped my lips together and inhaled the dank cellar smell through my nose. My ears strained for any sound. I'd almost convinced myself that my imagination was taking me for a wild ride when there was a creak as someone took a step down.

Whoever was up there seemed to be listening. A new idea came to me, more terrifying than facing a whole pack of hostile brats. If they shut and locked the door, I'd be trapped down here. One thing I knew for sure about this place: there was only one way out. I was ready to leap from under the stairs and stage a confrontation using my little blue light until a new sound caught my ear. It was the slick slice of a switchblade gliding out of its handle. Since fifteen-year-old Beth had flicked her knife blade out so many times during the nights in our shared room, that sound was forever cut into my memory. Change of plans. I stayed still. My legs and back began to ache, and I forgot about the hidden box.

Fear started to swell like a wave, and the dank cellar darkness became suffocating. I squeezed my eyes shut.

✦　✦　✦

After the social worker left, the red-haired girl named Beth was told to take us upstairs. She showed us the two large bedrooms, each with three bunk beds: six to a room. They were spacious, with simple furniture, and had big windows. Coming downstairs after unpacking, we saw dinner was being served. Several kids gathered quietly on the benches beside the long dining room table. The last thing we'd eaten had been cereal for breakfast that morning, so we eyed the roast, gravy, and steamy mound of mashed potatoes with anticipation.

"I imagine you're hungry," Hazel Frey said. She looked like a grandmother, with bland features and a helmet of gray-brown hair. We nodded and she smiled in a cold way. "That's too bad then."

I noticed that some of the children were looking at us with sorry eyes while others ignored everything but the food. "Come with me," Hazel said, and we went with her to the door next to the stairs.

She flipped a light switch, opened the door, and led us down. A single dim bulb above the stairs lit the way, and once we were at the bottom she pointed to an ugly quilt made of rough polyester squares.

"Just so you know, there's something the children who come here need to learn before anything else. That's the Seale House rule. We have only one and it's this: don't do anything that bothers me. If you break my rule, you skip dinner and spend the night down here. So you can see what it's like, you get to try it out your first night here."

43

Hazel turned and tromped up the stairs as we gaped after her. She slammed the door and locked it. The light went out, plunging us into darkness.

✦ ✦ ✦

I had tried so hard to forget the months we'd lived at Seale House. I told myself that some of the eerie occurrences inside these walls couldn't be real, but now as I crouched under the stairs, my ears and eyes straining against the relentless black, something happened that once again skewed my reality. There was a slight stirring of air at my back, as if caused by a movement in the dark. Someone or something inched in close behind me.

A chill tightened my scalp and the space under the stairs felt claustrophobic. For a few seconds I couldn't move, paralyzed by doubt and dread. My mind screamed: *It's not real!* But I could feel hot air ruffling the hair against my neck even as I sensed the skulking, nearly forgotten being from so long ago. Reason demanded that I reach behind me and prove nothing was there except empty space. And yet what if I touched something slimy or decomposing?

I shoved down a sob, frozen in place as the presence slowly sucked away my energy. Although the blood was roaring in my ears, I could still hear its breathing. Was it going to lunge and clamp the back of my neck in its jaws?

Forgetting the angry kids upstairs, now caring only about escape from this dungeon, I tumbled from beneath the steps. Seconds later a sharp pain seared my upper arm. I screamed and bounded up the stairs, trailing a piercing wail behind me that sounded unearthly, even to my own ears.

At the top of the stairs there was a gray outline of the open doorway and someone standing there. As I came up, screaming like a demon, the guy staggered backward. I slammed into him and he landed on the floor, but I kept moving. The sun had vanished and the fire in the front room was burned down to embers, but compared to the inky black of the cellar, I could see well enough. Now that I'd stopped screaming, I could hear others running at me from different directions. I lunged into the shadows next to the staircase that led to the second floor. From my hiding place I could see a boy with a switchblade jump to his feet and turn in an anxious circle. There was a shiny glint from his knife as he stabbed at the dark.

His blade should have scared me, but I studied it with detachment. Compared to the thing down in the cellar it seemed harmless. My upper arm throbbed with pain, and my throat ached as I forced myself to breathe quietly. Over the hammering of my heart I heard a low rumble, and for an anxious second wondered if the beast was going to come charging up the stairs. A flash of lightning silvered the windows, and I realized it was only thunder. Another storm had arrived at Watertown.

Wind rattled the eaves as three other kids gathered around their friend. I heard guttural cursing and it seemed wise to slowly back up the stairs. The years melted away and I once again recalled the cautious code Noah had taught me and Jack to help us avoid the creaky boards. I began counting silently to myself. *Four, five, six . . . move to the far left and step up. Seventeen, eighteen, back to the right with a giant step. Glance around the corner. If the way is clear, take the steps two at a time up to the landing.*

So far so good. Then I heard something from my past that pegged the needle on my already overstimulated anxiety meter.

"Jocey . . . ," a low voice called as the boy ascended the stairs behind me. "Jocey, where are you?"

five

ESCAPE

The smell of stale smoke filled the second floor. Both walls in the hallway were scorched, but one was burned through and part of the eaves had collapsed. Wind blew inside as I hurried past.

I slipped into the boys' bedroom, now empty except for a braided rug, a stool, and some cardboard boxes. As I silently closed the door an image came to mind of Noah and Jack motioning me to the window. Hurrying there, I glanced over to where the bunk beds had been.

✦   ✦   ✦

Beautiful Dixon, who was seven, sat up. His pale curls were mussed from sleep, the covers pulled up to his chin. There was worry in his eyes.

Across the room a boy huddled in a pile of blankets. He had the sallow face of a street kid who, in self-defense, had learned to keep his

*back in a corner. His cold eyes showed a soul sickness and fester-
ing cruelty. His real name was Conner, but we called him Corner
Boy.*

✦   ✦   ✦

Until that moment, I'd forgotten about him. All my therapy
sessions with good old Dr. Candlar, which had included
many details about the Seale House kids, and I hadn't even
thought to include Corner Boy. The part he'd played had
nearly destroyed me—he was the reason I ended up running away from Seale House. Yet I hadn't remembered him
until now. Were there other misplaced pieces of my past I'd
also lost?

I forced back the memories and raised the narrow window blinds. Lightning flashed and thunder shivered the
panes. My fingers flipped the old metal latch, but then I
paused at the sound of muffled voices in the hallway. I still
wasn't sure if that kid with the knife had really said my
name. How could he know who I was? Even creepier, why
had he decided to drag me into this ghoulish game of hide-
and-seek?

Only twenty minutes inside Seale House and already a
freakazoid kid with a switchblade was chasing me, I'd had
a run-in with the phantom in the cellar, and a childhood ghost reminded me of something I must have really
wanted to forget. It was too much, and I started to feel like
I'd fallen through some sort of time-warp wormhole in a
cosmic joke. I almost laughed until I tried to open the
window and it didn't budge.

Out in the hallway I could hear some doors banging open as voices wafted and waned like an angry wind. Shoving my full weight against the window, I got it to creak, but it didn't slide up. Another flash of lightning and the glass glowed bright, my reflected image vanishing for that second. Thunder followed and I shoved harder. Had Hazel Frey learned the truth about our secret exits and nailed this one shut? But if that was true, then why had the cloakroom door opened so easily? What if Seale House let me in but didn't want me to leave?

I grabbed the small stool with both hands. The lightning came again. I anticipated the thunder that would follow and swung hard. The stool hit with a crash that was swallowed by the boom. Glass flew everywhere, one piece slicing the side of my hand. It stung but wasn't serious. I knocked the shards out with the stool and climbed out onto the narrow ledge just as the bedroom door banged open.

The cold wind stole my breath. I pulled myself up onto the roof the same way Jack, Noah, and I had done dozens of times. Of course on those nights the moon usually lit our way and there was no strong wind. I scrambled up to the peak and walked carefully along, telling myself not to look down because that was what Noah had always cautioned. The wind tugged at my feet and whipped hair in my face, but I inched forward, determined.

I took in several gulps of air, refreshing after the smell of smoke and damp ashes. Glancing back, I saw the silhouetted shape of the boy, like a large, hunched-over monkey, scrambling up to the top of the roof. It skittered across the worn shingles with no difficulty at all. Was the kid insane, going that fast? I pushed myself forward, trying to hurry along the peak even though the wind made my legs tremble. I was making good progress toward the familiar place where the peak met a second overhang. Just then, the toe of my shoe snagged a curled shingle and I fell forward, landing hard.

Charred boards snapped and a portion of the roof gave way beneath my hands. I cried out, my arms flailing for a handhold as shingles and weakened rafters fell with a loud clatter to the surface below. Barely able to steady myself, I grabbed wood that crumbled away like blackened matchsticks. The dark maw threatened to swallow me. I backed away from the hole. If I hadn't slipped and hit that place on the roof with my hands, I would have stepped on it and fallen through the attic to the second, or even the first, floor below.

My pursuer laughed like a crazed hyena. The inhuman sound spurred me to clamber around the cave-in. Thankfully, the hole also slowed switchblade boy and gave me time to reach the second roof.

I crossed the next peak, then headed down the side. It was nearly impossible to see, as heavy clouds smothered the moon, but in an odd way it was also like reading a long-forgotten map. Next stop was the huge birch tree with branches that met the roof and made a natural ladder. Unfortunately, the map had changed in the years I'd been gone. I stood at the edge of the roof and shoved the wind-whipped hair off my face. Far below was a pitiful tree stump, all that was left of the big birch.

Before I could think what to do, I was pelted in the back by something hard. Spinning around I saw the boy throw a shingle at me like it was a Frisbee. I ducked and moved sideways. A third glanced off my shoulder, stinging, but it barely registered because just then a burst of wind lifted me off my feet. I lost my balance, fell forward, and hit the roof. Suddenly I was sliding down the steep eaves, rocketing earthward as my cheek, jaw, and hands scraped against the rough surface of the shingles. The hem of my shirt was snatched up, the roof scratching my stomach too, until my feet slammed into the gutter. It stopped me from going over the edge.

A white knife of lightning sliced the sky and thunder boomed overhead. I clung to the roof, my palms stinging. Another hyena laugh drifted down from somewhere above me and I sensed he was coming. I imagined his knife brought down full force through my back, puncturing my heart.

Scuttling sideways like a frenzied crab, I moved to the corner of the house and slid over the edge. Windy dust stung my eyes and my vision blurred, but I focused on the vibration of the guy's tromping boots. I swung my feet back and forth in the empty air, trying to feel for the oversize water pipe attached to the gutter. Once I connected, I let go with my right hand and grabbed it. Cautious, I transferred my weight to the pipe just the way I'd done years ago. It had been scary back then. Now it was terrifying.

I clutched the pipe and started to slide down, but it pulled away from its rusted fittings. Weighing quite a bit more than I did at age twelve, and also knowing the brackets were a lot older, it shouldn't have surprised me. And yet, when Seale House's water pipe tossed me away, I took it personally. Fear and anger collided as I experienced the gut-clenching sensation of falling. The pipe slowed my descent but not enough for an easy landing. I hit the ground hard, my hip taking most of the blow, and had the air knocked out of me. For a few horrible seconds I struggled to get my lungs working again, finally pulling in a painful lump of air.

I sat up, my body shrieking in protest as I studied the line of black sky and gray roof. If switchblade boy was up there, I couldn't see him. That worried me more than if he'd been shouting and waving his knife. I forced myself to my feet; my legs trembled from the shock of the fall. Thankfully, nothing seemed broken. I moved as fast as I could, but my legs felt like rubber. Heading around the side of the house, past evergreen bushes and beneath giant maples, I finally reached the front yard. I sprinted across the soggy lawn to the sidewalk.

Behind me the front door banged open so hard that one of the glass panes shattered. Over my shoulder I saw the kids scurry outside like cockroaches swarming from a hiding place. Some leaped down the steps two at a time; others hurtled over the porch railings. They were coming after me.

Six

THE ALLEY

I took off running, my gut screaming: *Get out of here!*

The kids chased me, and though I couldn't figure out why they were so hostile, I didn't dare stop and ask. I had long legs and a new burst of adrenaline, so I was able to keep ahead of them. Again I felt that strong blend of fear and anger. What did they want? Were they mad because I'd crashed their stupid campfire party?

Their boots clunked on the concrete behind me, but that was all. They didn't swear or yell at me to stop. Any of that would have made it less scary than this silent pursuit.

I turned a corner and sprinted across two unfenced yards, the grass making a squishy sound beneath my shoes. The wind died down, and the nighttime world now seemed a black-and-white canvas of abstract shadows. My heart and legs were pumping as I pushed forward and tried to ignore the scrapes that stung my face, stomach, and palms. I zigzagged my way through the neighborhood. My lungs felt like they were bursting.

I hit a physical wall, but hearing the footsteps behind me pushed me beyond it. I didn't dare stop because instinct said they meant to hurt me. Glancing behind I saw that even though they'd fallen back, they were still coming. What were they, mindless alien zombies?

The residential area merged into business streets. This end of Watertown had definitely received a facelift since I'd been here last. Although some of the buildings were familiar, enough had changed that I felt like a stranger. I desperately hoped my pursuers would get winded and fall back. Trying to lose them, I darted between buildings, through an alley, and around two more corners. After another block I couldn't see them, so I stepped into the deep recess of a door belonging to a closed art supply shop. The large awning made it dark inside the shadows, and I doubted anyone could see me. It was a good place to hide and catch my breath. My lungs burned as I swallowed and tried to shake off the tremors in my arms and legs. I couldn't explain, even to myself, why their chasing me had taken on a creep factor beyond anything I'd felt in a very long time.

I squatted down to rest and listened for the thump of approaching boots. The only sound I heard was distant thunder rolling away and the drone of a passing car or two. I shivered. My chest continued to heave and my lungs felt seared, but relief washed over me. I'd been able to elude those kids, which seemed a miracle. Like the blustery wind and thunder that had moved on without leaving rain, maybe they were all hot air, too.

I slowly stood and eyed the dark scene. My mind raced. What should I do now? Going to Seale House had turned out worse than I could have imagined, and I hadn't even been able to open Jack's hiding spot. That meant I'd gone into the cellar for nothing. Frustrated, I raked my fingers through my wind-knotted hair.

Careful to make sure no one was watching, I slipped from the doorway and stayed on the darkest parts of the sidewalk. After passing a long row of closed businesses, I turned down an alley and skirted a smelly Dumpster with mounds of soggy newspapers next to it. Glancing at every suspect shadow along the way, I darted across an empty street and ran down another alley. This one was darker than the last. Too late I saw that a chain-link fence and a jumbled mountain of cardboard boxes turned it into a dead end. I started to retreat.

"Why did you come back?" a reedy voice said.

Startled, I spun around. A gasp died on my lips as someone surfaced from behind a rusted Dumpster. Like a stalker in a bad dream, the boy who'd chased me across the roof now stood blocking my way. His build was thin and wiry; I was taller and outweighed him, but had no illusions as to any advantage I might have. Draped in nighttime gray, his face was hidden, though there was enough light from the street for me to detect a vicious glare. Behind him four others emerged like wraiths from the gloom. I backed away and scanned the alley. Buildings on either side were light-less, the steamy smell of fried rice and hot oil coming from nearby.

"Who are you?" I was surprised by how calm my voice sounded.

"You don't remember me?" His tone was hurt, though whether it was sincere or faked I couldn't tell.

"You seem familiar. Wait, I know. Did you star in the *Village of the Damned* remake?"

He pulled the switchblade from his pocket and pressed a button. The blade shot out, glinting wickedly in the dim light, and I said, "Guess not."

"I've missed you, Jocey." Strange shadows streaked his numb face like tears on a mannequin.

"Jocelyn," I corrected. "Which one are you? Martin or Georgie? Or maybe little Evie dressed like a boy?"

He moved closer until I could see his features more clearly. Looking past the heavy eye makeup and piercings on his lip and eyebrow, there seemed to be a familiar overlay. He'd been so little back then, a blond boy wearing Spider-Man jammies. A weird sort of sadness touched me.

"Georgie. You've changed a lot since the last time I saw you."

"So have you."

"I've been gone a long time. How did you know it was me?"

"You were standing across the street and then sneaked around the house. You went in the cellar. What other girl would do that but you?"

The others were inching closer, hesitant now because of our conversation.

"But why were you at Seale House? There hasn't been foster care there in years."

Georgie's face was still blank and he didn't answer. Now that I'd stopped running the cold had started to seep into my bruised joints. I shivered.

"What do you want?"

He lifted the knife like it was a prize. "Your heart."

"I'm guessing you don't mean that as a figure of speech."

"You shouldn't have done it, Jocey."

"Done what? I shouldn't have given you my dinner roll under the table? Or checked behind the toilet for earwigs before you went pee-pee? Maybe I shouldn't have said I was the one who chipped Hazel's china bowl so you didn't have to spend the night in the cellar."

Georgie took a step forward and I stepped back, hesitant dancers. He faked a lunge with the knife and I jumped.

"What's wrong with you, Georgie? You're not a killer!"

Maybe he was, though. The others were coming closer, and a sinking sense of my fate came over me, the heartsick surrender in a nightmare when there's no way out. Worst case scenario: I wouldn't wake up from this black dream. Georgie lunged with the knife for real this time.

I leaped away, barely escaping the blade. Stumbling into the waterlogged boxes, I fell backward and gazed up at Georgie. His mannequin features broke into a nasty grin, his eyes full of hate. He raised the knife. Desperate, I kicked out, my foot connecting with his knee. He howled and staggered back. I turned and scrambled over the boxes, going for the fence as the roaches swarmed. One of them slugged me in the back so hard that it knocked me against the chain link, which rattled.

Georgie raced forward as I tried to climb. The fence wire cut into my fingers, but I pulled myself up anyway. Glancing over my shoulder, I saw him swing his arm in a fierce arc. The deadly blade headed straight for my back and I braced myself for the blow.

A loud gunshot rang out and Georgie spun around like a marionette on twisting strings. He collapsed, his knife skittering across the pavement. One of the girls started screaming. I vaulted over the top of the fence and dropped onto some metal barrels with a painful thump. Rolling off, I crouched behind the barrels and peered through the jumble of cardboard boxes. At the far end of the alley there was the outline of a man backlit against the sulfur glare from the streetlight. I couldn't see his face or make out much else, but when he fired another shot the kids forgot their fallen friend and vanished. My heart hammered so fast that my breath came in tiny, terrified gasps. For just a second I studied the distant silhouette of the man who had saved me until he disappeared around the corner.

Rising and peering through the fence, I saw Georgie lying still. There was no longer any hatred in his eyes. Blood seeped from his head and made dark swirls on the pavement. For one tiny moment he was again the little boy who'd slept with an ugly toy dinosaur and been afraid of earwigs.

"Georgie," I whispered, his name catching in my throat.

I turned away and fled past Dumpsters and a parked delivery van. I tripped once, my knee smashing against the asphalt, but I jumped up, afraid to stop. I ran blindly.

The edges of reality began to evaporate and it seemed as if I were drifting on a tiny dissolving iceberg in a boiling sea. In time I found myself crouched once more in that darkened shop doorway with its umbrella awning. I was shaking.

An approaching siren screamed as a cop car zoomed past with flashing lights. By the time my mental cogs finally started grinding again, I knew that I needed to get moving.

Seven

STALKER

Once I was sure no one was watching me, I slipped through the shadows and began running again. I couldn't keep it up long, though. Fatigue overwhelmed me and it was all I could do to simply walk. I moved aimlessly, not knowing where I was heading. Although no one seemed to be following me, several times I jumped at harmless shapes in the dark. Buildings and shops became a blur. The rainless storm was gone and gray clouds were thinning against the black sky. The still air grew cold. I had on a long-sleeved shirt but no jacket. I rubbed my arms, wincing at my aches.

In time I found myself in a busier area of town; there was more traffic, and pedestrians traveled between shops or headed to bistros. Some of the stores began to look familiar, and then I noticed I was on Factory Street. As if on autopilot, I headed for Soluri's Pizza, happy to see it was still in business. The hearty scent of pizza hit me when I entered.

I made my way to the ladies' room. The girl in the mirror looked back at me with frightened eyes and a scratched, dirty face. It was clear that sliding down the roof had done more damage than I'd realized, since there was an ugly abrasion on my cheek and jaw. I ran water until it was warm, gently washing my scrapes. It stung and I grimaced, patting my skin dry with a paper towel. At least most of the dirt was gone by the time I was done, though the scratches looked worse.

Someone tried the locked door, startling me. I quickly worked at straightening my tangled hair with my fingers, but without much success. Leaving the bathroom, I passed a mother waiting with her little girl. At the back of the pizza place I scooted into the corner of a dimly lit booth. Couples and a few families were scattered throughout the place, eating or talking. I envied their associations and their pizza. I also wished I had more money left than two dollars, since I'd spent Noah's cash on the cab and Internet access. A waitress with short black hair came over, and I ordered cinnamon hot chocolate, the house specialty and all I could afford.

How many times had Jack, Noah, and I come here after leaving the library or running errands for Hazel? We loved this place. Pizza was always a favorite for my brother and me, but Melody seldom bought any. She was obsessed with watching what she ate so she could fit into her tight jeans. Whenever Jack and I had a chance to buy pizza, we did.

I recalled sitting in this same booth and playfully

blowing the paper wrapper off a straw. It had hit Noah in the forehead and we all laughed. On that day, the three of us were really excited. A local business had donated two computers to Seale House. There were no games installed on them, only operating systems and some basic word-processing programs. And, of course, Hazel would never think of buying any software or paying for Internet access, so there wasn't much we could do with them. Most of the other kids quickly lost interest, but we had decided to learn programming. That day we did some research on the library's Internet and checked out a couple of books. Jack and Noah were serious about it; I was just happy to be with them.

My thoughts were interrupted by laughter from a group entering the restaurant. As they came closer and made their way past occupied tables, my glance became an uncomfortable stare. There were three guys and two girls. And one of the guys was Noah. I didn't recognize the others but decided they must be some of the high school friends he'd told Jack about.

There was a stocky kid wearing a black T-shirt with RIT printed in orange on the front. A girl with long hair was hanging on the arm of a boy in a baseball cap. The other girl had short auburn hair, pretty skin, and prettier makeup. She was talking to Noah and smiling. He nodded at something she said, then glanced up, his eyes locking on mine.

Noah raised a questioning eyebrow. The girl stopped

talking and turned to follow his gaze. She studied me, her expertly lined eyes fringed with the best fake lashes I'd ever seen. A couple of seconds later her glossy lips tightened as if she were sucking on a lemon.

Aware of my own mussed hair, scraped cheek, and complete lack of makeup, a blush crept up my face. I gazed down at my mug of hot chocolate and didn't look up again.

A few seconds later I heard him say, "If this is your idea of stalking, it's not funny."

With the noise in the restaurant, I hadn't heard him approach. But there he was, standing by my table and studying me with a closed expression.

"I'm not stalking you!" I glanced over at his friends who were starting to sit down—all except the girl. She glared at us, her hands on curvy hips.

"Right," he said.

A flare of anger made me slide across the seat to get out, but Noah blocked my path. He sat down on my side of the bench, forcing me back. "Chill, will you?"

Scooting away from him, I folded my arms. "Go back to your friends."

"What happened to your face?"

I didn't answer and didn't make eye contact.

"Jocelyn?"

Reaching for the mug of hot chocolate, I wrapped my fingers around it and took a swallow.

"You're white as a ghost and that scrape looks bad. What's going on?"

"I'm not stalking you, Noah. How would I even know you'd be here tonight?"

"I always come on Wednesdays for the house pizza, and sometimes my friends do too. Jack knew that."

"Well, he didn't bother to tell me. Like I even care what you do."

The girl motioned to Noah to come back. She widened her eyes in an inviting way and mouthed something.

"Order without me," he called, and she turned around in a huff and sat down.

"Who's she?"

"Sasha."

"You two dating?"

"Not yet."

I glanced over at her stiff back. "I don't want to mess up what you've got going. Let me out and you can eat with your friends."

He shook his head. "They can do without me, and you should stay."

"Why?"

He studied me with an expression that was familiar and yet oddly out of place on his more mature features. "Jack's not around to look after you now. He wouldn't like it if I let something happen to you."

I shook my head with disbelief. "Neanderthal. Move so I can get out."

"What's wrong now?"

I just looked at him.

"Okay, Jocey, I'm sorry if everything I say annoys you! At least stick around for pizza. You can tolerate me that long, can't you?"

"Let's get clear about something. I only came in this place because I happened to recognize it from when we were kids. I didn't know you were going to be here tonight or I would've kept going."

"When did you get so touchy? You were a lot easier to hang with at twelve."

The waitress came back again and he ordered a medium pizza. After she left I looked at him. His unreadable gaze made me feel even more uncertain than last night.

He pointed at my face. "Are you going to tell me what happened?"

"I went to Seale House and it wasn't a good experience. I sort of . . . fell. Satisfied?"

"Why would you go there? Are you that determined to dig up old ghosts? Nobody even lives there now."

"Not unless you count the cellar beast."

I could tell he thought I was joking.

"Did you go inside?"

"Yes."

Noah raised his eyebrows. "It's probably not even safe in there because of the fire."

He was right about that. I was still shaken by how many close calls I'd had. Most of all, I was horrified by what I'd seen happen to Georgie. Thinking about the shooter made me even more worried for Jack.

"You okay?"

"Yes." I decided to ask him something I needed to know. "I've been wondering who told you about Jack's accident. That he was . . . gone."

"Oh. Well, I didn't find out right away. Jack didn't come online for a couple of days. He just wasn't there, you know? At first I thought maybe he was busy working, but then ISI sent me a report about what happened."

The waitress dropped off a drink for Noah and he took a gulp.

I said, "I should've called, but I just couldn't."

"That's okay."

"At least ISI was decent enough to tell you."

"Yeah." He stared down at his drink. "A week ago I quit working for them."

"You did? Why?"

"Mainly because when Jack died, it was like letting the air out of a life raft. Without him, I didn't want to stay. I mean, we found our love of computers together in the first place, right? Both of us were so excited about programming. And then about how ISI was interested in us. Now that he's gone, it's not the same."

Noah could be so difficult and prickly at times, but his loyalty to my brother really touched me.

A few minutes later the waitress brought over a steaming pizza layered with sausage, ham, and glazed onions. Noah dug in, lifting a piece that trailed cheese. He glanced at me. "You want some, don't you?"

My pride battled my stomach and quickly lost. I grabbed a slice and ate. For a while we were too busy chewing to talk.

There was a burst of laughter from his friends and I glanced over at them. Sasha was talking with a lot of energy, smiling at the stocky guy who seemed uninterested in her flirting. Maybe it was apparent to him she was trying to make Noah jealous.

I reached for another slice, starting to feel better now that I'd warmed up and wasn't so hungry. In the sane setting of the restaurant, the bizarre events at Seale House and in the alley seemed almost unreal. I considered telling Noah what had happened to Georgie. Right away I tossed the idea. He hadn't seemed to really believe me about the Jason December letter, and I didn't have the energy left to try and convince him of anything else. Once I was full I just sat there, ignoring the throb of a beginning headache. Distracted, I picked at a piece of shingle grit embedded in my palm.

Noah caught hold of my hand, moving it closer to the light. "Your palms are chewed up, too? All this from just one fall?"

I pulled away and grabbed my mug, finishing off the last of my drink. He was still studying me with uncertain eyes as I set it down. "Thanks for the pizza, Noah."

"You need to get something on those scratches, especially the one on your face. I have a tube of antibacterial gel at home."

I didn't answer and he added, "I think you'd better spend another night at my place."

A slow pounding in my temples grew—bad headache was on its way. I wasn't sure what to do, because the last thing I wanted was to impose on Noah again. But if I was going to go back to Seale House in the morning, I needed a safe place to stay overnight.

He looked into my eyes. "I can see you're trying to think of a way to turn me down."

"Am not."

He dug some ones out of his wallet for a tip and slid out of the booth. "Let's go."

I paused for a couple of seconds, watching him stop at the other table and say a few words to his friends. The guy in the baseball cap glanced in my direction and smiled, though his girlfriend glared at me for her friend's sake. Noah left them, heading to the cashier, and I admitted to myself it would be stupid to let pride stop me from having a safe haven for the night. Scooting out of the booth, I hurried past his friends, not looking at them, and followed Noah to the parking lot.

This time I got to sit in his passenger seat, which was much more comfortable than my last ride. Driving away from the center of town, we didn't talk. He played the radio, and I watched the dark scenery stream by. My thoughts swirled in a slow eddy of disquiet. Who killed Georgie? Had that man saved me from Georgie's knife, or was he shooting at me and missed, hitting Georgie by accident? Most of all, what about Jack? My brother had faked his death for a reason, and now I knew for sure that something serious was going on.

Tomorrow I would head back to Seale House and check out Jack's hiding spot. A slight shiver passed through me. When I did go back, I would be better prepared. I finally decided it was best not to worry about the cellar any more tonight; I'd save that for tomorrow. In the warmth of Noah's car I even tried to convince myself that the scary stuff in my old foster home must have been triggered by childhood fears.

Once we got to his place and went inside, Noah said, "You look tired. Why don't you turn in?"

"Thanks."

"Don't forget to use some of that antibacterial gel on your face."

I headed to the bathroom and the first thing I did was toss down three ibuprofen. Then I doctored my scraped face and hands the best I could. Going into the room where I'd slept last night, I dug one of Noah's old T-shirts out of a dresser drawer and tossed it on the bed. It was clean and didn't have the smoky smell from Seale House like my other stuff. I took my clothes off and threw them in a corner. Eager to collapse between the sheets, I reached for the shirt but paused when I caught a glimpse of myself in the mirror. There were welts and bruises in several places on my skin. In the muted lamplight I examined the growing bruise on my hip where I'd landed after my fall, as well as the other bumps and cuts. Then I glanced down at the sore on my upper arm and sucked in a startled breath.

Moving closer to the mirror, I recalled the sharp pain as I'd rolled from beneath the cellar stairs. I stared at it and all my terror during those minutes rushed back.

Outlined in clear purple bruising was a giant bite mark.

eight

THE DEAL

The road twisted away like a white-gray ribbon, the landscape heavily draped in nighttime shadows. Our truck rattled along as we drove near the edge of a steep cliff. Above us the moon was a lopsided orb and the sky shimmered with stars.

My mind couldn't process all my worries. Our mother, Melody, was muttering to herself in partial sentences as she drove, blurting out bits and pieces of regret, anger, self-satisfied revenge, and heartache. Sometimes she laughed with vengeful derision, at other times she wept or sang odd little songs that weren't musical. During the years past, even in all the bizarre ranges of her emotions, I'd never seen anything like this. It scared me. Even more frightening—Jack was sick and couldn't help me with her.

He was slumped against the passenger door, asleep with his head resting on the window, his breathing shallow. His fever was so high that his forehead was red. I wished he would wake up and be himself again, because he was the one who knew what to say to Melody.

Jack was always the calm voice of reason who managed to keep our mother's dark fears away. I was only the witty jester who tried hard to make Melody laugh. When she did laugh, and when she was happy, it was better for all of us.

The old pickup shuddered at the high speed and jerky turns. Peering through the cracked windshield, I noticed red rust on the hood that seemed to be inching closer. A chill went up my spine as I sat between sleeping Jack and pitiful Melody. It was now clear that the red on the hood wasn't rust at all, but blood. The dented hood was stained with it, and that stain was coming at us like creeping fingers. The air we rushed through picked up a drop, which then hit the windshield. Another followed, and then more, until it was like red rain splattering the dirty glass.

Melody didn't slow her one-car chase, but she screeched louder, more determined than ever for us to keep going. She turned on the squeaky wipers, smearing the blood until we were driving blind. The truck started to shudder as if it had a sudden heart attack, and the tires whined as they hit the shoulder. We flew over the edge of the cliff, out into the black night. I opened my mouth to scream, but my terror was so high pitched that no sound came out.

✦ ✦ ✦

The dream jerked me awake. I lay still with my heart thrumming away as it always did following that nightmare. After a few deep breaths, my pulse started to calm. It was morning. Light filtered through the ivory curtains. The sky had cleared and cheery larks performed in the nearby trees, a total contrast to my dark dream.

I crawled out of bed and headed for the bathroom. All my aches and pains made me wince. After downing more ibuprofen, I took a long shower and sluiced away the sweat caused by the bad dream. The shooting from last night went through my mind again, more terrifying than my nightmare, and once more I wondered who the dark man at the end of the alley was. How had he happened to be there just as Georgie's knife was ready to rip into me, and why had he killed him?

There seemed to be no answer. I sighed in frustration and shut off the water. Toweling myself dry, I checked out my face. It looked a little better but not great. Then I examined my other bruises and scrapes and the mark on my arm. A night's sleep hadn't made it look any less like a bite, and I tried to remember when I'd had my last tetanus shot. My guess was about four or five years ago.

I decided to worry about it later and got dressed in my same sage-colored shirt and wrinkled jeans. More than ever I missed my luggage and my stolen car. I had worked for months to earn enough money to buy that battered little Civic, and I wondered if I'd ever see it again. Plus what would my foster parents think when they found out? I hadn't planned to tell them about this trip upstate, but now I'd have to. They would be upset that I'd come here on my own, and disappointed in me for lying about going camping with my friends. Disappointment from Marilyn and Brent was worse than being grounded.

I left the bathroom and followed the smell of food and

the sound of Noah's voice. The smell was delicious, the voice angry. I found him in the kitchen. His boyhood interest in cooking had obviously continued, and for some reason I found this comforting. The Noah from my past had spent a lot of time preparing meals, sometimes even taking a double shift, and we were always glad when it was his turn to cook. Seeing him working at the stove made it seem like the old Noah had come back, at least until he swore and then shouted into his cell phone.

"I said I'd take care of it!" He disconnected, shoved the phone in his pocket, then turned and caught sight of me. His scowl deepened. "Eavesdropping?"

"My favorite hobby."

He pointed to the table, which was set with purple plates and glasses filled with orange juice. I sat down as he scooped scrambled eggs into a shallow bowl and came to the table. Seeing the strips of bacon on a plate close to me, I understood what the delicious smell had been. Bacon was another food Melody never let us buy. It was sweet revenge that because of my height, which she'd only made fun of, I could eat whatever I wanted and not worry about weight the way she had.

I took several pieces of bacon, some toast, and a helping of eggs. After one bite I said, "Delicious. I'm glad to see you still like to cook."

He didn't answer, just chewed in silence, and I wondered if he was mad because of the phone call or mad at me for listening in. There sure wasn't much of the boy I had once known left in Noah. He seemed so much harder.

Not only that, but when we were kids, I'd been slightly taller. Since we'd been apart he'd grown and actually had a couple of inches on me now. He had also filled out in the chest and arms, with muscles I hadn't seen five years ago.

As kids, there were two things about Noah that had always intrigued me. The first was the low sound of his voice, which had mellowed even more now that he was older. Even when he was angry, the tone of his voice drew me to him. The other was his eyes; they were intelligent in a thoughtful way, and the color was amazing. I'd noticed them that very first day at Seale House, even before he came down to the cellar and the three of us became friends.

His eyes were a shade of brown that wasn't chocolate or coffee, unless you added a whole lot of cream to the cup. But saying they were light brown didn't explain them at all. Maybe if I could only pick one word, I'd say *warm*. He could be angry or upset and scowling like a murderous vampire, but still that color called to me in a dozen different ways. I've never seen anyone with eyes like Noah's.

"Jocey, if I help you out with a bus ticket, will you go back home?"

I pulled my gaze away from him and looked down at my plate, dismayed to see I'd eaten nearly all my bacon and hardly tasted it.

"That eager to get rid of me? You're the one who insisted I come back here last night."

"I'm not trying to get rid of you. It just seems like your grief over Jack is keeping you from thinking straight."

"I get it. To you I'm just a big problem. Maybe that's all I ever was. Jack's annoying sister who tags along."

"You know that's not true."

"Third freak, third wheel."

Instead of denying it, Noah smiled and shook his head.

"What?"

"Not a freak anymore, are you? Remember how those girls at school teased you?"

A quick memory took me back to the misery of my school year in this town. "Nessa, Monique, and Tabby? And who was that other one . . . Geena?"

He nodded. "If they could see you now, I guess they'd shut up fast. You're prettier than any of them ever dreamed of being."

"Why are you acting so nice?"

"Not nice, just honest. We were always straight with each other, weren't we?"

"Yes."

"So when I tell you to go home and deal with your grief, you can see I'm being honest."

"Do you think the envelope from Jason December is a fake? Like some sort of sick joke?"

"I don't know what to think."

I put down my fork and stood. "Listen, Noah, I appreciate your putting me up here for two nights and cooking this breakfast. But I need to keep looking for Jack."

"How will you do that with no car or money?"

He was right, and though I hated to ask for help, it

didn't seem like I had much choice. "Any chance you'd give me another loan? I'll pay you back when I get home. I have a small savings account." I showed him my crystal watch with its turquoise jelly strap, the only thing of value on me. "It cost almost a hundred, new." I didn't add that it had been an early graduation gift from Jack.

"It's not my style."

"Okay. Thanks anyway."

"Giving up so easily?"

"What do you want from me, Noah? Just to keep on playing some stupid game? Because if that's all you want, I'm tired of it."

"Calm down."

"You talk about trust, but trust is the last thing you're willing to give. You don't believe the Jason December envelope is from Jack. But I promise you I didn't make it up."

"I never said you did."

"Then who sent it to me? Did you?"

"No. Of course not."

I didn't say anything else, just stood beside the table and stared down at him. At last he shook his head and shrugged. "I've tried to think who sent it. I can't figure it out."

"Did you tell someone else about the Jason December codes?"

"No."

"There are only three people who knew that name: you, me, and Jack." Grabbing the envelope out of my pocket, I threw it on the table. "Look at the facts, why don't you? It has a Watertown postmark, mailed to me in Troy. That's why I dropped everything to drive up here. What else could I do? I had to try and find out if he might still be alive."

"He's not. I read a copy of the accident report that ISI got from the police."

"Which could've been faked."

"But why?"

"Maybe he's in serious trouble but can't contact us directly. He sent me that envelope for a reason. I have to figure out why."

Noah seemed to be going over my points, putting the facts together. He picked up the envelope and examined the postmark. I almost held my breath, hoping so much that he would accept what I'd told him.

He pushed away from the table and stood. "Okay. What do you want?"

"I need to go back to Seale House. If Jack left me a message, it'll be there in his hiding place."

"What hiding place?"

"One that only Jack and I knew about."

His eyebrows drew together. "I thought we shared everything."

"Not this."

"So the two of you had a secret I didn't share. No big surprise, I guess. Tell me something, and don't lie. If you look there and find nothing, will you accept Jack is gone for good?"

"Guess I'll have no choice."

"All right then, I'll help you."

Relief washed through me. "I need some cash for a taxi, a flashlight, and a screwdriver." I went over to the counter, grabbing a knife from the butcher block. "And this."

"Put that away. Hell, Jocey, you're making me nuts!"

"Please don't swear."

Noah crossed the room, standing beside me and encircling my wrist with his fingers before taking the knife away with his free hand. The warmth of his touch startled me. For a couple of electric seconds he stared into my eyes and neither of us said anything.

He let go of my wrist, turned to the counter, and put the knife back in its block. "Tell you what. I'll drive you to Seale House myself and we'll both look in your secret hiding place. When you see there's no message from Jack, you go home. Deal?"

"Sure."

"But no knife. And you help me do the dishes before we go."

nine

SEALE HOUSE

"Just so you know, I think it's a mistake not to take a weapon with us," I said as Noah parked his Jeep Cherokee in front of Seale House.

"Try not to let your childhood fears get to you."

He turned off the ignition and we got out of the car. Overhead, a white jet stream left a swelling gash across the cheek of the sky. Wind whipped my hair in my eyes and made me grateful for the lightweight fleece jacket Noah had loaned me. He wore a similar one but in a different shade. It made us look like one of those disgusting lovesick couples who show their commitment by dressing alike.

We walked up to the wide porch. The memories of Seale House seemed even more alive to me than yesterday. There were so many children, like Georgie, who dotted the landscape of my Watertown past. But besides Jack and

Noah, there were three who stood out most in my mind: the one I feared, the one I feared the most, and the one I feared the most for.

The first of these three had been Angry Beth, the oldest girl in the foster home. I couldn't even guess how many times I'd tried to talk to her, ending up having one-sided conversations I was never sure she even listened to. She was like a simmering tea kettle on the verge of shrieking, and she desperately wanted to hurt someone. We were all relieved when she finally decided to start hurting herself instead of us.

Corner Boy, the one I'd feared the most, had been forgotten until yesterday. Thinking about it now, I admitted there were lots of reasons to try and forget him. And the child I'd been most afraid for had been seven-year-old Dixon, a beautiful but damaged little boy who followed me around like a lost puppy. One of these three, I knew, was dead. The other two had vanished from my life on the wretched, snowy evening when I ran away.

Noah and I climbed the steps and crossed to the front door, which was still ajar after last night's chase. He went inside and I followed. My eyes and ears searched for any sign of the cockroach kids. Walking past the ashes of their dead fire, Noah paused to glance at it. By the time we reached the cellar door my mouth was dry.

"It sure smells in here," he said, meaning the smoke.

"I know. Want me to carry the screwdriver for you, since you've got that big flashlight?"

"No. You'll end up holding it like a weapon. I don't want you to panic and stab me in the butt."

I scowled at his back and made a rude comment, but secretly I knew he had a point after what happened the last time I was walking behind him with a sharp tool.

"You said it's down here, right?"

"Yes."

He opened the door and turned on the flashlight, which did a much better job of lighting the steps than my little LED had.

"Noah," I whispered, creeping down the stairs after him, "it might be a little late to bring this up, but there's something down here. It bit me on the arm."

"Thanks for the heads-up."

"I mean it. I'm not making this up!"

By now we had reached the bottom steps. "Since you're being such a wimp, Jocey, let's look around first."

"No, that's okay . . ."

Ignoring me, Noah walked through the cellar and shone his flashlight beam across every inch. He even unveiled the fake Christmas tree with its few remaining ornaments and a broken candy cane. Next he headed to the loamy graveyard, where Dixon had been sure the corpses of bad kids were buried. A minute later he returned with a bored expression.

"There's nothing dangerous down here, unless you count the poisonous mushrooms growing in the dirt back there."

"Okay." I tried to look self-assured but wished I'd never

told him about the now-absent cellar beast. I turned to Jack's hiding place below the stairs. "Under here."

I climbed beneath the steps and asked for the screwdriver. This time he handed it to me. I pointed at the boxed-in bottom step, and Noah shone the light on it. This revealed something my little LED hadn't: fresh hammer marks. Although the piece of wood that made up the facing had many old marks on it from when Jack had opened and closed it years ago, there were also fresh scrapes. Noah didn't seem to notice, but it gave me a little bit of hope as I used the screwdriver to pry it open.

Finally the board came off, and he aimed the light inside so I could see. "Look, Noah!" I reached in and pulled out Jack's beat-up metal lockbox. "I told you!"

"Uh-huh."

I suddenly became aware of how close he was crouched behind me in the tight space under the stairs, and I felt even more flustered. Why, I asked myself, was I getting nervous just because he was kneeling so near, even if his breath did stir the strands of hair resting against my cheek? At least he wasn't the cellar monster.

"So you found an old container. That doesn't prove anything."

He backed away and we both came out, studying the locked box. We were about to head up the steps when a noise stopped us. From somewhere overhead came a crazed howl that lasted for several seconds, followed by the sound of someone walking around.

A hiss of irritation threaded its way through me. "Not again!"

"What do you mean?"

"Turn off the light!"

He did and we were plunged into darkness, but that didn't stop Noah. He grabbed my arm and whispered, "Come on. Let's go see what's going on."

I thought about Georgie and his creepy friends. Georgie was dead, but I figured the others were still plenty dangerous. "I don't think we should."

We were halfway up the stairs when we heard the door ahead of us slam and a lock turn, accompanied by a long sob. We were trapped in the cellar. Fear rose in me, worse than acid, and I wanted to scream but my throat closed up. Little croaking sounds emerged that would've been humiliating if I hadn't been too terrified to care.

Breaking away from Noah's grasp, I surged past him and up the stairs, fumbling for the knob. I started to pound on the door but the sudden light from Noah's flashlight stopped me. He turned me around to face him, and in the illumination of the beam his features looked elongated, reminding me of his vampire phase.

"Stop panicking."

"We're trapped down here! They locked the door!"

"I know. Slow your breathing or you're going to hyperventilate."

He reached down and took the screwdriver. "Hold the flashlight."

I took it from him and did my best to keep it steady,

embarrassed by the tremors that shook my hands. As he worked I strained my ears for any sound, but whoever had wailed and locked the door was silent now. I just hoped they weren't waiting on the other side with more evil plans.

Noah finished taking the knob apart in record time. I was impressed. "Why didn't you ever teach me that?"

"I didn't figure it out until after you left."

He opened the door, shining his light into the next room. No one was there. We didn't hear any voices, but there was the sound of a door closing and we both looked into the kitchen.

"Stay here," he said.

"Oh, come on!"

Noah handed me the screwdriver. "Be my backup in case they come this way. Feel free to stab them in the butt."

His fearlessness irritated me as I stood in the dining room, watching him walk off and wondering why he'd never been afraid. All of the Seale House kids had lived with varying degrees of fear, from Corner Boy's fake bravery to the quivering terror of little Dixon who came and sat on my lap at the first sign of trouble. Every one of us had been sinking in emotional quicksand, and every one of us had looked to Noah for safety.

Hazel Frey ran Seale House like a military commander. Charts ruled every task. They listed all of our rotating chores, homework shifts, what we ate for meals, and even when and how long we showered. Heaven help the kid who misread the chart or messed up. And though the social workers praised her for such organization, I'm sure they didn't know how fast and cruel her punishments could be. To Hazel, foster parenting was an income and nothing more. I don't believe she had even a drop of kindness in her brittle soul. She put on a good show for the social workers though, since they never seemed to figure out the real reason we worked so hard at weeding the flower beds or shoveling the snow.

My mind drifted along that path as I waited in the gloom of the unlit room. Where was Noah? My eyes started to react to the strain and I closed them for a moment.

✦   ✦   ✦

"You're a liar," Corner Boy whispered in my ear, startling me awake. "No one believes you."

It was a humid summer night and some of us older girls had been allowed to sleep on the covered porch at the back of the house. I'd been in such a deep sleep that it was like swimming up from the bottom of a murky pool. His breath in my face stunk. I knew he never brushed his teeth, only pretending to do it when Hazel checked the boys during their nightly ritual.

"Get away from me." My voice was thick with sleep.

A sliver of moon peeked just beneath the eaves. Its rays covered the other sleeping forms in watery light but didn't dispel the shadows on Conner's face. No breeze stirred the air, and except for distant crickets the night was still.

"You shoulda told her the truth!"

I felt confused, still hardly awake. I'd told Hazel the truth, just not the "altered truth" Conner had tried to blackmail me into saying.

"Your boyfriend is still sleeping upstairs. So is your brother. Who's gonna stand up for you now, ugly?"

He lunged at me with his hands, his long, dirty nails digging into my face.

✦ ✦ ✦

My eyes flew open, my cheek stinging. Where was I? I found myself in another part of the house—not where I'd closed my eyes. A dizzying nausea welled in me; I struggled to squelch it. How had I ended up in this room? I'd been downstairs waiting for Noah to return, and my eyes seemed to close for only a second. What was happening?

Had Corner Boy's hostile ghost somehow managed to transport me, or had I fallen into a strange fit and traveled up here like a sleepwalker? Panic surged through me, and I turned around. The door was open. I stumbled toward it. At the threshold I stopped, grabbing the doorjamb to steady myself. My face felt hot with fear, and my heart was galloping away like a horse in a death race. Still, a stubborn determination took control of me. At that moment I hated Seale House as much as I feared it, and I also loathed the feeling of dread that had been my frequent companion all those years ago.

"You're not going to win!" I whispered.

If Seale House had transported me here to the second floor, then I was going to face whatever it had to dish out—bite marks and all. Forcing myself to turn back around, I studied my surroundings. At first it seemed to be an unfamiliar room with nothing more than faded wallpaper and water-damaged furniture. These windows let in more light than the downstairs ones, but the film of soot on the glass filtered the morning rays and turned them gray. A small circular table with a warped top sat near the center of the room. Flowered chintz curtains drooped from their rods, matching the soggy overstuffed chair in the corner. Some parts of the walls were charred, and the room reeked of smoke. Turning in a slow circle, it was suddenly clear where I was. I sucked in a startled gasp. This was Hazel Frey's private room, the last place on earth I wanted to be. It was nearly as frightening as the cellar.

I thought I smelled the sweeter reek of marijuana and wondered if Hazel had been the one to start the fire by falling asleep with her toke. Why had Seale House brought me to this room that had been a forbidden place during my childhood? Then, before I could even come up with a theory, there was a creak behind me. Spinning around I saw someone standing in the hall, just outside the doorway. It was a girl with bleached yellow-white hair and eyes so darkly shadowed and lined that for a second it seemed they were empty sockets.

"This is getting old," I said.

Her heavy eyeliner was smudged and tears had left stain marks on her cheeks, the makeup of a sad clown. I tried to guess her age and figured if she'd been friends with Georgie she might be fourteen. She looked younger, though.

"Why'd you come back?" she asked.

"For some answers."

The girl nodded as if we were on the same page. "Who killed Georgie?"

"How would I know? Someone just showed up and started shooting."

"I think it's your fault."

"Everything usually is."

"What's in the box?"

I looked down. My hands were clenching Jack's dusty metal box. I'd forgotten I was still holding it. "I don't really know, but you can't have it."

She pulled a long chain from her pocket as she stepped through the doorway and began swinging it back and forth. Soon it was whizzing through the air in a blur, making a deadly figure eight. Staring at me, she came nearer. I, of course, backed up.

"Your face is bleeding," she pointed out.

"Is it?"

"Just a scratch, but I can take your eye out with my chain. Do you believe me?"

I did believe her. I watched the chain, which was now whirling like a propeller.

"Give me the box and you get to keep your eye."

There was a quick movement behind her, and a fist slammed into the back of her head. She staggered forward. The spinning chain fell limp as her knees hit the floor. Noah strode forward, snatched the chain from her hand, then grabbed her neck, jerking her to her feet.

"I'm counting to three. If I see you again today, I take you out."

He let go, shoving her away from me. Like the startled cockroach she was, she skittered around him and through the door. Once she was safely out of range we heard her howl with rage and spew some filthy language in our direction.

"I thought I told you to stay downstairs," he said.

Having caught a glimpse of the same dangerous Noah who had choked me in his garage, I didn't even know what to say. Being around the kinder side of him last night and this morning had lulled me into forgetting how tough he could be.

"Your cheek is bleeding. What'd you do, bump the scrape?"

"Something like that. Did you see anyone else?"

"No. She must've been the one we heard, because I checked everywhere. The house is empty. Why are you in Hazel's room?"

I lost my nerve to stay and figure out what was in Seale House's nasty bag of tricks. "Let's just get out of here, okay?"

"First open the box."

"I can't. It's locked."

He took it from me and set it down on the small trinket table that had lost its trinkets. Picking up the screwdriver from the floor where I must've dropped it, he shoved it in the latch and popped the lid open. The two of us bent over the box as if we'd become those long-ago kids focused on solving a mystery. I picked through the contents: marbles in a yellowed ziplock bag, a few dusty coins, Magic cards, tokens from an old gaming parlor, a pair of black lacquer chopsticks we'd bought from a Chinese shop, and beneath it all a brown envelope. With shaking fingers I picked up this last item. It was blank except for two words written in the top left-hand corner: *Jason December.*

ten

THE MESSAGE

I insisted we leave Seale House before opening the envelope, not explaining that I was afraid of being transported to the cellar or roof against my will. We headed for his Jeep and sat inside, out of the wind. I put the battered metal box on the floor and stared at the brown envelope for a couple of seconds.

Lifting the flap, I pulled out two sheets of square paper printed with strange groupings of letters in several directions.

"Look, Noah. It's a ciphertext."

I eagerly studied the letters and bits of words. There was no obvious message, but that was to be expected. Turning the papers around, I tried to form a few sentences but it was useless. Whatever clues might be hidden there, they wouldn't be easy to figure out. I also knew that even though it would probably take time to find the answer, it wouldn't be impossible.

Noah took the papers from me, examining each one. He didn't say anything, just rotated them one at a time and stared at the writing with his mouth in a grim line. I knew he was struggling to accept the obvious truth: Jack had left us this clue, which meant he must still be alive.

Ti woL   OL   x   N   eNd   prOg   aN   wHe
Me   əd iN RC   ot waM   op   How
     Tow   R so flN G   e   kNo st
DyL not F   O   LL   Yo   th
eX   mEL NɥM

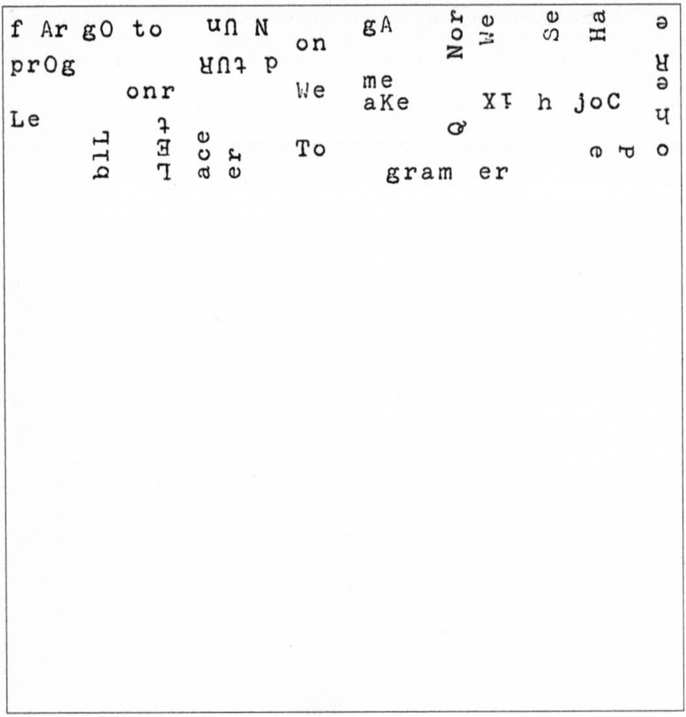

f Ar gO to   u∩ N   gA   ᴎo   ǝ   ǝs   ɐH   ǝ
                        on   ≷ǝ   ᴚ
prOg   ᴚ∩ʇ p   ǝ
        onr   We   me   XI h ɔoC   ५
Le   aKe   ᵞ
        ll   ǝ   To   ǝ �070 o
        q   ꓛ   ɐɔ ɹǝ   gram er
                 ⊥

Noah handed back the papers. "I know you've got it in your head now that Jack is alive, but think it through, Jocelyn. He could have hidden that box under those stairs a long time ago. Maybe months or even years ago."

"I'm glad I don't have a yellow balloon."

"What?"

"Because you'd try to pop it, wouldn't you?"

Putting the paper and the puzzle pieces back in the envelope, I opened the car door and the breeze rushed inside. "Thanks for your help."

"How are you going to get home?"

"I'm not going home. I only agreed to leave if there was nothing for me in Jack's hiding place, remember?"

"So what're you going to do? You don't have any money, or a car."

I paused, having forgotten about that in my new excitement. "I'm not going to worry about it until after I decode this."

Noah turned the key in the ignition and started the engine. "Close the door."

"Why?"

"You're going to need my help."

He was studying me with those warm brown eyes, though his expression wasn't very warm. I looked away. "It's been so hard. I think about my brother all the time. Every morning I wake up and feel like a ton of bricks is crushing my heart. Then the envelope came."

"I know."

"You don't, or you wouldn't want to take this away from me."

"I'm just being a realist."

"When were you ever a realist, Noah? When you were dressed as a vampire or a ninja? When you played Luke Skywalker and I was Chewbacca? You and I have lived in a world of make-believe our whole lives."

"We were kids back then. It's time to grow up, Jocey." He rubbed the place between his eyebrows as if he had a headache. "I'd like to believe Jack is alive just as much as you. But if he's not and this is all some big hoax, we'll both be taking another painful hit."

I understood what he meant, relieved to at least see the human side of him again. I closed the door. "You're right. I do need your help."

He put the Jeep in gear and we drove away from Seale House in silence, my fingers occasionally stroking the envelope like it was a treasure. We got back to his place and Noah led me into his computer room. It was small, dominated by a computer desk with a ton of tech accessories.

"Give me the papers," he said.

I handed them over. Noah ran them through a scanner and then pulled up a computer program I wasn't familiar with. He set it to analyze the letters as text.

"Where'd you get that?"

"A programmer friend of mine made it and let me have a copy. It's a really good decryption tool. This might take a while, though."

I grabbed the papers from the scanner and sat down at a small worktable next to the desk. As I picked up a notepad and pencil, Noah pushed himself over in a wheeled office chair. "You think you can solve it faster than my program?"

"I'm just playing around. Do you remember the treasure hunt the two of you made up for our thirteenth birthday?"

"Sort of. When was that?"

"July first. Did you know that Jack and I were born in Toronto? That means we have dual citizenship until we turn eighteen this summer. Our birthday falls on Canada Day, a big holiday there."

"I didn't know that."

"I always loved it if we happened to be in Canada on our birthday. They had parades and fireworks. Anyway, we turned thirteen the year we were staying at Seale House. I gave Jack a book of logic problems, his favorite kind of puzzle. But that was nothing compared to the quest you guys sent me on. Remember that?"

"Yeah. You were so excited."

"It was the most fun birthday ever. Even if it did take me all afternoon to figure out the clues. Neither of you would give me any hints. You know, I still can't believe you hid one of the secret messages in Mr. McCloskey's backyard. His dog almost bit me." I paused and smiled, remembering that marvelous day. "It was worth it, though."

"For a bunch of dollar-store junk we called presents?"

My smile faded and I studied Noah, wondering how he'd gotten so jaded. "To me, it was all treasure."

"I guess we look at things differently."

"I guess. You live with a bunch of books and computer stuff. But you're alone. Are you happy, Noah?"

"Don't start playing head games with me. You won't win."

The computer beeped and we looked at the monitor. The program displayed a diagnostics box that declared *no match found*. Noah scooted over to the computer, punched a few keys, and the screen cleared. "I've got another older decryption program, but it's a lot slower. And if this one didn't crack it, I'm not sure my second one can."

I turned back to the paper. Picking up the pencil I began jotting down the few small, unrelated words that were scattered throughout. As the computer processed the data, Noah began to work beside me with his own pencil, scribbling notes and anagrams. It gave me a sense of dèjá vu to work out clues together.

Next I wrote two new lists of word fragments that started with capital letters and lowercase. Nothing made sense. Then I grouped them based on the direction they were written. Again, nothing. I worked through several variations, and also read them backward. All I got was gibberish. More than an hour passed, and Noah left to make lunch while I continued to work. I was starting to get a headache but couldn't tear myself away to go find some ibuprofen.

He set down a tray of drinks and ham sandwiches. "Still biting your nails, I see."

"No calories at least," I replied, though I dropped my hand to the table, self-conscious.

We ate in silence, my eyes constantly straying to the encryption. "Why did Jack make this so hard?"

"Maybe it's all a deception."

I glanced up, noticing how his eyes were focused on my face and not the papers. It almost seemed like he was more interested in analyzing me than the clue. "What for? Just to lead me to a dead end? Jack wouldn't do that. He always had a purpose to what he did. There's a message in here somewhere. I just need to figure it out."

When the computer program came up with nothing, Noah closed it. "I'm sorry, Jocelyn."

"It's not really surprising, is it? Jack didn't leave this clue for your computer. He left it for me."

Noah picked up one of the papers and studied it thoughtfully. Laying it back down on the table, he folded it in half, parallel to the words, and creased it.

"What are you doing?" I reached for the paper but he snatched it away.

"I've got an idea."

"Then print a copy! Don't mess up the original."

"Stop fussing, will you? Just watch."

He folded it a second time, so that the row of words became the only visible part of the paper. He then made several other folds with the narrow strip, always making sure the letters stayed visible.

"You're doing origami?"

"No. Don't you remember making a shuriken?"

Watching him crease and fold, I recalled lunch hours spent on the playground and quiet times in the school library. The three of us created messages by folding two papers into small pointed packets.

"Chinese throwing stars?"

He nodded. "Our school's note-passing craze, weren't they? Except, of course, we usually put the writing on the inside. Work on that other sheet of paper if you remember how. Make it a mirror image of this one. You were right when you said Jack wouldn't give you a code that takes a decryption program. He'd make sure you already had everything you needed to figure it out on your own. I should've taken myself out of the equation."

He waited for me to finish, then grabbed my folded piece of paper and laid it crosswise atop his, working to insert the points a little like the way flaps on a cardboard box are when you layer them closed. If done right it would make a star with four points. I leaned in, eagerly watching and giving bits of advice that annoyed him.

He completed the star and we both looked at it with disappointment. The letters that were still visible didn't make sense. "You realize you've just ruined those papers."

Noah ignored me, taking it apart. He switched the two strips and made it back into a shuriken.

His smile was smug. "There." He turned it so I could read the writing.

Each abutting edge of paper formed half a word, and now that it was put together four words jumped out at me:

        P e a c e
        T o w e r
        N o r t h
        W e s t

Just then the stale air in the room felt too warm. "The Peace Tower! That's where we went on our big field trip, right? Anybody in Mr. Montclaude's French class got to go."

I remembered our excitement at having a day off from

school and riding the bus across the Canadian border. Ottawa was just north of Watertown. We spent the day touring Canadian Parliament, where French was often spoken. It also included a trip to the top of the Peace Tower.

Noah said, "But that's at least a couple of hours' drive."

"So? It's where we're supposed to go."

"And do what, exactly? Find Jack? Think he's been sitting on a bench all this time? Just hanging around, waiting for you to decipher this clue and show up?"

I was determined not to let him burst my yellow balloon. "Do you have a passport?"

"Yeah, but what about you? They won't let you across the border without one."

I stood up, digging in my jeans pocket and pulling out two cards. "I always keep ID on me, just in case. I learned that the hard way the last time Melody took off. See? My driver's license and a passport card."

I held the second one out for him to examine. "This will let me cross any U.S. border. My foster parents got it for me a couple of months ago so we could visit Niagara Falls."

Noah blew out a long, exasperated sigh. "You're determined to go to Ottawa?"

"Yes. And you, of course, are going to drive me there. You're just as interested to see where this leads as I am. Think of it as a fun road trip."

Flipping the star over, I missed whatever rude comment Noah made because on the back were more words.

```
S e e
H a L L
O L b I L
R C
R
```

"Look at this!"

"What's the Hall of Olbil?" he asked. "I've never heard of that."

"I don't know, but if it's important we'll figure it out when we get there." I picked up the star and put it in the envelope with the puzzle pieces. Then I smiled at Noah. "Thank you for figuring it out. I don't know if I could have."

He returned my smile though his eyes were still somber. "You're welcome."

This was progress, as was his willingness to drive me into Canada.

Once we were in his Jeep, we rode in silence, the strong east wind making tree branches and flower baskets sway. Some of the areas of Watertown we passed through were familiar to me, others seemed unknown, yet everywhere we went there were whispers of memory.

"Why did you stay here?" I asked.

"It's where I grew up."

"Exactly. So why not leave?"

"I didn't want to."

I just stared at him. "Come on, Noah. We talked about getting out of here all the time. Remember how we picked our favorite places to go? Jack's changed every other week.

Sometimes he wanted China, other times Scotland or Greece. But your dream was California. You said you wanted to live on a warm beach and never shovel snow again."

"So? You always wanted that place on the Canadian shore. You've never been there, have you? Where was it you were going to live?"

"Charlottetown, on Prince Edward Island."

"Oh right, because of all those books you were reading. It didn't happen, though. Instead, you ended up living in New York the same as me. Life never turns out the way you think it will when you're a little kid."

"That's sort of fatalistic, don't you think? We still get to make choices. When I turn eighteen in a couple of months, I'm going to do a lot of things I've always wanted to. And I'm definitely not going to stay stuck in one place my whole life."

Noah rolled his eyes. "You're sure Miss Chatty today, aren't you?"

I didn't like the nickname given me by Angry Beth any better now than I had all those years ago. However, the retort on my lips was replaced by a startled yelp when a large rock, thrown from a passing vehicle, slammed into the windshield.

eleven

THE TOWER

The three cockroach kids looked out of place in the light-blue Ford Focus they were driving. Not that they should've been driving at all—they were probably underage. I didn't have much time to think about that because another rock crashed into the windshield, leaving a quarter-size chip. Noah braked. I caught a glimpse of two black-haired boys hanging out the side windows, the rubber tubes of their slingshots flapping in the air. They grinned like demons and flipped us off as their car sped away.

Noah pulled the Jeep onto the side of the road. We both stared at the cracked windshield. He grabbed his cell phone and entered the car model and license. Then he called the police and made a complaint. He was on the phone for a bit and I waited while he gave all the information. Ending the call he turned to look at me. "Is there something you want to explain?"

The way Noah skewered me with his glare made me feel like a worm on a hook. "What do you mean?"

"At Seale House this morning, I figured that girl showing up was just a fluke. But now another attack? Why do I get the feeling there's more to those kids trying to take you out than just coincidence?"

"I ran into them last night when I was looking around, okay? They're the ones who built a fire in the front room. I think they might've started the first fire too, but I'm not sure."

Peering down the road, I kept an anxious watch for the blue Ford in case it came back. "Do you remember Georgie? He was with them. Of course, he wasn't a cute little boy anymore. And he wasn't exactly happy to see me, either."

"No kidding."

"He tried to stab me."

When this confession caused no reaction from Noah, I decided to get it over with. Plunging in, I gave him a quick recap of what happened. Retelling it forced me to think about the unknown shooter as well as Georgie's fate. Even though Georgie had tried to stab me, the memory of his death tightened my stomach in a queasy knot.

"And you waited until now to tell me this?"

"At first you didn't seem to believe me about the Jason December envelope. I was afraid to tell you this other stuff."

He put the Jeep in gear, pulled back onto the road, and accelerated. "There wasn't anything in the news about a kid being shot. In Watertown, that kind of thing would be big."

"Maybe the police are keeping it quiet."

"Don't be ridiculous."

Frustrated, I slammed my palm against the dashboard. "Fine! I made it all up, along with those kids throwing rocks at your windshield."

Noah didn't say anything else for a while as we drove along, me sitting in the passenger seat with my arms folded and him watching the road. I pretended not to care.

He shoved a CD in the player and we let the music separate us. My thoughts drifted to school and Ms. Chen's English class. I'd already gotten an extension for turning in my essay on Mary Shelley. I was supposed to finish writing it during spring break and e-mail it to her before Monday, but the rough draft was still in my netbook. Which was in my car. Which had vanished.

I decided not to think about it since there wasn't anything I could do. Instead, I listened to Noah's music, realizing how similar his tastes were to Jack's.

The traffic grew heavier and slowed as we approached the border. We waited in one of the lines inching forward to the booth ahead of us. The man at the window asked to see our passports and then asked a couple of basic questions as to why we were coming into Canada. Noah told him we were planning to tour Parliament and we'd be back by nightfall. After wishing us a nice visit, he motioned us through.

I slumped against the seat. More relaxed now that we

were on our way to the Peace Tower, I closed my eyes as stress began to ebb away. Soon drowsiness took its place. I fought it for a while, but finally gave in.

Waking a while later, I sat up and rubbed my forehead.

"Where are we?"

"About half an hour from Ottawa. Let's stop and get some snacks and drinks."

We pulled off at a small roadside market and bought a few items. Ten minutes later we were back on the road, driving past lush trees until we reached the outskirts of the large city. The April weather had warmed, and as we got closer we passed several helmeted bicyclists in spandex. Driving into Ottawa, Noah had to keep putting on the brakes because a small bus ahead of us was stopping for passengers.

Driving in the slow stop-and-go traffic, we made our way to the massive government buildings in the heart of the capital of Canada. I gazed out the window at the towering structures and carved stonework. Many of the copper roofs were green with age, the same hue as the Statue of Liberty. I thought that Parliament and its Centre Block seemed more like English castles than government offices.

"I forgot how impressive this is."

"Yeah," he agreed.

"Have you been back here since our field trip?"

"A couple of times. Ottawa has a lot more sports and entertainment than our little town."

Our goal, the Peace Tower, rose from the front of the Parliament building. It had four clocks, one on each side. It also had a carillon, an observation deck, and the Memorial Chamber honoring those who had died in Canada's wars.

The traffic worsened this close to Parliament, but Noah finally found a parking spot several blocks away. We got out and he put money in the meter. I kept the brown envelope with me, paranoid about leaving anything in his car now that mine had been stolen.

We headed down the sidewalk, passing two white cop cars with blue and red stripes. RCMP, I remembered, meant Royal Canadian Mounted Police. A minute later we went through a wide wrought-iron gate and around the Centennial Flame, where an eternal flame burned in the center of the flowing water. Nearing the tower I looked up, studying the imposing carvings. Gargoyles stared back at me.

"Where do you want to start?" Noah asked.

"Since the clue says 'north west' I'm thinking we should try the observation deck."

We entered through the visitors' door that was around the corner from the main entrance into the Parliament building. After waiting in line, we reached the monitored area. It was similar to airport security. We had to empty the stuff in our pockets into plastic bins, send our shoes and everything we were carrying past an x-ray scanner, and walk through a detection gate. Then we headed up two flights of stone steps. We passed by the center court, which was full of amazing carvings, stonework, and stained glass.

"It's like a medieval castle in here," I said.

We hurried up the steps that veered sharply along the interior of the tower and paused to look down through arched windows at the center rotunda. At the top we came to a line of visitors waiting for the single elevator that went up the tower. There were several people ahead of us chatting in French with their tour guide. After a few minutes we went in with them. Noah showed me the long, narrow window at the back of the elevator, which let us see some of the bells of the carillon as we ascended.

The tower was a lot taller than any other building in the area and gave a great view of Ottawa and Parliament Hill. From the observation deck there were five vantage points, including one that looked down on the copper roofs of the Centre Block. However, only one view interested me, and that was from the windows facing northwest. We walked over and looked out.

In the distance, the wide Ottawa River was dark gray-blue with sunlight glittering on its surface like scattered diamonds. Directly across, on the far side of the water, was a small city. From this distance it appeared as a miniature model and was built right up to the brink of the river. I recognized it. "That's Gatineau, Quebec."

"How do you know?"

"We stayed there for a few days before we came back across the border and ended up at Seale House."

From this far away everything seemed so small and insignificant, yet one of my most painful memories came from that place. I didn't want to explain this to Noah.

"Do you think Jack wants us to go there?"

"I can't see why. It was so long ago, and we were there just a couple of days. I don't remember the address and wouldn't know where to look."

I stared down at the buildings in Gatineau. During our field trip to the Peace Tower, Jack had recognized the Quebec town and pointed it out to me. But that conversation hadn't really been important, so what was Jack trying to tell me now? The only thing I could think of was the field trip itself, and how we had stood in this exact spot, unaware of the girls pushing in behind us.

✦ ✦ ✦

"Get out of the way, beanpole," Monique said. "You're blocking the view."

Nessa laughed. "Yeah. Be considerate of us normal-size people." Two others, Tabby and Geena, joined in with jeering comments.

I turned to look down at the four petite girls with their long hair and shimmering eye shadow. "Oh, I'm sorry. I thought you were still in the restroom stuffing your bras with toilet paper."

A few of the boys laughed, including Jack and Noah. Nessa's eyes narrowed. "You don't even wear a bra, do you, freak?"

"Nope."

"I don't think you ever will. In fact, I think you're just a boy who dresses like a girl."

"At least I'm not a girl who dresses like a prostitute."

Outraged, Nessa swung her purse at me, but Noah stepped in and blocked it with his arm in an impressive move. Her face turned red and she aimed for his head. He snatched the purse from her and sent it sailing across the floor of the observation deck. Along the way it scattered lipsticks, tampons, and a comb. With a screech, she called him several obscene names and then went chasing after it.

✦   ✦   ✦

During our school days in Watertown, our freak-dom had become set in stone. The name *freak*, which cruel kids at our small school had labeled Noah, was extended to Jack and then me. They'd meant it to be hurtful, but we embraced it and wrapped ourselves in the layers of friendship that built a protective force field around us. Noah was the first freak, Jack was the second, and I became the third.

My brother was so impressed that a boy like Noah, who was a bit older, was willing to be friends with him. He admired Noah's brains and fearlessness, silently grateful for his friendship. Now, though, I grasped something else. It wasn't just us. Noah himself had been desperate for someone to hang out with. An outcast at school, and living in a household of withdrawn and wounded kids, he'd been hungry for friendship with someone on his own level. Someone who wouldn't think he was weird for pretending to be a vampire or ninja but who would, in fact, jump in with full acceptance of whatever strange paths he decided to take. No wonder that friendship had been so easily renewed when Jack and Noah started chatting online.

"Remember what happened during our field trip here?"

I asked, still studying the view. "You stopped Nessa from hitting me with her purse."

"Yeah. Just one of the many times I had to step in because your mouth got you in trouble. Do you think being here has something to do with that?"

"I don't know."

I looked to the left and then the right, as far as the glass would let me see. There was nothing special in either direction. I turned away from the view and glanced around the observation deck. My eyes searched the surrounding area, hoping for a clue, but there was no hiding place. Finally I got the paper star out of the envelope.

"Any suggestions, Noah?"

We both studied the front of it and then the back as I flipped it over. "Why are those words spelled in part caps and part lowercase?" Noah asked.

"Jack's writing was like that through all the rows of letters."

"Yes, but when we put the shuriken together, 'Peace Tower' and 'North West' looked right. There were capitals at the beginning of each word. But the stuff on the back isn't like that."

"True." I peered at the code.

```
S e e
H a L L
O L b I L
R C
R
```

Turning it upside down I laughed. "This is *so* Jack! Look, 'OLbIL' isn't a word at all, it's a series of numbers: 7 1970. He couldn't write numbers right-side up in the column of letters. We would've noticed them before making the star. He wanted us to fold the paper into a shuriken so we could find the other words first."

"Think it's a date? Maybe July 1970?"

"Could be."

"Come on, let's go." Noah turned and headed for the elevator.

"You know where the hall might be?"

"No, but I know where numbers are important."

As we rode down in the elevator, the carillon tolled four gongs that rang through our confined area. The vibrations seemed to pass through me with foreboding. Why, when hope was riding high, did I have an unexpected sense of warning? Even after the last gong hammered its way through the elevator and then faded to silence, my intuition told me to leave the tower and do it now.

I tried to tell myself to ignore it, yet the fear didn't fade. Instead, it washed over me even stronger. The inside of the elevator suddenly grew dim and the air suffocating. I wanted to cry out a warning but my lips were sealed together, as if stitched shut by an undertaker's thread.

It was then that the walls began to collapse inward. They pushed down on us and compressed the air—even the molecules grew dense. The walls themselves started to pulsate, the elevator changing. As I watched, it became like the internal organ of some malevolent entity. Viscous matter

113

surged around us, and everyone in the elevator panicked. A woman beside me screamed, trying to claw her way out.

Hysteria rose inside me as Noah disappeared into the gelatinous mass. Unable to move, I was engulfed by steaming tissue.

twelve

FLOWERS

"What's wrong?" Noah asked. "You look upset."

He was standing in the lobby just outside the open elevator doors, and other than gazing at me with a puzzled expression he seemed fine—no wounds, no missing chunks of consumed flesh, not even a few pieces of gummy tissue still clinging to his cheek. The elevator walls were no longer made of pulsing jelly but of flat brown paneling, just the way they should've been.

Noah and the other passengers had all gotten out, clearly unaware of what had just happened. I watched the woman who had, only seconds ago, been screaming in agony. She stopped to snatch a brochure from her large handbag and then wandered off like any tourist. Noah stared at me as I stepped into the small lobby, my body still stiff with fear. Something so bizarre had just happened in that elevator that I couldn't wrap my head around it, and I knew there was no way of explaining it to him. He was obviously unaware of what I'd seen, but if I tried to tell him he'd probably drive by the closest mental clinic and boot me out without bothering to slow down.

Struggling to shake off the apprehension that clung to me like an icky odor, I walked through the foyer, faking detachment.

"Are you sick?" he asked.

Ignoring his question, I turned around and stared back at the elevator as the doors closed. It looked harmless and normal. Noah touched my arm. "What's going on? You're shaking and you look like you're going to throw up."

"I'm okay. Just got a little claustrophobic."

"Claustrophobic?"

"It's nothing. Let's go, okay?"

He studied me a few seconds more and then shrugged. "Whatever. This way."

I followed him through the open door of the Memorial Chamber, relieved he'd dropped it. Though my heart rate had slowed, my limbs still felt weak and my head was buzzing with confusion. I told myself to just keep moving.

"Since we're looking for a date," Noah said, "I think this might be the place to start."

Gothic arches and high stained-glass windows made the room look like a small chapel inside a cathedral. I remembered this place from the field trip. There was a beautiful carved altar on a raised stone dais in the middle of the room. It had a glass-topped case of etched brass with small statuettes of angels kneeling in each corner. Going up the steps, I looked inside the case: *The First World War Book of Remembrance*. Other glass cases on lower stone stands were placed in a semicircle around the room, with a handful of people looking at them. In total, there were seven books that recorded the Canadians who had fought and lost their lives in each of the wars. The center one focused on World War II.

Noah whispered, "Out of those numbers Jack left us, I don't think the first 7 means July. I think it means the seventh book."

Nodding in agreement, I followed him past two elderly women to the second altar from the right. "This one," he said. The nameplate declared: *In the Service of Canada, The Seventh Book of Remembrance.*

"According to the inscription, it was started in 1947."

"And it lists every serviceperson that died during peace-time activities."

Remembering snatches of the tour guide's lecture during our field trip, I knew that the pages were more like pieces of art than just leaves in a book. The names of the lost were printed in calligraphy-style font and the pages were decorated with heraldic illumination and beautiful watercolors. Peering through the glass, we saw the book was opened to a page with the names of those who had died in 1956.

"May I help you?" a raspy voice said from behind, startling me.

We turned around and stared at a hobbity little man

with unruly tufts of white hair. He was short, barely coming up to Noah's shoulder, and had the largest earlobes I'd ever seen. His red jacket stretched over a small potbelly, and a name tag with a maple leaf on it was pinned to his lapel. His name was Stuart.

Noah pointed to the case. "Is there a way to turn the pages and find a different date?"

The man beamed at us, pushing up the glasses that had slid down his nose. "So nice to see young people interested in their past!" He dug inside his coat pocket and retrieved a pair of white cotton gloves. "What date and name are you interested in?"

"Nineteen seventy, with the last name of Hall."

"Very good." He pulled on the gloves like a doctor preparing for surgery. "A relative of yours?"

Noah shrugged. "We're not sure."

Stuart nodded and then launched into a tour guide dialogue about the history of the books, spewing details that rattled past my head. It was difficult for me to focus on what he was saying, mainly because I still felt so shaken. The elevator experience had faded a little but continued to bother me. The gong of the bells had warned that time was ghosting away from us, and it was doubly important to find my brother. The danger he was in seemed more serious than ever.

Stuart retrieved a small brass key from his breast pocket, unlocked the case, and lifted the glass lid. "Not too close, now. Wait until I'm finished, and then you can look."

He hunched over the book, a protective gnome, his gloved fingers gently turning the pages. Noah smiled and leaned into me. He whispered, "You'd think he was defusing a bomb."

Very aware of how close we stood, I smiled back at him until he casually pulled away.

"Ha!" Stuart said with triumph, then glanced around and lowered his voice as if embarrassed he'd forgotten to be quiet. "Here it is."

He replaced the protective glass, locked it with the key, and then motioned to us. "Theodore Gregory Hall, 1970. Is this the one you're looking for?"

"I'm sure it is," Noah said as we stepped closer.

"Then I'll give you a moment to yourselves." He looked in the direction of a middle-aged couple who had just stepped into the chamber.

"Thank you," I murmured over my shoulder, turning back to stare down at a page edged with a scrolling gold border.

Noah bent over the glass. "But why this name? Does 'Theodore Hall' mean anything to you?"

I shook my head. "No, but the name just above it does. Remember the field trip? When we were here last time, the three of us stopped to look at this book and it was on this page. We saw that name."

"Roswill Herbert Flowers?"

"Yes. And then Jack asked the teacher about it." I stared at the page, trying to remember his question.

"Oh, right . . . Wait a second. Did it have something to do with Watertown? Like Flower Avenue?"

We looked at each other and said at the same time, "The library!"

Noah tapped his finger on the glass. "Jack asked if this was the man the library was named after. But Mr. Montclaude explained that was someone else. A governor, I think."

I envisioned the plaque on the front of the large building that I had entered dozens of times, including once yesterday. "Roswell P. Flower Memorial Library."

"That's it."

Excitement crept into my voice as it came together. "Then this is the clue! Now all we have to do is go back to the Watertown library."

Noah turned away from the case to stare at me. He didn't say anything.

"What's wrong?"

"You're joking."

"I'm not."

"Don't tell me Jack sent us on this stupid road trip all the way to Canada just to send us back down to New York!"

From across the room Stuart turned in our direction with an anxious stare. "Shh," I whispered, moving closer to Noah. "Of course that's what he's done. Don't you remember how his clues always led us crisscrossing back and forth?"

He shoved his hands in his pockets and scowled. "This is ridiculous! Besides, what are we supposed to do when we get back to the library?"

"Find a book written by someone named Theodore Hall, of course."

Noah scowled, his lips drawn into a tight line.

"Please don't be angry."

Shaking his head, he gave a weary sigh. "Let's get out of here, okay?"

He caught my arm and led me to the stairs. I glanced down at the way his long fingers comfortably slid to my wrist and then curled around my hand. Although Noah seemed hardly aware of his casual touch, I couldn't help thinking how twelve-year-old Jocey would have been thrilled.

We headed out the main front doors of the Parliament building and passed a throng of touring Tibetan monks in orange togas. As we left through the main gates, Noah glanced down at our linked fingers and looked almost surprised.

We walked past shops and cafés. Red-and-white maple leaf flags hung from balconies and flagpoles, and cars inched down the packed road as drivers searched for places to park. All kinds of shoppers and tourists passed us. A dark-skinned man wearing a sombrero and a suit made entirely of zippers got a nervous glance from a woman in a tailored business suit. We heard a bagpipe playing; in the distance was a guy in a kilt and full Scottish attire. People stopped to watch him play and put cash in his copper bucket.

A block-long flower market, its framework heavy with bright hanging baskets, caught my attention. Workers with watering cans and misting bottles catered to the plants, and the sweet scent of flowers drifted on the breeze. I wished we could stay longer and play tourist.

Once we got in the Jeep, it took us another half hour to get out of Ottawa. Noah sulked for most of the drive back to Watertown, and I couldn't blame him. Jack had always gotten a little too caught up in making outrageous clues for his treasure hunts, but this was extreme. Why did my brother have to make every clue so difficult and involved? Not impossible, though. He never made it impossible.

I promised Noah that once I got home I'd send him some cash for the gas, or that Jack would reimburse him. It didn't seem to help his grouchy mood, and he cranked up the music. After that I didn't say anything else, just watched the sun sink behind the trees.

My mind wandered back to Seale House. No matter how I tried to shove down memories of that place, one insisted on surfacing: my last night there.

In the dull setting of my childhood, that single evening stood out—all harsh sounds and flashes of color:

The radio playing.

White snowflakes falling outside the kitchen window.

Dixon's blue-and-yellow pajamas.

His cry of terror.

The red of Hazel's furious face.

A reedy voice reciting an awful poem.

Angry Beth hissing demands.

Fists hammering on the cellar door.

The heavy gun in my hand and its deafening blast.

Noah's betrayed voice: "If I ever see you again, I'll kill you."

+ + +

Finally, we entered Watertown, and it was a relief the trip was over. We drove down Washington Street and pulled into the parking lot of the Flower Memorial Library. It was unchanged from five years ago: a large, elegant building with marble facing, an octagonal dome on top, and a series of double columns in front.

"When Jack and I lived here, I loved this place."

Noah didn't answer.

We got out of the Jeep, stiff after the long ride, and went up the steps. A plaque on the double doors showed the hours. "They're not open much longer," Noah said.

"What time is it?"

"Eight forty."

We found a bank of computers and sat down. I pulled up the library catalogue and did an author search for Theodore Hall. A long list of writers with the last name of Hall came up, but none of them was Theodore.

"It's not here," I said.

"So I see."

There were a lot of authors named Hall whose first names started with the letter *T*, and I clicked on them all. There were a variety of book titles, including novels. Others were nonfiction about everything from sports to history. There was even a picture book. None of the subjects related to Jack though, and I knew he wouldn't have left it so unspecific.

"What now?"

Noah shrugged.

A new idea came to me. "Do you remember Theodore Hall's middle name?"

"No. We should've written it down."

I closed my eyes, trying to visualize the memory book. A few seconds later my eyes flew open. "It's Gregory. Theodore Gregory Hall."

Clicking back several pages to the list of *G* names, I saw there were several Gregory Halls. But when I checked, none of their books seemed right, either. "Jack wouldn't put a clue in just any old book, especially not ones about dog training or weight loss."

Scrolling up the list there was the name Greg Hall, and I clicked on it. Three nonfiction books came up:

> *The BASIC Conversion Handbook*
> *Neuro-Linguistic Programming*
> *Revision Control Reference: A Guide for*
> *Application Source Codes*

"Programming books," Noah said.

"Yes! And what about that last one? It's got the same three letters as the clue on the back of the star: R C R. I'm sure that's it!"

I glanced at Noah. He was studying me more than the screen and gave a grudging smile. "Smart girl."

I enjoyed hearing the phrase that had, in the past, been his positive appraisal of me. I was also relieved his earlier irritation had softened.

After copying down the reference number, I exited the library catalogue. We were ready to go find the book when an unexpected voice behind us startled me.

"Hello, Noah. Who's your girlfriend?"

thirteen

CONDOLENCES

The guy standing behind us was in his early twenties, and for no reason I could explain I felt an upsurge of anxiety. He looked down at us and instinctively I stood, wanting to be on an even level with him. Though he was a stranger, for an odd second or two it seemed like I should know him.

He had a shaved head. Pale lashes and eyebrows gave him a mildly surprised look, and he grinned at me with swaggering self-confidence. Some girls might have found him attractive, but I didn't. Maybe it was the rubbery tan of his skin that reminded me of Silly Putty, maybe it was just my gut instinct, but I sensed he was not someone to be trusted.

"What are you doing here?" Noah asked. It wasn't until he spoke that I saw he, too, was standing.

"Our boss wanted me to come see you, but you're a hard guy to track down." Turning to me, he introduced himself and offered his hand. "I'm Zachary Saulto."

I looked down at his tan-pink flesh and just stood there.

Noah shifted his weight to move slightly in front of me, and Saulto dropped his hand, though his smug smile stayed in place.

"Tell Sam I don't have anything else to say. I thought that was clear the last time we talked."

"You may not want to talk to us, but maybe Jocelyn does. So what brings you to Watertown?"

"How do you know me?" I asked.

"I work for ISI, the company Jack interned for. I'd like to offer my condolences about your brother." His smile was replaced by a falsely sympathetic gaze. "He was a great kid who did good work. I can't tell you how sorry we are that he's gone. He was a brilliant programmer."

"Thank you."

"It's nice to finally meet Jack's beautiful sister." His eyes seemed to glint with an insider's joke.

"Let's go, Jocelyn." Noah took my arm.

"Don't you want to hear what I have to tell you?" Saulto asked him.

"No. In case you've forgotten, I don't work for you anymore."

Saulto stepped forward, blocking our path. "You signed a contract when you came to work with us, you know."

"So sue me."

"We don't hire losers at ISI. And in my book, a quitter and a loser are the same thing."

"Save your sports talk for the handball court."

Saulto leaned near, the thick muscles of his chest

straining the fabric of his blue shirt. "Think about Jack," he said in a quiet voice.

I studied the guy's glass-hard eyes and said, "What do you mean?"

Saulto's smile emerged again and he pulled back. "Sorry. I didn't mean anything by it. Very nice to meet you. Jack never said much about you, but I wish he had."

A low bell chimed, and over the loudspeaker a woman's voice announced the library was closing. Noah led me away from Zachary Saulto. He didn't follow, but a glance back showed he was staring at us.

"What was that about?" I asked as we rounded a corner.

"Nothing. The guy is just full of hot air. Let's go."

"But we still have time to find the book by Greg Hall."

"No. We don't."

I stopped walking and he turned to look at me with barely concealed irritation. "The library is closing. We'll come back tomorrow."

I couldn't accept the idea of waiting all those hours before getting the information we were so close to. I started to backtrack. "I'm not leaving. Go ahead if you want, but I'm staying. I'll hide in the restroom and come out when it's clear if I have to."

When I started walking away, Noah caught up with me and grabbed my shoulders, turning me around. "Listen, Jocelyn, now is not a good time. Whatever clue Jack left, he meant for you to find and no one else. You don't want to go looking for it right now. Understand?"

He must have read the anxiety in my eyes because his grip softened and so did his voice. "The library opens at ten. I promise I'll bring you back here first thing tomorrow."

Glancing past Noah, I saw Zachary Saulto round the corner and head in our direction. Suddenly his advice about Jack's clue being for our eyes only made sense. I gave in, walking with him through the glass doors.

fourteen

CONVERSATION

We bought Chinese takeout, and by the time we were back at Noah's place, it was getting late. We sat at his kitchen table, dishing the food onto our plates. I was tired, and all my aches and pains from yesterday started to surface. I dipped my egg roll in hot mustard, thinking about how much the three of us had loved Chinese food. I remembered the meal Noah and Jack made for New Year's Eve, and how we'd laughed at Jack's awkward use of his new chopsticks. The memory should have been pleasing, but instead a melancholy mood crept in.

"You're quiet. What happened to Miss Chatty?"

Shrugging, I ate a forkful of rice.

"I promised we'd go back to the library tomorrow."

"Yes, I know. I was just thinking about my brother. You two chatted online all the time, but you never got a chance to get back together."

"We planned to meet up for real, but stuff kept coming up. Like when he got strep throat. I wanted to come see you both, and I regret not making it happen."

"Until Jack found you online, he missed you a lot. Both of us wondered what happened after we left Watertown, but it bothered him the most. I think he felt he owed you, in some weird way. You were the guy always taking care of us kids. The one who kept Seale House running."

I stared down at my half-eaten egg roll. "The last time we were together, he told me you were his closest friend."

"Nothing can unite two people like early morning insomnia. It was a bond Jack and I had that you never did. You always slept like you were dead. But at three or four in the morning, when no one else is awake, it's a lot easier to open up."

I had a fleeting memory of rousing from a nightmare at Seale House and going in search of Jack, only to find him and Noah out on the roof. They were looking at the moon with an old pair of binoculars they'd found in the cellar.

"In the early mornings," he said, "when I couldn't sleep, I'd get on the computer. Jack was usually already there. We started talking about all kinds of stuff. I think it's easier over the computer than face-to-face. Guess I ended up knowing him better during this last year than even when we were kids. One thing we almost never talked about, though, was you."

"Because you were still mad at me?"

"No, of course not. Jack just made it clear that talking about you, other than in the distant past, was off-limits. He didn't want to discuss your current life or what you were up to. I don't know why exactly. I sort of figured he was being protective. Maybe he thought I was still upset about how you left Seale House. It wasn't until a few weeks ago that he started to be more open to my asking about you."

This was unexpected news. "Why did you want to talk about me?"

"You were important to me, Jocey. The only girl from my past I ever cared about."

I didn't say anything. I didn't know what to say.

"Jack told me about all the moving you two did. About your mother and what life was like. It wasn't hard to figure out why you two ended up in the system."

"What about you? Did you finally tell Jack why you were sent to Seale House? You used to insist your father was Count Dracula and he was forced to leave you behind because Professor Van Helsing seriously burned him with a cross."

Noah shrugged. "That's because the truth isn't very interesting. My mother was a drug addict whose dealer got her pregnant. She didn't really want me. I guess back then it seemed less hurtful to make up a story instead of telling the truth."

I felt ashamed at having forced him to this confession. Also, it made me a bit insecure to see he had moved on and no longer let his past define him the way I still did.

"Can I ask something else, Noah?"

"Sure."

"I feel confused, like there are missing puzzle pieces. And I'm not talking about the ones Jack left me. I've been thinking about what happened today with Zachary Saulto. He works for ISI the same way you and Jack used to, right?"

"Yes. He was sort of my supervisor and sent me work. I didn't talk to him much in person, though."

"Why did he say, 'Think about Jack'? What does that mean?"

"I don't know."

"But why did you quit working for them? And don't tell me it's just because Jack died."

He paused and it seemed as if he crossed a mental line. "You understand my work for them, right? I mostly customized the security program we'd already written."

"The same thing Jack was doing."

"They'd send us new programming assignments and we'd specialize the coding for different companies who purchased the software. But then something happened. Jack sent me a strange e-mail the day before his accident. There was just one sentence. It said that some of the ISI programmers had written back doors into their security codes."

"Back doors so someone could secretly get through a company's security?"

"Yes. Which means they wouldn't really be secure."

"Is that illegal?"

"If they didn't tell their clients, it is. I'm guessing ISI wouldn't want anyone knowing about it or they could get sued in a big way."

"But Jack never said anything to me about that."

Noah shrugged. "Maybe he didn't get the chance."

"So how did he learn what other programmers were doing?"

"I don't know."

"Would the people that run ISI have been threatened because Jack found out? Would they have tried to stop him from talking?"

"There's no way to know that either. But when he died, the whole thing made me nervous. I decided it was time to quit programming for them."

Noah's cell phone rang. He looked at it and said, "It's the police department."

He had a short conversation and then disconnected. "That was Don Iverson. He's a police detective and kind of a friend of mine."

"You're friends with a cop?"

"Don's okay. He was the officer in charge of closing the Seale House foster care program. And he's sort of kept an eye on me ever since. He even helped me become an emancipated minor so I could live on my own and not end up in another foster house."

"Sounds like a good guy."

"Yeah. Anyway, seems the police picked up some

kids for underage driving. They might be the same ones who rocked my windshield. Don asked me to come down to the police station and identify them. Want to come?"

I stood and started clearing off the table. "I'm tired, and I'm not really interested in seeing those brats again."

"Okay. I'll probably be back in about an hour."

After Noah left, I downed some painkillers and soaked in a tub of hot water. As I relaxed, my mind wandered across the day's events, including the strange experience of finding myself transported to Hazel's upstairs room. What unique and frightening powers did Seale House possess? Had those same dark powers somehow followed me into the elevator of the Peace Tower? That idea was so weird I shoved it aside, the same way I had tried to shove aside the memories of other abnormal incidents from my past in Watertown. I told myself none of it had been real.

Was it all in my head, like some sort of magician's trick? And yet a nagging voice persisted: what about Georgie's death? I'd seen the silhouette of the shooter who killed him, and the angry girl this morning confirmed we'd seen the same thing. Even the rocks thrown at Noah's windshield by Georgie's friends helped prove it. I examined all the bits and pieces that refused to fit together, believing if I could only figure out the "why" of it all, then I'd understand everything else.

With weary resignation, I finally let the water out of

the tub. I toweled off and scrounged another of Noah's T-shirts to sleep in, wishing for the tenth time that I had my luggage. Outside, the wind picked up, sighing softly against the house and whispering at the windows. More relaxed, I turned off the light, climbed in bed, and fell into a deep sleep.

The next thing I remember was being inside a tangled dream. There were two images familiar to me. One was an old woman, the other a scary man in a dark room. I had dreamed about the woman for a few years but about the guy only recently.

In my dream the woman was very old, her skin thin and clear as vellum. Wisps of white hair lay on her forehead and temples, and she wore a silver cross against a purple blouse. As we stood looking at each other, a deep ache filled me and yet instinctively I knew she wasn't the cause of it. Maybe she was only the witness.

Her fingers were bent and veins lined the back of her hands. She gently reached out, touching me, first at my temple and then at my heart. Although she said something I knew was really important, the dream didn't let me understand her words. Before I could puzzle them out, she faded into a murky fog and I found myself pulled into a small dark room.

I was reclining on what felt like a dentist's chair as a heavyset man approached me. There was a glaring light behind him that outlined his buzzed head, but his features were in shadow. He held up something sharp. "Don't be nervous." His voice was surprisingly gentle. "This won't hurt too much."

It was then that I heard Jack's voice. "Jocelyn, wake up."

I opened my eyes and lay in the dark, trying to calm myself. Jack's voice faded back into the dream, though for a few seconds it had seemed real, which only added to my confusion.

I stared up at the dim ceiling and tried to calm my nerves. Listening to the low moan of the wind, I wondered if Noah was back yet. The house was quiet, so I guessed he was still gone. As the last of the dream began to fade and I started to relax, a sound distracted me—a faint creak as if someone was in the room with me and had just shifted his weight from one foot to the other. Startled, my eyes searched the blackness in the corners.

Shadows climbed and scurried across the wall: headlights. As I lay there my nerves stayed taut, refusing to accept that my anxiety was just a remnant of the dream. A slight movement caught my attention, and I sucked in a startled breath before realizing it was just the curtains. They were stirring slightly in the breeze. But the window hadn't been open!

I threw back the covers and lunged for the door. A dark form flew at me from the shadows and slammed me back onto the bed. I struck at him but a blow from his fist made my head reel, and within seconds he was pressing me beneath his full weight. One hand cruelly twisted my hair and pinned my head to the mattress, the other squeezed my throat in a painful grip.

His shadowed face was directly above mine. As his fingers tightened on my already bruised throat, his voice snarled, "Tell . . . me . . . where . . . it . . . is!"

fifteen

GETTING CLOSE

He twisted my hair with his fist, and my scalp was in agony. The fingers and thumb of his other hand dug into the sides of my throat as he put increasing pressure on my Adam's apple. Frantically I clawed at his arms and hands, but he continued to choke me. He seemed some kind of psycho phantom in a hooded sweatshirt, with oily hair hanging in his face.

"Tell me where it is!"

When he eased up enough for me to pull in a breath so I could answer, I let out a hoarse scream. He cut it off mid-screech.

A couple of seconds later a fist hammered on the bedroom door and Noah shouted. The guy squeezed tighter, cursing me with such anger that his spit hit my face. In a panicked flash I knew he was going to kill me before Noah could get through the door, but this thought was swept away by a frightening sensation. I felt his hand getting hot. It scorched my neck as if an electric current flowed between us. He snarled like a demon werewolf. Then, just as Noah kicked the door in, he leaped off the bed and dove through the open window.

Noah stumbled inside. After a quick check to see if I was okay, he headed out the window. I listened to footsteps running down the driveway. On trembling legs, I made it over to the window. An engine roared to life. Shoving the curtain aside, I peered out at the dark street. There was the screech of tires and a car, with no headlights on, drove dead center at Noah. He jumped out of the way. The car zoomed past and disappeared down the road.

I left the bedroom, more stable on my feet by then, and met Noah at the front door. He came in and locked it; he was out of breath.

"That car almost hit you!"

"Yeah. But it didn't." He looked at me and then his expression grew anxious. "You're hurt."

"No, I'm okay." My voice was hoarse, and because of his worried gaze I walked to the nearby mirror. He flipped on a lamp and I caught my breath. The flesh on my throat was a mess—charred and peeling.

Noah took me by the arm and led me to the couch. He hurried to the kitchen. I heard water running. A few seconds later he came back with a wet towel that he carefully placed on my throat. The cold was soothing. "Rest for a minute," he said, heading back to my room.

I heard the window close and then saw him checking

other rooms. After he'd secured the house he came and sat beside me. "Who was that, Jocelyn?"

"I don't know, but this is twice someone tried to choke me. It's getting really old. You know nothing scares me more than that."

He looked uncomfortable. "I'm sorry about what I did to you in the garage. I'd been on edge ever since quitting work. When I figured out someone was hiding in the back of my car, I thought Zachary Saulto was having me followed. I was furious."

It became clear Noah was more concerned about what ISI might be doing than he had let on. He added, "Of course, I had no idea it was you. Jack never e-mailed me a current photo of you, even though I asked."

I liked the fact that he'd asked Jack for a picture of me. Why was my stupid brother so overprotective? It wouldn't have hurt him to send Noah my senior picture.

He stood, went to the windows, and checked the locks. "No one should've been able to get in. The doors were bolted. So were the windows. I'd just come inside when I heard you scream."

"That guy kept saying the same thing over and over: 'Tell me where it is.' Tell him where what is, Noah? What did he want?"

The frightened sound of my voice made me feel ashamed, but I couldn't help it. Something horrible was happening all around me, and the more I tried to figure it out, the more puzzling it became.

"Did you see his face?"

I shivered, rubbing my arms, my head resting against the back of the couch. My poor scalp was still aching, and I wondered how much hair the attacker had pulled out. "No, it was too dark."

Noah went and got a fleece throw, covering me.

"Thank you."

He sat beside me again. "Any chance it was Zachary Saulto?"

"No. This guy wasn't bald. He had longer hair. That's all I noticed, except he had garlic breath. Not really helpful, is it?"

Noah reached for the damp towel. "Let me take a look at this. Does it hurt?"

"A little. Not as much as it should, I guess." I didn't add that this scared me even more, since I knew lack of pain from a burn meant it was serious.

Using the corner of the damp towel, Noah carefully wiped my throat. His fingers pulled away thin, charred pieces of skin and he leaned in, his face close to mine. I studied him. Noah had grown into the lean features that once made him seem awkward. Now he had a sharp-edged look that was compelling, especially with the dark stubble on his chin and jaw. The boy I'd known hadn't even needed to shave. Though I'd secretly been in love with him back then, he had now become far more mature and masculine than I ever could have imagined.

Sitting on his couch that way, with his fingers gently touching my neck, was strangely sensual—except for the nasty little reminder of how a couple of days ago those same fingers had choked me worse than the scary guy tonight. Just then I didn't want to think about that, instead focusing on his brown eyes. For a couple of seconds I even fantasized about him pulling me into his arms and holding me the way I'd always dreamed. What would it be like to press my mouth against his? Would he be shocked if I kissed him?

His eyes met mine and I blinked, wondering if he'd read my stupid girly thoughts. I focused on his grim expression and all the fantasy stuff vanished right out of my head. "Is it bad?"

"Not for you. Jocelyn, this charred skin isn't yours. It's his."

"What?"

I stood and hurried back to the mirror. He followed. Gazing at my reflection I saw that my throat was red, like it was sunburned, but only in the outlined shape of a large hand. I turned to stare at Noah. My voice came out a whisper. "What's going on?"

He gave a slow shake of his head. "I've got no answers. Come sit back down. You're really pale, and I don't want you passing out."

He guided me to the couch and I slipped beneath the blanket, pulling my legs up under me. Noah went into his bathroom, then came back and sat beside me on the couch. He unscrewed the cap on a tube of burn ointment. "Lean your head back."

I did, this time staring up at the circles of muted yellow lamplight on the ceiling. He carefully applied the salve to the red area. It was cold, letting me mentally outline the hand that had felt so hot on my skin.

"There." He put the cap back on the jar. "You'll be okay."

I sat up. "Will I, Noah? All these years I've worked so hard to convince myself that the crazy stuff at Seale House was nothing. Maybe just my overactive imagination. I grew up and started living in the real world where logic rules everything. Logic sets boundaries, and I like that. But now it's like I'm twelve years old again and have no control in my life. Things are happening that I can't explain."

I grabbed my sleeve, yanked it up, and showed him the bite mark. "Courtesy of the Seale House cellar."

Noah peered at it with a concerned expression.

I said, "Tell me something. Do you think there's a chance Corner Boy is still alive?"

"No. How could he be?"

"I don't know. But it makes me wonder if whoever attacked me in the cellar was the same guy who came here tonight."

Noah said nothing at first, only stared at the bite mark. "Why didn't you show that to me before now?"

I shrugged, pushing my sleeve back down.

"Jocey, it seems like that guy got burned worse than you. Is there any way you might have sent that heat at him to protect yourself?"

"You mean like superpowers or something? That'd be nice. Think I'll develop x-ray vision next?"

"Okay, so it was a dumb question. I guess if you could do that kind of thing, you would've done it to me in the garage."

"Considering how weird this all is, it's not that stupid to ask. But in my life before and after Seale House, I've never seen stuff like this. So how could it be me?"

Pausing, I thought over the strange dream I'd had before being attacked. Noah must have noticed something in my expression. "What is it?"

"Probably nothing . . . except that right before that guy attacked me, I heard Jack's voice. He told me to wake up."

"You can't really believe Jack came to you in a dream."

"It's not as lame as your superpower theory, is it?"

"Guess not."

"Is there any chance tonight's visitor was one of the kids who rocked your windshield?"

He shook his head. "I just identified them at the police station. They'll be having a little vacation downtown until their parents bail them out."

"Then I'm running out of ideas. Why did that guy keep asking where 'it' was? I don't have any idea what 'it' is."

"There are a lot of lunatics in this world."

I sighed and closed my eyes. "Yeah, and I've already met my quota. Besides, this isn't just one more random weird thing. I think it's all tied together."

"Me too."

I opened my eyes to study his concerned face. We sat together, listening to the ticking clock, the gentle creaks as the house settled, and the wind anxiously tapping its fingernails against the panes.

"Noah, I'm scared."

"Then maybe you should forget about the Jason December clues and go home."

"How can I? Abandoning Jack isn't an option."

"He wouldn't want you to be in danger."

"No, but what happened tonight proves I need to find him. The fact that things are getting scary means we're getting close."

sixteen

CATCHING UP

Noah retrieved my pillow and gave me an extra blanket so I could sleep on the couch—both of us were reluctant for me to spend the rest of the night in the other room. Despite my protests he also sacked out on the nearby recliner. Except for a lamp in the corner, the rest of the lights in the living room were off. It was dark enough to sleep but light enough to still see.

More than once the frightening image of the intruder invaded my sleep and jerked me awake. Each time I glanced over at Noah, asleep in the recliner, and felt a little calmer. He rested beneath a crazy quilt sewn in shades of brown and faded gold. I remembered it from Seale House, and when he first pulled it out I was a bit surprised that he'd somehow gotten hold of it.

Eventually, after many starts and stops, exhaustion forced me to sleep. Sometime later Noah touched my face and said my name, waking me. His blurry image was leaning over me, and as I blinked and looked up at him, he asked if I was all right. He brushed my cheek and there was wetness on the back of his fingers. "You're crying."

"I don't know why." I wiped the tears from my face, embarrassed. Although I'd been in a deep, dreamless sleep, a heavy sense of sadness still lingered over me. I felt vulnerable that he'd seen it, but Noah's expression was only concerned.

Sitting up, I looked at the clock next to the mirror. It was nearly four. "I didn't mean to wake you."

"You didn't. I've been up."

I rubbed my neck, slowly moved my head to the side, and then winced.

"What's the matter?"

"That guy pulled my hair so hard he hurt my neck."

Noah sat down next to me. "Let me give it a try." His fingers began to slowly massage the painful kinks.

"Have you been awake long?"

"A while, yes. It's the early morning hours like this, when I can't sleep, that I miss Jack the most."

"I miss him all the time." I said it so softly I wasn't sure he heard me.

"Being around you sure brings up a lot of memories from when the three of us were kids."

The tension in my neck began to ease. I let out a slow breath, now wide awake even though it was still dark outside. "Yeah, I know. It's strange the way life takes its twists and turns. Think it was fate that brought the three of us together?"

"Chance, maybe. I don't believe in fate."

His thumbs moved in circles on the knots, slowly releasing the pain. His touch did more to me than he knew, and I couldn't help but respond to the warmth of his hands. "Guess you're right. It wasn't destiny that threw us into the foster care program. Just worthless parents who never should've been allowed to bring their babies home from the hospital."

Noah chuckled, but the sound was mirthless. "You got that right. From what Jack was telling me about your mother, I'm kind of surprised she didn't abandon you at the first chance."

"There were probably times she wanted to. But I think she was more afraid of living without Jack than being stuck with us."

"What do you mean?"

"Melody's life was a cycle of dating, mating, and breaking up. All her relationships were doomed because she was so wacked. Once the guys she got with saw what was hiding under her pretty looks, it scared them off. Even the decent ones couldn't make it last. She dragged us with her on that never-ending quest for men because she was dependent on Jack. He helped guide her through depression about her unhappy childhood."

"I don't have sympathy for people who blame their lousy behavior on what happened when they were kids."

"Me either. But Melody did have a hideous childhood. She grew up in poverty and abuse on a dirt farm in Nebraska."

I didn't say anything else. Melody's escape had come when she was fifteen and met her cousin's friend, Calvert. He was fresh out of jail, only a few years older than she was, and involved in a lot of bad stuff. They ended up running away together, and Melody often talked about how he'd been the one true love of her life. He eventually abandoned her at a truck stop and took off with a woman in a red convertible. It broke her heart. That happened three years before we were born, and though she never talked to us about our own father, the relationship with Calvert was the one Melody could never let go of. She would retell the story when depression swept her down to its darkest place, and Jack was the only one who knew how to talk her out of it.

These days, whenever I thought about my mother, which was almost never, there'd always be this little knot of loathing wrapped up in relief that she was dead and forever out of my life.

"One time I asked Jack why you were so touchy about swearing," Noah said. "He told me it was because of all your mother's low-life boyfriends. You hated their bad language. That true?"

"Yes. I despised the brainless jerks Melody always fell for. I despised her, too, and everything she did. My main goal in life was to make sure I never ended up like her."

"So you're still a virgin?"

I moved away from his hands. "Thanks. My neck is okay now."

He raised his eyebrows. "I didn't mean it as an insult."

"I'm a virgin, yes, though I'm not sure why I'm supposed to be ashamed of that. Those slobs who dated my mother only cared about one thing. After I grew up and saw the same pathetic reaction from guys, it was a big turnoff."

"Not all of us are like that."

"Not all, no. I've dated a few nice boys. Though if things got serious, I ended it. I didn't want to involve some poor guy in all the stuff I was carrying around."

"Excess baggage, you mean?"

"More like three suitcases, a couple of steamer trunks, and a carry-on."

He smiled when I said that.

"What about you, Noah? It's not like you have anyone, either. You live here by yourself. You don't even own a pet."

"I've had a few girlfriends, but it never lasted. I get bored."

"That's the problem with trying to fit into normal society, isn't it? After you've walked a crazy high-wire like the one we were on, the rest of the world with its safety net seems so unexciting. I don't like pretending I'm the same as everyone else. And I hate lying about my past to whatever guy I start liking."

"Why would you do that?"

"I'm ashamed, of course. Admitting my mother was the world's biggest tramp and that I never knew my dad is humiliating. It wouldn't exactly inspire any of the boys at my high school to ask me on a second date."

"Then you're dating the wrong kind of guys, Jocey. Your mother's choices don't have anything to do with who you really are. Do you despise me because my mother was a cold-hearted drug addict knocked up by her dealer?"

"No, of course not."

"Was it Angry Beth's fault her older brothers molested her? Or Dixon's, because his mother left him alone in a filthy apartment for days?"

An image of Beth slipping a knife under her pillow came to mind, and for the first time it seemed more sad than warped. Then there was little Dixon who followed me around, clinging to anyone who would be kind to him. How many nights had he sat on my lap while I read him his favorite story? I'd nearly forgotten that ragged old book, *The Gingham Dog and the Calico Cat*. He'd begged me to read it to him all the time. We'd done that for so many nights he'd ended up memorizing the words. The sad feelings returned and I pulled the blanket closer.

"Noah, how'd you learn that stuff about them?"

"I was the only one Hazel trusted to clean her office, remember? When I was in there I looked at the files. Just so I'd know what to watch for."

"Did you look at mine and Jack's?"

"No. After that first night in the cellar, when we became friends, it didn't seem right. We'd built a little trust then.

You two listened to my vampire stories, and Jack talked about his Artemis Fowl books. Besides, I could see you didn't have any weird behaviors that might be dangerous."

"Always the caretaker, weren't you?"

"Someone had to be, in that place."

He was right. We'd lived in a world that spun on an alternate axis, where everyone's life was off-balance and nothing was predictable. During the last few years I'd tried to forget what it had been like when life took a group of frightened children through the looking glass, into a world of lunacy. Noah had been our strength.

"'The time has come to talk of many things,'" I murmured. "'Of shoes and ships and sealing-wax, of cabbages and kings.'"

"'And why the sea is boiling hot and whether pigs have wings,'" he finished with a smile in his voice.

I sat listening to the quiet, comfortable in the intimacy of the early morning hours and understanding why it was easier to share thoughts now than in the daylight.

Noah stretched and asked, "Are you hungry?"

Surprisingly, I was. I nodded and he said, "How about I fix us an early breakfast?"

After taking more pain medication, I went to the kitchen and helped him. He fried ham and made pancakes. While we were eating, the glow of early dawn slowly began to lighten the windows. I studied the pearly, overcast sky.

"You don't eat enough," Noah said when I turned down a second pancake.

"It's so early. I never eat breakfast until after nine. Let's just get ready so we can be at the library when it opens, okay?"

"Okay," he agreed around a mouthful of ham, then plopped another pancake on my plate. "All I'm saying is that you could use an extra five pounds."

"Stop mothering me. It's creepy."

"Fine! I'm going outside to grab yesterday's mail."

He left the kitchen and I poured syrup on the pancake, taking a big bite. Then I heard Noah call my name. I found him standing by the open front door, staring out at the driveway. Leaning around his shoulder to see what he was looking at, I gasped.

"Is that your car?" he asked.

Seventeen

ANOTHER CLUE

I stared at my tan Civic. The car sat innocently in the driveway, and I could hardly believe it. I looked around the quiet neighborhood. It was deserted except for an elderly man dragging a garbage can out to the curb. We walked over to my car. Peering through the window, I saw my backpack on the floor of the passenger side. My makeup bag and netbook were still on the backseat where I'd left them three days ago.

I took the key out of my jeans pocket and headed for the trunk. Noah held out his hand. "Let me do that."

"Why?"

"We don't know what's in there, do we?"

Something grisly inside my trunk came to mind. Still, no way I'd let him think I was chicken. I ignored his upturned palm and shoved the key in the trunk lock, opening it. There was nothing in there but my suitcase. Noah lifted it out while I grabbed my stuff from inside the car. We went into his house and he locked the door. I looked through my backpack; nothing had been stolen.

I checked my cell phone. There were several texts and a photo from the friends who had asked me to come camping with them. They were standing together, making I-love-you and rocker hands.

There was also a voice message from my foster mom, Marilyn, checking to see how I was doing. I shot her a quick text saying I'd hiked to a place that got reception, but I'd probably be out of touch for the rest of the time. Not to worry, I was okay. Lying to her stank, but if I ended up bringing Jack home, I knew all would be forgiven.

Noah asked if anything was missing from my suitcase. I quickly searched through it.

"Not that I can tell. And everything's still in my wallet, including credit cards and cash. That doesn't make sense. Why would someone steal my car but not take anything?"

"And why did someone bring it here last night?"

"Was it a threat, or just an anonymous good deed?"

"I don't think someone doing a good deed would've left it without knocking on the door, because it's upsetting not to know how it got here. So whoever brought it back wants you to know they're on your trail. Which means it's not safe to stay here anymore. Especially after you were attacked. If you want to change your clothes, do it now. I'm going to pack a few things. Then we need to get out of here. You've got ten minutes."

"Okay." I watched Noah, amazed that he wasn't even a little upset. If anything, his mood seemed lighter, like this was exciting instead of dangerous.

I took my suitcase to the bathroom. Though I was relieved to have my stuff back, everything now seemed suspect. I wondered if the thief had gone through my clothes. He or she probably had, even though it all still looked the same. It felt like I was being forced to play a game that I didn't want to. Then I reminded myself it had been my choice to come here in the first place. I could have tossed the Jason December letter and called it a cruel joke, but I hadn't. Driving up here may have opened the door to all sorts of weirdness, but if I really loved Jack and wanted to find him, then I needed to be tough.

After my attitude adjustment I changed into clean clothes, head to toe. Since the weather was even cooler and the sky overcast again, I pulled on a dark gray long-sleeved shirt and my favorite jeans. I ran a brush through my hair, wincing at the pain, and then quickly put on some makeup. The scrapes on my face had practically disappeared by the time I was done, and my eyes stood out with the smoky shadow and pencil I'd applied. Feeling more like myself I smiled, until I saw the red marks on my throat. The outline of my attacker's hand was still visible and it bothered me. Digging through my suitcase, I pulled out a long Chinese scarf with streaks of plum and green, and beads on the ends. I wrapped it around my neck a couple of times until it hid the burn.

I finished packing everything together and headed to the living room, where Noah was busy putting stuff in a duffel bag. He looked up and stopped what he was doing, studying me. I felt a little uncertain under his stare. "Is something wrong?"

"Don't leave anything behind that you might need. I'm not sure when we'll make it back here again."

"That sounds serious."

"It is." He wore a cheerful expression in contrast to the words.

We made sure the house was locked, and after a quick discussion about which car to take, I gave in. We put our bags and his laptop in the backseat of his Jeep. Noah smiled at my obvious worry. "Just think of this as an adventure."

We stood together in his garage for a few seconds, almost on the same spot where I thought he was going to choke me to death. I was still afraid, but this time for different reasons. He tucked a piece of stray hair behind my ear. "Let's go."

We climbed in his Jeep. He turned the ignition over and pressed the garage door opener. The mental image of bullets flying in through the back windshield came to mind and I scrunched down in the seat.

He peered over his shoulder as we backed out. "You know, if someone was going to shoot you, they had plenty of time when you were standing in the driveway looking at your car."

Embarrassed, I sat up and didn't say anything as we drove out of the subdivision and onto the main road leading back into town. A couple of times I turned around and looked behind us but didn't see another car.

Noah flipped on the radio. Music from a quirky English group came through the speakers. He hummed along.

"What's going on?" I finally asked. When he raised a questioning eyebrow I added, "Where's the angry Noah who bites my head off? You're actually happy."

He chuckled, though the sound was tinged with irony. "So I'm feeling okay with all this. Is that a problem?"

"It's as if you've been taken over by aliens."

"Look, Jocey, the bond between you, Jack, and me was always foursquare. So here's the truth. In light of the two pieces of solid evidence, I'm just very relieved to know you're not crazy. Don't look at me like that. What would you think if you were in my place?"

"I'd believe whatever you told me. We always believed each other."

"That was years ago. Since we met up again, you've told me some crazy stuff. I had this suspicion you were making it up and maybe even planted that clue in Seale House yourself. But last night that guy attacked you. And your car showed up in my driveway this morning. Proof you were telling it like it is."

"So you're on my side now?"

He looked at me for several long seconds. "I've always been on your side. And just knowing Jack is probably still alive is huge. If he faked his death, he did it because he didn't have a choice."

"That's what I've been telling you."

On the way back into Watertown, we passed the Urban Mission with its huge mural painted along one wall. There were colorful swirls and abstract faces floating across a background of deep reddish pink. I remembered it from the last time I was here.

Instead of heading straight to the library, Noah took several meandering turns, his eyes frequently checking the rearview mirror. After another ten minutes we pulled into the parking lot of the library. We headed through the doors and he turned back, his eyes scanning the handful of people coming in after us. He seemed satisfied and went to the information desk while I walked over to a directory. A cute guy wearing rimless glasses and a library name tag came up to me. He smiled and offered to help find what I was looking for. Noah came back and chased him off with a mean scowl.

"Stop playing Dracula," I said.

"Then don't talk to strangers."

I bit back an annoyed reply as we took the elevator upstairs. I pulled the piece of paper out of my pocket that had the book's file number and felt a renewed sense of excitement. We found the programming section and Noah checked the numbers. He took a thick book off the shelf and we looked at the cover: *Revision Control Reference* by Greg Hall.

"This way." He guided me to an empty table behind several tall shelves where we could have some privacy.

We sat down and he slid the book over to me. "Flip through the pages."

I did, finding a business card sandwiched close to the spine. "This must be it."

I closed the book as Noah and I read the small card together. There were five groups of letters printed all in capitals: U TREC ALERT LEGAL RYLA

"Which means what?" he asked.

"An attorney named Ryla? Hang on while I grab a phone book."

It took me just a minute to get one from a librarian and come back to the table where Noah sat studying the card.

"You really think it's a lawyer?"

"No, of course not, but when it comes to deciphering Jack's codes the first rule has always been to pyramid it. Start with the broadest guess and narrow it down. This way we won't miss something. Make yourself useful and try to anagram those letters, will you?"

Noah took the pen and paper I handed him. "Why couldn't he just leave us a note that said 'meet me at the bus depot' or something?"

"I'd never follow a note like that, because it wouldn't be from Jack." I glared at the useless Yellow Pages. "Under the listing for attorneys there's only a Rylund but no Ryla. Think it might be a first name?"

"Probably not. If he wanted 'U' to 'TREK' your way to a lawyer, wouldn't he have spelled it with a 'k' not T-R-E-C?"

"Okay, then look at it backward. What's CERT? Is it short for 'certain' or you have bad breath, pass me a Certs mint?"

Noah chuckled as I grabbed a nearby dictionary and tried looking up CERT and RYLA but found nothing. He tapped me on the shoulder and I looked up to see he was peering so closely at the card that it was only a few inches from his face. At last he handed it to me. "Take a look at the decorative border."

Turning the card to the light, I brought it close to my face the way he had and squinted at the pale-gray edging that was barely visible. If I held it just right I could see the border was a line of tiny symbols:

$$\male + \male - \female : + \female - \male - \male + \male - \female : + \female - \male - \male + \male - \female : + \female - \male - \male + \male - \female$$

"A male and female equation," Noah said.

I lowered the card and reached for the pen and paper, copying it down. "It's repeated. He used the colon to separate the main five symbols, the way he did on the lantern clues that one time, remember? Okay, so what do we have when we add a female, subtract two males, add a male, and subtract a female?"

"Hollywood relationships?"

I looked up at him and laughed in surprise. "Noah, you made a joke."

"It happens once in a while."

It was so rare I wanted to write down the date to remember it. However, deciding not to say anything that might set our touchy relationship on edge, I just smiled and turned back to the equation. "There are lots of possibilities. How do we know what it means?"

"Come on, Jocelyn, you're the one who was always inside Jack's head. You should know what he meant. Is he talking about relationships here? Are some of the people in that equation you, me, and him? If so, who are the other two? And is RYLA a woman's name?"

"No, I don't think so. To Jack, clues were about clues. He would use the border equation to tell us how to solve the letter clues."

Noah studied the symbols and then grinned with pleasure. "Think about the field trip. Why did we get to go?"

"Because of French class with Mr. Montclaude."

"Yes. And remember what he stressed all the time? Masculine and feminine articles, because the nouns are gender specific. French basics of 'le' and 'la' are what I'm guessing. Translate those male/female symbols on the paper."

I did as he suggested and ended up with: +la, −le, −le, +le, −la. Taking the pen from me, he added the first 'la' in front of U TREC and put it all together.

"Lautrec, I'm guessing."

"What's that?"

"It's a who, not a what. Toulouse-Lautrec, the painter."

"Good thing you always liked studying art in school." I'd never understood his interest in painters.

"Now, let's subtract 'le' from 'alert' and we have . . ."

"Art!" My excitement began to grow. "Take away 'le' from 'legal' and we have 'gal,' then add the 'le' for 'g-a-l-l-e' . . ."

"Gallery," Noah finished. "Minus the 'la' from the end of RYLA and with the other letters it becomes gallery."

"Lautrec Art Gallery."

"I've seen that before. I think it's over by the Paddock Arcade."

I let out a slow breath and smiled at Noah. He smiled back with a very pleased expression. It was a special moment, reminding me again of that remarkable day in the pine tree when we solved our first Jason December letter. "So it's not far then?"

"No. And at least he's not trying to send us back to Ottawa."

As we drove, my anticipation increased. "Have you been inside the Lautrec Gallery?"

He shook his head. "And I can't figure out why he's sending us there. It wasn't even around when we were kids."

The wind picked up, scuttling wool-gray clouds across the sky and churning the leaves on the trees. It took a couple of passes down Holcomb Street before we found it. The small gallery was a converted house of tan brick with dark-green awnings. Paintings in the windows were elegantly mounted on cloth-draped easels. Noah parked and we made our way across the street. A bell jangled when we opened the door and entered. I smoothed my hair with my fingers.

Looking around, I saw that the gallery had an old-world look. The dark wood floor gleamed, and there were art pieces and antiques everywhere. A tiered display was topped with brass sculptures, and paintings closely covered walls that were papered in watered silk. Moving deeper inside the shop we heard someone say, "I'll see who it is."

A boy came hurrying through an arched doorway, a cluster of paintbrushes in his hand. He wore a gray shirt the same color as his eyes, and his hair fell in loose gold curls. He looked young, only about nine, though I knew he was twelve. I remembered what a pretty child he had been, and now—despite the awkward preteen years—he was still beautiful. Dixon stopped where he stood, a surprised smile spreading across his face.

eighteen

DIXON

Cold rain during the last week of May seemed a mean trick. With the promise of summer so close and school getting out soon, we should have been able to wear shorts and flip-flops. But not here, in upstate New York, where cold seeped its way down from Canada. I couldn't wait to be free of the stifling classrooms, the harassment from snotty girls, and teachers who gave out boring worksheets.

I was on the bottom bunk doing my math homework. Across the room Beth sat on her bed, alternately reading a book and sending sly glances at me. Every so often her hand slid under her pillow, caressing the knife I knew was hidden there. I ignored her and worked on my fractions.

I sensed someone standing nearby and looked up to see Dixon staring at me. His eyes were brimming with wetness, which he blinked hard to hold back. Tears, he knew, only annoyed Hazel Frey, and in the cruel pecking order of foster care they were also a sign of weakness. During Dixon's few months at Seale House he'd learned not to let the other children see him cry, but seeing sympathy in my eyes, it was hard for him to keep back the tears.

"What's the matter?"

He held out a bruised finger that had deep teeth marks on it. His hand was small and the imprints large, so I knew it hadn't been done by one of the little kids.

"Who bit you?"

"The n-new boy," he whispered, stuttering.

"Do you mean the one who sits in the corner?"

Dixon nodded.

I got off the bed and headed down the hall to the boys' room. Conner was sitting in the far corner, his knees hugged to his chest, his eyes scanning the others in the room. Jack and Noah sat on the top bunk, making notes from their programming books, while Georgie and Spence were building a tower with Legos. I walked up to Conner but he ignored me and picked at a scab on his knee. I'd overheard the social worker tell Hazel he was thirteen, which was hard to believe. A lifetime of hunger and abuse had stunted his growth, and he was the size of a ten-year-old.

"If Dixon did something to bother you," I said in a strong voice, crouching down, "then tell him to leave you alone. In this house we don't hurt each other. And we especially don't touch the little kids."

Though he refused to make eye contact, I wasn't willing to move until he responded. He looked dirty even though the social worker had forced him to take a bath and put on clean clothes before coming to Seale House. There were dark shadows under his eyes and his cheeks were sunken. Bland, thin strands of hair lay limply on his brow, and there were bruises on his scrawny arms and shins. I began to feel sorry for him. He looked so pathetic sitting in the corner, his face an unmoving mask.

I didn't ask him "why did you bite?" since "why" was a word that shouldn't be used with foster kids. "Why" brought up a bucket-load of garbage from the past that most of them didn't want to share and the rest of us didn't want to hear. Simple commands were best. "Don't bite," I stressed again, my voice kinder this time.

I stood and started to turn away when Conner flew from his crouched position and latched on to me, his teeth sinking deep into my upper arm. With a yelp I staggered back, dragging him with me. I slugged him hard on the side of the head and the impact broke his hold. Pain shot up my arm but there was barely time for disbelief to register because he slammed into me, this time knocking me down. He clawed at me, his teeth snapping in my face. I managed to hold him back, but although I was taller than him, he had the wiry strength of a lunatic.

Suddenly he was jerked away and Jack slugged him on the jaw. It didn't seem to faze Conner, who unleashed a flurry of kicking and scratching so wild it took both Jack and Noah to control him. It wasn't until Noah had his arm around Conner's neck in a chokehold that the boy finally stopped fighting.

"We don't act like that around here." Noah tightened his grip. "Understand?"

Conner looked at us with bulging eyes before giving us a sullen nod.

"Okay, let him go," Jack said.

Conner scuttled back to the corner as the three of us walked over and stood in a semicircle looking down at him.

Noah stared at Conner. "If you don't like it here, then run away."

The boy laughed, the sound reminding me of the screech of a howler monkey I'd once heard at a zoo. "Changing my plans now!" His high voice was creepier than if he'd talked in Darth Vader's low rasp. "Was gonna get out of here tonight, but now gonna stay. Stay until I get back at you!"

He looked up at me, his expression blank. I expected to see hatred or fear but there was nothing there, as if his face were a plaster mask covering what really lay beneath. It was downright spooky, and worry began coiling inside me.

"Better watch out for your little dog too," he said in his girlish voice, his eyes moving past me.

I turned and saw Dixon standing in the doorway, his eyes wide with fear. I left the room and guided him away from the door. Jack and Noah followed. "Stay away from him," I said to Dixon as we stood together in the hall. He quickly nodded.

I looked down at my arm. Conner's teeth had bruised and partially torn my flesh. The others anxiously studied the bite mark, too.

"That one is crazy," Jack said.

"The stinking little Erv shouldn't even be here," Noah said, calling Conner by the private slang we often used.

"Maybe we should talk to Hazel."

"She won't listen. He's another eight hundred bucks a month."

"And now that she's sucking more coke up her nose, she needs every dollar she can get," I added.

"Shh!" Noah glanced down the hallway to make sure no one else was around and then looked at Dixon.

The little boy slid his hand inside mine as Jack said, "Noah and I will just have to keep an eye on Corner Boy. We're bigger than he is, and there're two of us. Three when you're around, Jocey."

Noah nodded. His dark expression showed he was resigned to the task. Dixon moved closer to me and I slipped my arm around his thin shoulders.

That night at the dinner table Conner sat down on the end of the bench, sliding his plate close to him. He began shoveling food in his mouth with his hand. Annoyed, Hazel demanded he use his fork. The boy grudgingly did so until she looked away, when he would hold the idle fork in his right hand and grab food with his left. Other than that, he seemed subdued enough. I wondered if being forced to spend last night down in the cellar, in Hazel's tradition, was enough to keep his behavior under control.

After dinner and dishes, when the light was growing soft in the rainy twilight, Dixon sought me out where I was reading, a shy expression on his face. He handed me a piece of paper with a drawing on it. There was a girl riding a unicorn, flying past stars and the moon. "That's you."

Whenever he showed me his artwork I was always surprised that a little boy could draw like that. I smiled. "It's really nice. One of the best you've done. Though I think this girl is too pretty to be me."

"No, that's you."

He was also holding his ragged book, and I lifted him onto my lap. "You start first, and I'll help you with the words you don't know yet."

My chin rested against the softness of his curly hair as he opened to the first page and started reciting the memorized words. " 'The gingham dog and the calico cat, side by side on the table sat. 'Twas half past twelve . . .'"

I glanced up from the ancient book's faded picture as Conner slowly passed by the door. His eyes washed over us like oil sliding across the surface of water.

✦ ✦ ✦

"Noah?" Dixon came closer.

"Hi. It's been a long time. What are you doing here?"

The boy smiled. "I live upstairs with my mother. This is her shop." He turned to me and his smile faltered. Peering up into my eyes, he slowly exhaled my name. "Jocey?"

For a couple of seconds I held my breath. Would he be mad at me, like Georgie? Finally I said, "You recognize me?"

Dixon ran forward and grabbed me in a hug around the waist. I was touched, and I laughed.

He let go and took a step back. "You're so grown up! But your blue eyes are just the same, the way I always drew them. Wow, Jocey, you turned out real pretty."

I smiled. "It's nice you think so. You've grown up, too, though I'd recognize you anywhere."

A woman came through the archway. "Dixon?" In those two syllables I could hear her uncertainty.

Noah and I turned to look at her. She had marble-shaped eyes in a narrow face, though stylish black hair and mascara helped offset her homely features.

"Mom," Dixon said. He set the paintbrushes on a table

and motioned her near. "I want you to meet my friends, Jocey and Noah. I knew them back at Seale House, before I came to live with you."

She glanced at us with a troubled expression, but Dixon didn't seem to notice. "Where do you go to school?" I asked, wanting to make it less uncomfortable.

"Right here. Mom homeschools me."

I glanced around the art store with its antiques, knowing it was a place other children would probably not be invited to come play. What was it like for Dixon, alone for hours with this older woman and not going to a regular school with other kids? Was she good to him? Her eyes were cautious as she studied us.

"Jocey was like a big sister to me," Dixon said. "She looked out for me."

Her face relaxed a little.

"Do you still draw pictures?" I asked.

He nodded with a look of shy pride. "Mom gives me art lessons."

She looked at him with fondness. "He has a lot of talent."

"I'm not surprised. I remember the unicorns you used to make, Dixon. You drew better at seven than I did at twelve. You must really like taking lessons."

He nodded again, the smile still on his face. Beneath it I caught a glimpse of the pain that had always been so much a part of him. "Hey," he said. "Where's Jack?"

Noah and I glanced at each other. "You haven't seen him? He didn't come here ahead of us?"

"No. Why would he do that?"

"Oh. Well, a little while ago he . . . disappeared. That's why Noah and I are here. He left us a few clues we've been following. We're trying to find him and thought he came to see you."

"Clues? Like the games you played at Seale House?"

"Yes, a lot like that. And one of them led us to this gallery. When I saw you, I kind of guessed he'd visited you before we got here."

"No. He hasn't, but I wish he would. I'd sure like to see him again."

Noah's eyes scanned the walls that were packed with artwork. "This is a nice gallery. Care if we look around?"

His mother followed Noah's gaze. "That's fine, though I need Dixon to help me with something."

She turned and walked away. Dixon followed. "I'll be right back," he said over his shoulder.

I looked at Noah. "So why were we supposed to come here? Just to see Dixon is still alive and okay? I mean, I'm really happy he is. But what is Jack doing?"

"I don't know. If you ask me, that's been the question from the beginning. It's his game now. At this point we can't do much else except play along. Let's look around and see if he left us a clue."

"Like what? I know nada about art, and even less about antiques."

"You don't need to. Just look for something that doesn't belong."

We started checking out the pieces we passed. There were lots of still-life paintings: bowls of fruit, flowers, that kind of thing. The rest were landscapes and portraits. There were also delicate tables, spindly chairs with satin seats, figurines, and other stuff I'd never waste money on. The more I wandered around in this confusing place, the more I wanted to slug Jack on the arm.

After several minutes Noah motioned to me. "What about this?"

I walked over to where he stood. An acrylic painting hung in a corner. It was a narrow abstract, about eighteen inches long, six inches wide, and hardly noticeable. A combination of splatters and swipes in muddy colors, it wasn't something I'd ever hang in my room.

"That's ugly. And the artist wants a hundred dollars for it! I could've painted that with a blindfold on."

"Exactly." Noah looked amused. He pointed to the initials in the bottom-right corner. "J. D."

"Jason December!"

He removed the painting and we both looked at the bare spot, then at the back of the frame. It had a cardboard backing sealed with tape, but nothing else. Noah carried it up to the counter just as Dixon's mother came through the archway. "Can I ask about this?"

She looked a little embarrassed. "That was a special request. It came in the mail a few days ago with a cashier's check for a hundred dollars. There was a note asking our gallery to hang it for a week. If it doesn't sell, I can take it down. I've been promised another check for the sale price."

I wondered why Jack was throwing around his savings like that.

Noah said, "I'm guessing artists don't normally pay you to hang their work."

"No," she admitted.

"But doing that would be a smart business move," I added in a supportive voice, wondering how many sales she managed to make in a month. Still, Dixon dressed nice enough. Digging my Visa card out of my wallet and handing it to her, I said, "We'll take it."

I was a little worried that I'd reached my limit on the card, but it went through and she handed me the receipt to sign.

Noah said, "Do you happen to have the mailer it came in, so we can check the postmark?"

"Sorry, that got thrown out."

The front door opened and another customer came in. It was an attractive guy with olive skin who looked about thirty. He wandered to the far side of the shop.

After I paid for the painting, Dixon's mother started to wrap it in brown paper but Noah stopped her. "Don't bother. We'll take it like that."

"Can we say good-bye to Dixon?" I asked.

She glanced at the arched doorway behind her. "I'm sorry. He had to run an errand for me."

I was disappointed, and she must have seen. She added,

"Can you understand? It took almost two years for his bad dreams to stop. So many nights he woke up screaming. I don't want it to start again."

"Sure," Noah said. "We understand."

I nodded in agreement, feeling sad for Dixon.

We walked away and she left the counter to talk to the other customer. He was one of those guys that practices being casual in his good looks. He was dressed in soft, loose-fitting slacks and a collarless cotton shirt. His brown hair, on the longer side, had gold highlights and was combed back from a face with strong features. The guy's stare followed me. Noticing his hand, I was startled to see a gauze pad on his palm.

We headed through the door, my spine stiff with tension as the wind snagged my scarf and lifted it. I turned to Noah. "That must be him, from last night!"

"I know." His free hand went to the small of my back, guiding me across the street.

He unlocked the Jeep and tossed the painting in the backseat. We heard our names being called and Dixon ran to us. "Are you leaving?"

"We have to," Noah said, his eyes on the gallery door.

"Oh." The boy's voice sounded unhappy.

It pulled me back in time to when he was little. "Are you going to be all right?"

He nodded. "My mom is kinda shy around people she doesn't know, but she's real good to me."

Dixon's mother came to the window, watching us with an anxious face. For most other kids, such a possessive mom would have made me concerned, but this was different. Because of all the neglect during his early years, Dixon was sort of an emotional black hole. No matter how much attention and affection was poured into him, I knew it would never be enough. So maybe that sort of smother-mother was what he needed.

"I'm happy for you, then."

Noah climbed in the driver's seat. "Bye, Dixon. It was good to see you again."

The boy took a step closer to me. "Jocey, before you take off I want to tell you something. I know everyone was mad at you that night about what happened. I wasn't. You did it to save me. After I left Seale House I ended up in a better foster home. That's how I met my new mom. She was their cousin and liked me right away. I came to live with her and now she's adopted me." There was a sort of pride in his voice I'd never heard before.

"That's great. I've wondered about you a lot, Dixon."

"Really? I worried when you ran away that night. I never got to see you again and thought it was my fault."

Noah opened my door from the inside and called my name. I glanced up. The long-haired guy had stepped outside the gallery and was walking to his car. "It wasn't your fault, and don't ever think that, okay? Promise?"

"Promise."

I gave him a hug and his thin arms went around my

waist. "Take care of yourself," I whispered, finally breaking away and slipping inside the Jeep.

I shut the door and Noah shifted into gear; we sped away. I kept my eyes on Dixon until he went back inside the shop.

nineteen

THE PAINTING

Noah treated the streets of Watertown like a racetrack, and I was surprised he didn't cause an accident or get pulled over by a cop.

I kept my eyes on the road. "So you saw the gauze pad on that guy's hand?"

"Yes. Have you seen him before, other than last night, I mean?"

I shook my head. "Why are we running away instead of confronting him? He didn't have a gun."

"Don't count on it. If Paul Gerard is armed we probably wouldn't see it."

"You know him?"

"Yes. And a face-off wouldn't be helpful. There's no way to make him tell us why he attacked you or what he wants. My black belt skills won't stand up against him."

"You have a black belt?"

"Martial arts. Remember Don Iverson, the detective? He got me into it, because he wanted to keep me from spending so much time on the computer. Jack didn't tell you I studied martial arts?"

"Sure, but I just didn't know you were that into it." I couldn't help but smile. "You became the black ninja after all."

Bracing myself as he ran a red light, I looked over at him. "Noah, slow down. You're making me nervous. So who's Paul Gerard?"

"He worked for ISI as a specialist."

"Is he a programmer?"

"No. He does other kinds of security. His job included giving orientations to new people the company hired. That's when I met him. Of course, all of that was before he quit."

"He quit too?"

"Left more than a month ago because ISI had a problem with him. But I don't know what. I think he might have embezzled money from them. Though if that's true, they kept news of it from getting out."

"Sure, since a security company wouldn't want their clients to know they can't protect their own assets. That could lose them a lot of business."

"Just one more reason I'm glad I bailed."

"But what does Paul Gerard want from me? What's the 'it' he kept asking about?"

"How would I know?"

I touched the scarf covering my throat. "Do you have any idea how he burned me?"

"No . . . except when we met he talked about the deep martial arts stuff that's way out there. I guess he even studied at a monastery in Nepal. Or said he did, anyway."

"Are you talking about like what happens in movies?"

"It might just be made up. But when he was here training me, I invited him to my dojo for a sparring session. He's very skilled. Even the owner of the dojo was impressed."

"Great. So I stand no chance if he comes after me."

"I think Gerard is trying to intimidate us. He wanted to make sure we saw him just now, to let me know who attacked you last night."

I stared at the road, feeling that old creeping depression as Noah drove past the city limits and headed in the direction of Wellesley Island State Park. Situated along the St. Lawrence River, and part of the Thousand Islands region, it was green and lush.

We turned in and traveled for several miles. After looking in the rearview mirror, Noah slowed and pulled onto a narrow roadway. He followed it through thick groves of trees to a picnic area, then turned the Jeep around, facing back the way we'd come. With the overcast sky it was too cold for visitors so there were no other cars. Noah turned off the ignition.

He grabbed the painting from the backseat and used a pocketknife to slice off the back. Taped to the canvas were three things: a small plastic bag holding five puzzle pieces, a narrow strip of red paper covered with letters, and a key.

EED	TH
CAU	
WAS	EDS
	STO
GW	OU
BE	E
HO	WE
	ER
RA	TY
AR	NIN
EW	EL
R	KH
SS	WHA
BRI	IX
FSH	HAZ
LIA	TIN
GRA	NOT
LE	OS
SO	OF
E	TS
AT	IS
TT	TW
OU	RES
TH	THA
HE	RY
NE	INK
TI	TA
*C	

We examined everything. The paper was the most interesting. It was about a half inch wide with groups of letters in blocked printing.

"There's more on the back," Noah pointed out.

I flipped it over, seeing different letters. "They look like chopped-up words."

He scrunched down in the seat. "Here we go again."

"What do you mean?"

"How much longer is this going to go on? It's one thing to send us looking for clues like we were kids again. It's another when it involves somebody like Gerard."

I studied his dark expression. "You've never been afraid of anyone, Noah. Not even those senior bullies who chased us with lit cigarettes. Why are you afraid of this guy?"

"I'm not afraid for me. I'm not the one Gerard tried to strangle."

"Oh."

"I can probably defend myself okay. But it's going to be hard to try and keep you safe if Gerard wants to hurt you. Don't you get it, Jocelyn? He's all hot to get his hands on whatever it is that Jack is sending us on this crazy chase to find. Which means we're damned if we get it, damned if we don't. Either way, Gerard will come after both of us in the end."

My worry took a giant step forward in this scary game of Mother May I. "What are we supposed to do? Should we just drop all this and make a run for it?"

"No. We need the final prize. Whether it's Jack or something Jack left you. Otherwise, we've got nothing to help us figure out what's going on."

He took the strip of paper from me, holding it between his fingers and examining both sides.

"It's a scytale," I said. I could almost hear Jack's voice from all those years ago.

✦　✦　✦

"See? It's a simple system developed by the Spartans during the fifth century. You just take a strip of paper and wind it around a rod like this pencil. Make the paper overlap. Then you write across it and leave a message."

Noah and I bent close, watching him at work. He wrote one or two letters on each overlapping edge of paper, slowly turning the pencil to write several lines:

"Monique is stupid, Tabby is dumb, Geena is a crybaby, Nessa sucks her thumb."

We laughed as Jack unwound the strip of paper and laid it out flat on the cafeteria table. The letters now made no sense because they weren't in their original order.

"And one really cool thing is you have to use the right size of rod.

If you write the letters around a thin paintbrush but wrap it around a pencil that's fatter, the letters don't line up. You can't read it. That's how the Spartan soldiers got their battle plans back and forth. The messenger would run miles with the strip of paper. He'd give it to a captain who had the same-size rod as the guy who sent the letter. If the messenger got captured or killed, the enemy couldn't decode the words."

✦ ✦ ✦

Tree branches swayed in the wind like the arms of hula dancers, while thick clouds passed across the face of the sun. Birds flew and dipped above us. How pleasant it would be to come here for a picnic when the sun was shining and no bad guys lurked in the shadows. I wondered if there might ever be a time when my life was not haunted by the past or threatened by the future.

Noah grabbed a pencil from the glove box and wrapped the strip of paper around it, but no message appeared. "It wouldn't be that easy, would it?"

"Nope."

"But there wasn't a scytale rod hidden in the back of the painting. And what about this key? It looks like it might be to a post office box. Except whatever number was on it has been scratched off. Why would he do that?"

I shrugged. "Probably because if Paul Gerard is looking for the clues Jack left, then he wanted to make sure only we could decipher them. He wants us alone to read the message."

Noah watched the movement of the swaying branches. "So all we have to do is find the scytale rod."

"Yes."

He started the Jeep and we headed out of the park, driving past willowy trees, ferns, and giant clovers the size of a baby's fist.

"Where are we going?"

"To get something to eat. It's one o'clock and I'm hungry."

I didn't understand how Noah could think about food when we had an unsolved clue, but I didn't say anything. Soon we were back on the main road heading into Watertown. He parked behind a restaurant and opened the door.

"Do you think it's safe for us to stop here?"

"Nothing is safe, Jocey, but for now we've lost Gerard. Besides, I've had time to think it over. He isn't going to try and kill you until after he gets what he wants."

"That's reassuring."

Inside the restaurant, the hostess seated us at a booth and gave us menus. I looked around. "I think I remember this place. Didn't we come here when we skipped school and went to see a movie?"

"I'd almost forgotten that. It was my first time eating here. They have the best roast beef sandwiches."

The waitress came back and Noah asked me if he could order for both of us. I let him. After she left he said, "Why was it we skipped school that day?"

"It was September and school had just started. I hated being back. For one thing, there was that nasty group of girls. They were walking around with their glittery T-shirts and new little boobies."

I stripped the paper off my straw, fiddling with it. Noah studied me with an interested expression. "They were rotten to you."

"To all of us, really. I used to wonder what was wrong with them. Here we were just poor foster kids. They came from decent homes and had whatever they wanted. All I wanted was to be left alone with you and Jack."

"Yeah, I know."

"On that day when we skipped, remember how hot it was? Everyone was groaning because normally it would've been a lot cooler. We were trying to find some shade during the lunch hour. Those girls had their little electric fans, misting themselves with spray. Of course I was so busy doing *Star Wars* dialogue with you and Jack that I didn't even see them coming."

"*Star Wars* dialogue?" he asked.

"Don't you remember? Jack and I were testing that amazing memory of yours. All day long, if anyone talked to you, you could only answer with a line from the original trilogy. He made a bet that you couldn't pull it off. A week's worth of dish duty was the prize. You were doing great. Except I think you got in trouble with Mr. Farlen for saying, 'Will someone get this walking carpet out of my way?'"

I laughed at the memory. "He wouldn't have been so insulted if it wasn't for the bad toupee he wore."

Noah smiled and his eyes took on a faraway look. "That's right."

"During lunch break, when we were outside, you responded to any question with a *Star Wars* answer. Some of the other kids were starting to pay attention. They'd throw out a silly statement and you'd come back with the coolest stuff. Monique and the others couldn't stand not being the center of attention. They showed up and called us geek freaks. Then they went off to fix their hair."

"Jack was furious. He stomped over and chewed them out."

Now that we were talking about it, more images from that day came to mind. "We were all mad. Even Beth, who'd been standing with us. Remember how their bangs caught on fire?"

Noah nodded. "They were putting all that hairspray on with the hot sun shining down on them. Their hair just ignited. It was hilarious. They were screaming and slapping themselves in the head. Someone threw a carton of milk on Nessa to put her out."

"And then the lunch lady showed up and shouted at everyone for laughing."

During all the noise we'd slipped through the fence and taken off. There was going to be an assembly after lunch, and we knew no one would miss us. We went to the movies and then came to this same restaurant to eat.

Noah leaned back with folded arms, smiling. "That was a great day."

"It was. But the thing is, until I came to Watertown I never saw kids' hair just catch on fire like that. Or curtains that put fires out once they started. Or walls warp like in a bad dream even though I was awake. Sometimes hidden things would disappear, and the kids would be so frustrated. Beth used to get furious when her secret switchblade vanished from under the mattress. It showed up in her dresser drawer or other places. Sometimes I found it under my pillow, and that happened to Jack and Dixon too."

I looked through the restaurant window, not seeing the road outside but instead a distant memory. "Worst of all, one time I dreamed about being down in the cellar and getting attacked. The next morning I found bruises. Until I lived at Seale House, stuff like that only happened on TV."

I turned back to Noah, and there was reluctant acceptance in his eyes. He said, "I hate to admit it, but you're right. Something strange was going on. At first I tried to ignore it, but it seemed to get worse over time."

"Any theories?"

"Maybe one, but it's really out there."

I leaned forward, intrigued. "Tell me."

"A couple of times I wondered if someone in the house had abilities."

"What kind?"

"Maybe some sort of mental powers."

"I just don't see how that makes sense," I said. "From everything I saw, it seemed to me that the problem was Seale House itself. It was like the more controlling and mean Hazel got, and the more dangerous Conner acted, the more the house became that way too."

He took a drink and then stared down at the ice cubes

in his glass. "I guess we'll never really know. Besides, five years is a long time. If stuff happened back then that we couldn't explain, maybe it's not worth trying to figure out. Especially now that Seale House is half burned down. I'm just happy to be done with foster care. We should forget about it."

"That's what I've been trying to do ever since I left. Until Jack decided to drop me right back in the middle of it."

The waitress brought the food, cutting off our conversation, which seemed all right with Noah. The aroma of the roast beef sandwich and fries made me hungry.

We ate in silence until I pushed my plate aside. Opening the brown envelope, I dumped out the five puzzle pieces. Two were edges and I snapped them together. "This looks like a sidewalk."

"Is that all you're going to eat?"

"I'm full. You can have my fries if you're still hungry." I focused on the jigsaw pieces, trying to find other matches and disappointed when they didn't fit.

He said, "Back when we were kids, you could put away more food than either Jack or me."

"I was also taller than you. You've caught up and then some, if you haven't noticed. It's nice, by the way, not to look down on the top of your head anymore. I got tired of seeing your dandruff when you were a kid."

I scooped the puzzle pieces back into the ziplock bag and turned my attention to the red strip of paper that we were sure must be a scytale. I grabbed the straw from my drink and wiped it off. After wrapping the paper around the straw, it was soon clear this wasn't the right size either.

"This is so stupid! Why give us a scytale with no rod?"

Noah's cell phone buzzed and he answered. "Hi, Don, what's up?"

I assumed it was his detective friend, Don Iverson. "What?" Noah's eyebrows drew together as he listened. His face grew anxious. "Okay. I'm on my way."

He stood, pulled some cash from his wallet, and dropped it on the table. "Let's go."

I followed him from the restaurant, hurrying to catch up. "What's the matter, Noah?"

"My place is on fire."

twenty

CHARRED

Noah drove fast. We didn't talk much along the way, and I couldn't blame him. I gazed at the road winding through the trees as it led to his neighborhood.

We got to his street and saw emergency vehicles, a fire truck and two police cars. Some of his neighbors stood across the way, talking to each other and nodding with concern as they watched. Massive black plumes of smoke billowed skyward, blown at an angle by the wind. It caught and scattered ashes through the hazy afternoon air.

Driving closer, it became clear that the detective's statement about his home being "on fire" hadn't given a complete picture. It was a lot worse than that. The walls were still standing but badly charred. The windowpanes had exploded, and much of the roof was either blackened or caved in. Compared to this, Seale House's fire was just a little barbecue. I glanced at him with concern. He looked stunned.

"Noah . . . I'm so sorry!"

As we pulled around the fire truck we saw that the garage was more intact than the rest of the place. It seemed that the heaviest damage had been at the back of the duplex. The vacant other half was also seriously charred.

The garage door was partway up and an emergency vehicle blocked the entrance. Saying nothing, Noah parked on the far side of a police car. We got out and walked up the driveway. The smell of smoke stung my nose, and I knew that the black cloud was rising from water-doused wood, not from an actual fire.

His books, DVD collection, computer, and everything else must now be worthless rubble. If there were a few things that hadn't been burned, then they were probably either heat-warped or ruined by water. Until now, I hadn't really thought about how important Noah's little duplex was to him. Nobody, except foster kids who were bounced around like an unwanted dodgeball, could understand just how much it meant to have a home and permanent belongings. My heart ached at the ruin, and from his expression I could see he felt like he'd been slugged in the stomach.

"Noah," a man called, and we turned to see someone approaching.

"Don," Noah answered in a depressed voice. He gave a curt nod to his friend.

At first I was surprised someone so young could be a police detective, though as he came closer I saw this was an illusion. He was probably ten or fifteen years older than he looked—one of those men with a slender build and young features. If it wasn't for the gray at his temples, I would have put him in his late twenties.

"We need to talk, Noah," Detective Iverson said in a clipped voice. He glanced at me, doing a speedy assessment. "Who is this young lady?"

I quickly introduced myself, using my foster family's name. "I'm Jocelyn Haberton, visiting from Troy, New York."

Noah hardly seemed to notice. "Jocey, this is Detective Iverson." His eyes continued to scan the ruined duplex.

The policeman nodded at me. "If you'll excuse us, I'd like to talk to Noah alone."

"That's okay, Don. She's been staying with me and we're good friends. She can hear whatever you have to say."

The detective thought this over, looking at me again. I didn't think he approved of a girl staying with Noah.

"Yesterday when you came into the police station and made a complaint, you said you had no idea why those teenagers threw rocks at your windshield. Is that the truth?"

"Of course. Don, why are you here if this is just a routine fire?"

"Not routine. Neighbors heard a loud explosion. The back part of your house, farthest from the garage, has the most damage."

"A bomb?"

"Seems like it."

Noah and I looked at each other, shocked. Paul Gerard

had attacked me last night and then come to the art gallery today. It was too much of a coincidence. He had to be the one who set the bomb. I could see the same conclusion in Noah's eyes.

The detective was closely studying us. "What is it?"

Noah glanced away. "A bomb. Why would someone do that?"

"You tell me. Who would have a reason?"

"I don't know, Don. I've lost everything, haven't I?"

"I believe so. At least you weren't inside. You might have been injured or killed. And it's fortunate the other half of the duplex was empty."

Noah tried to hide the major sense of loss he felt. "I'm so sorry," I repeated, as if those pathetic words could somehow ease the misery of losing all his possessions.

"What's going on?" Noah asked as his eyes scanned the emergency vehicle parked in the driveway.

Iverson glanced back at the garage. "You and I have known each other for almost five years now. I've kept a watch out for you since those first troubles at Seale House. You know that. I helped you stay out of foster care, like you wanted. You've even been to my home and had dinner with my family."

A shadow of concern crossed Noah's face. "Yes."

"And I've been pleased you could turn things around and make a better life for yourself. Especially since the odds were against you. But if it wasn't for the kind of young man I know you are, we wouldn't even be having this conversation."

"I don't understand." For the first time Noah was more focused on his friend than on the house. "Am I in trouble because my house caught on fire?"

"Come with me."

We followed him up the driveway and past my car, which had a damaged hood. The heat had caused the tan paint to bubble and the windshield to crack. My poor little car! I'd worked so hard to earn enough money to buy that Civic, and I took good care of it. Now it looked awful. What would Brent and Marilyn say, since they'd been nice enough to put me on their insurance? Would this cause our rates to go up, even though I hadn't been responsible for the damage? I dreaded driving back to Troy and showing them.

Skirting the large emergency vehicle, we ducked under the half-open garage door and went inside. Several policemen worked in one corner. Coming closer, Noah and I peered down at the object of their focus, and I gasped. All worries about my car went right out of my head.

One of the forensic officers began snapping pictures of a singed but recognizable corpse. It was Georgie.

twenty-one

INTERROGATION

The minutes crept by as I sat on a hard bench at the police headquarters while Noah was in a room being questioned. Detective Iverson had asked me for identification, and luckily I still had my high school photo ID card in my wallet. I'd been able to go by my foster family name of Haberton in our small town of Troy, and though the police ran a computer search nothing showed up. However, if they learned my real name, Jocelyn Harte, then they might find a whole file on me under the local foster care system. Worst of all, I'd gotten in big trouble my last night at Seale House. Jack and I had left Watertown the next day, but after five years, was I still listed as a runaway?

Seeing Georgie's body had been horrid and forced me to relive what happened in the alley. I figured at least Noah must finally believe me about Georgie getting shot, though there was little satisfaction in that. Detective Iverson was grilling Noah in another room. What if he slipped up and told the police I'd seen the shooting? How would I be able to explain everything that happened? Cold dread filled me. I rubbed my arms and winced at the spot that was still sore from the bite.

The door finally opened and Noah came out with Don Iverson. Neither said anything. I walked with them until we were in the main lobby, where the detective glanced at me, then turned a long stare on Noah. I studied him too. Just then he seemed so young to me, a guy who always acted mature for his age but inside was still a kid who'd been through a lot.

"This is far from over, Noah," Don said. "You're not to leave the area, understand?"

"Yes." He was trying to look calm but it was an act and it showed. I felt even sorrier for him.

"You'll call me if anything else happens." It was an order.

"Sure."

"Wait here, then. I'll have an officer drive you back to your car."

"Thanks."

After one last look at us, Iverson left. I exhaled with relief. "What happened?"

Noah glanced at me and kept his voice low. "He questioned me, okay?"

"What did you say?"

"Hell, Jocelyn, what do you think? I lied to cover your butt. If they knew you were with Georgie when he died, they'd run your prints. Which are probably still in the computer from when you were in foster care. Then you'd be screwed, right?"

I didn't say anything, feeling a little numb. An officer came to get us. Noah and I sat in the back of the patrol car. We rode in silence, looking at the long afternoon shadows predicting sunset. Noah's withdrawal made me feel dejected, and the closer we got to his place the more I dreaded seeing his ruined duplex again. I wanted to say something that would help him feel better, but with the cop listening in, it was too awkward. Instead, I reached out with hesitant fingers, sliding my hand into his. He didn't look at me, but after a second or two his fingers closed around mine.

The officer dropped us off and drove away, as Noah and I stood in front of his place. The street was empty, except for a distant garbage truck banging its way up the street. We walked through the open garage and I averted my gaze from where Georgie's body had been. Noah reached the door leading into the house and opened it, the smell of char stinging our noses. I started to offer more words of sympathy but he stopped me. "Stay here."

I didn't argue but waited in the garage, feeling exhausted, thirsty, and depressed. He wasn't inside long. After he came out, I trailed him back to the road where he'd parked his Jeep hours ago. "There's nothing left?"

"Nothing worth trying to save."

I stopped on the sidewalk, watching him kneel down and check the underside of his car. Next he looked inside, soon surfacing with a small black transmitter from beneath the dashboard.

"Did Gerard put that there so he could follow us?"

"Who else?"

He walked over to a neighbor's trash can, tossing the transmitter in a cardboard box full of junk. We stood on the sidewalk and watched the garbage truck amble toward us until it stopped and picked up the trash. As the truck drove away, Noah climbed in the Jeep and turned over the engine. I continued to stand there, looking at him through the passenger window. He pushed the button and it rolled down. "Are you getting in or not?"

"Do you want me to?"

"No. I want to go off by myself and give Gerard a reason to get rid of me for good."

"Oh." I opened the door and climbed in. He drove away from his place, not looking back. I picked up the brown envelope that I had hidden between the seat and the gear console.

"I was afraid they were going to arrest you," I confessed.

"Don still believes in me. He said that even if I'd killed that kid, the last thing I'd do is leave the body in my garage. Let alone start my own house on fire. What he wants to know, and what I didn't tell him, is who tried to frame me."

"Maybe you should have. Someone needs to stop Gerard."

Noah shook his head. "There will be time for that once we get what Jack wants us to find. But if the cops get involved, I'm afraid it'll all unravel. We'll never figure out what's going on."

Soon we reentered the Watertown city limits, passing

familiar buildings. The sun began to set, turning the clouds a fiery ocher.

"Where are we going?" I asked.

"Back to Seale House. We need to find the rod that'll work with the scytale clue."

"I don't want to go there, Noah."

"We haven't got a choice. There has to be some sort of dowel that's the right size to wrap the paper around. The only place I can think it would be hidden is at Seale House."

We drove along in silence, watching the sky change from bloody to muddy, a reflection of our moods. Opening the envelope, I drew out the red strip of paper and unfolded it. I stared at the mystifying letters printed on either side. Jack had always planned out every detail and supplied us with whatever was needed to solve his clues. This was so unlike him.

We turned onto Keyes Avenue. Noah pulled up in front of Seale House and shut off the engine. He pointed to the red paper. "Better bring that with us, so we can try it out on whatever we find."

I studied Seale House, backlit as it was against the discolored sky. Its pillars and brickwork caught the hues of sunset and cloaked the porch in shadows. "This can't be right. It doesn't make sense that Jack would set it up this way."

Noah sighed. "Try to get your nerves under control, will you?"

A tiny idea blossomed in the back of my mind. I unsnapped my seat belt, knelt on the seat, and reached into the back.

"What are you doing?"

"I think I know what Jack wants us to use as the rod." I grabbed the metal box from the floor. Turning around, I plopped down and flipped open the lid. I picked up one of the black chopsticks and looked at him with a triumphant smile.

"Don't tell me we've had the rod all this time?"

"Of course we have! Jack wouldn't have done it any other way."

I wrapped the red paper around the end of the chopstick, letting each layer overlap a quarter of an inch so that the correct letters matched up. We slowly rotated it, reading the words that slanted diagonally around the stick:

> CHEATGRASS RAGWEED NETTLE BRIAR
> BE CAUTIOUS OF SHE WHO WAS THE LIAR

Unwinding the paper, I flipped it over and rewrapped it around the chopstick to read the other part of the clue:

> TARES OF HAZEL WEEDS THAT STINK
> HER STORY IS NOT WHAT YOU THINK

We looked at each other. This was the most surprised I'd been. "Jack wants us to see Hazel?"

"That can't be. What are those numbers on the bottom?"

I rotated the scytale farther and we read: TWO SIX NINE

"We're probably going to need them to find Hazel, just like we needed the name of the Lautrec Gallery to find Dixon."

Noah shook his head. "It seems to me there's a huge difference between meeting up with Dixon again and going to look for Hazel. Jack's sense of humor is getting old."

"I can't imagine him wanting us to see her again either. But he must have a reason."

"Yeah. Like he's gone off the deep end."

"Don't say that."

"This is crazy, Jocelyn! It's not fun anymore, if it ever was, and I'm tired. I've lost everything." He swore softly, and I could hear the hurt in his voice.

"Jack didn't mean for that to happen. I know it! You're his best friend, Noah."

"Yeah? Well, a best friend doesn't take you on a trip down memory lane when your past was hell. When I finally see him face-to-face, I'm just as likely to slug him as hug him."

I felt wretched. The sun had sunk beneath the horizon and twilight was growing deep around us. Seale House looked even more threatening in the lengthening shadows. "At least we don't have to go in there now."

He looked away and rested his wrist on the steering wheel. I studied the outline of his profile, drawn to him more than any guy I'd ever met, even when he was angry. He wasn't as handsome as a few of the boys I'd dated, but there was something in his features and the curve of his mouth that pulled me in like a magnet.

I forced myself to stop drooling over him, not wanting him to look at me and see how I felt. "So, what do you want to do now?"

Noah never had a chance to answer. A shot rang out, cracking the back windshield.

With a cry I ducked down as Noah turned over the starter so hard it made a grinding noise. The engine roared and he stepped on the accelerator. The Jeep leaped away.

twenty-two

SHADOWS

In the thirty minutes following the shooting, I saw areas of Watertown I'd been completely unfamiliar with. Noah, however, seemed to know nearly every road and alley. We traveled a twisting path, sometimes driving fast, sometimes slow, even parking for a while behind a grocery store where we could see if someone was following us. In time it grew dark and thick clouds masked the face of the moon.

"Paul Gerard has to be the man who killed Georgie," I finally said.

"I agree."

"But why did he save me from Georgie's knife when he's so against me?"

"Hmm. Well, maybe it's because if you die, there goes his only chance to track down your brother."

"Oh."

"He must've stuffed Georgie's body in his trunk and

afterward dumped it in my garage. Then he set off the bomb."

"I'm sure you're right. What I can't figure out, though, is how he found us again. You got rid of that tracking device."

"Because I was careless. I drove back to our old neighborhood and was focused on the scytale."

"I should never have come to you for help. I'm sorry, Noah."

"Stop apologizing, will you? Besides, we can't be totally sure it was Gerard who shot at us just now. Seale House is a gathering place for Georgie's friends, and I'm wondering if it was one of them. Did you notice any of those kids carrying a gun?"

"All I've seen so far is a switchblade, a chain, and slingshots. You'd think if they had a gun they'd have shown it off before now. Of course that doesn't mean they couldn't have gotten one. In a way, it'd be a relief to think it was one of them. Then Gerard wouldn't seem so all powerful."

"He's not all powerful." Noah was trying to reassure me, but his voice wasn't convincing.

Gerard had managed to get inside Noah's locked house, and then he had stood there watching me while I slept. I could still feel his choking grasp and the heat from his hand that left the burn on my throat. A shiver ran through me. I reached for my jacket in the backseat and pulled it on. "Noah, I need to use the bathroom and get a drink of water."

"Me too, and it's time for dinner."

We stopped at a fast food drive-through. "It's not safe to go inside?"

He shook his head. "The lights are too bright and it's like a fishbowl. Don't worry. I've got a place where we can hang out." He handed me one of the drinks.

Ten minutes later we were in an older neighborhood off Leray Street. The area was lined with oversize trees. Noah pulled up in front of a small town house that had a FOR SALE sign on the lawn. He got out and went to a keypad, punching in numbers that made the garage door slide up. Driving inside, we parked next to an older Toyota. He turned off the engine, then grabbed a flashlight from under the seat.

"Where are we?"

"A place I agreed to keep an eye on until it sells. Stay here for a minute." He got out and pushed a button to close the garage door. I watched him disappear inside the house.

I slumped down in the seat. Princess Leia would be so ashamed of me. Although I'd been willing to take on the make-believe role of a complaining Chewbacca during our childhood charades, I'd always secretly dreamed of grabbing a gun, kissing the guy, and shooting Stormtroopers just the way she had in the DVD we'd replayed dozens of times. But at the moment I was so drained and stressed, and in such need of a bathroom break, that I didn't much care if he went off and did the male let-me-check-it-out thing.

The small overhead light in the garage door opener shut off, plunging me into darkness. I sat listening to the wind and breathing in the scent of fast food growing stale. Noah didn't come back right away. I tensed, wondering if Gerard really was all powerful. What if he somehow knew Noah might come here? I opened my door. The car light dispelled some of the gloom and I stepped down. I shut the door and darkness returned. With some irritation I told myself that the next time Noah said "stay here" I'd slug him on the arm.

A flashlight beam preceded him as he stepped through the doorway. "It's clear." He opened the back end of the Cherokee. "Grab what you need and let's go inside."

We packed a bunch of stuff through the door, the beam from his flashlight leading the way. "There's no electricity or furniture, but at least it gives us a place to rest for a while. The bathroom is around the corner."

I used the tiny LED on my keychain to make my way there. Afterward I found Noah in the empty front room. He was eating one of the chicken sandwiches we'd ordered and tossed me mine. I opened the wrapper and took a bite, surprised by how hungry I was. Glancing around the room, I saw that the flashlight gave off just enough light to see the corners. Nothing was hiding in this small place, and if the carpet was old at least it seemed to have been recently cleaned. There was also the faint scent of new paint, but it wasn't too bad.

"Whose house is this?"

"Just someone I know."

"And he won't mind us crashing here?"

"She won't care, no."

I thought this over, wondering if Noah was talking about one of his old girlfriends he broke up with because he found her boring. After we were done eating he went into the hall and rummaged around in a linen closet. His flashlight sent jiggling beams back at me. He returned with several old quilts. "It's good the painters didn't throw these out. They won't be much to sleep on, but at least they'll give a little padding."

Noah tossed me two, both timeworn and smelling slightly of stale smoke. He unfolded and layered his blankets, making a padded cot. Grabbing a couple of shirts from his duffel bag, he fashioned a pillow. "Better do the same. The batteries in this flashlight aren't going to last all night."

I untied the scarf from around my neck and exchanged my jacket for a comfortable sweater. Then I did as he suggested, making my own place to rest and finally stretching out. Once this was done, he doused the flashlight and darkness engulfed us. Staring at the ceiling I said, "No way I can sleep."

"After everything you've been through, I figured you'd want to crash."

"I keep thinking about the fire. And Georgie's body, just tossed there like that." A slight shiver passed through me. "Then there are the clues. I want to figure them out, but my brain is too fuzzy. I know I can't."

"Wait till tomorrow."

"Yes, you're right." I felt discouraged and in need of

reassurance. "You know, in spite of everything, I still believe Jack is alive. Do you?"

"Honestly, Jocelyn, I don't know what to think. After the first clues it seemed you were right. But this has gone on too long. I just don't see why he'd be leading us on like this."

A car drove down the street, its engine a low purr and its headlights briefly changing the darkness to a muted gray. I turned on my side, trying to get comfortable in this unfamiliar place. I studied Noah. He must be homesick.

"So, since neither of us is sleepy," he said, "how about you tell me what you've been doing this last year?"

It secretly pleased me he was interested. "Not much to tell. Going to school in the morning and doing an internship in the afternoon takes up a lot of time. Plus my foster family likes to plan outings on the weekend. I help with the younger kids when we go. Jack used to come a lot of the time too." Sadness washed over me, but I didn't want Noah to see. "And if I get a chance, I also like to hang with my friends."

"What are they like?"

"Cool, in their own way. Mostly tomgeeks."

"Tomgeeks?"

"Not tomboys exactly, but girls into geeky computer stuff. Get it?"

He smiled. "Yeah. You'd fit right in with that. Any guy friends?"

"A few. There's a group of us. I was supposed to go camping with them."

I wondered if they were having fun roasting marshmallows and talking about their favorite computer games. "Sometimes we have what we call geek-togethers at one of their houses. A couple of the guys network their computers for multiplayer games. Except we won't have a chance to do that for a while. After the break we'll all be busy getting ready for graduation. Between senior projects and finals coming up, we won't have any free time."

Noah studied me.

"What?" I said.

"You've changed a lot since the days we were together. I mean, in some ways you're the same and I see the old Jocey. But you're different, too. More self-confident."

I smiled and shrugged. "It helps being able to live in one place. I guess some of the things I'm happy about would be small stuff to other kids. I like eating dinner at the table with a normal family, even if they're not really mine. I like having my own room. Clean clothes and decent shoes when I need them. And not being on the free lunch program. I don't mind being in foster care, as long as it's with someone like the Habertons."

"Can I ask you something I've always been curious about?"

"Sure."

"How did you and Jack end up at Seale House? I never asked when we were together. Back then no one wanted to talk about why social workers put them in foster care. It was something I wanted to bring up with Jack when we were chatting, but the timing never felt right."

Swirling patterns of light slid across the wall as another car drove by. Finally I said, "It was because of Erv."

Noah slowly sat up, staring at me through shadows. "Jocey, you're not telling me that Erv was a real person, are you?"

twenty-three

TRUTH

"Noah, don't go in there," Georgie warned, "'cause Juliann just Erved all over the bathroom floor."

"Thanks for the warning." Noah looked at Jack and me and said, "This flu keeps spreading, we'll be mopping up Erv five times a day."

We laughed and he couldn't figure out why we thought vomit was funny. To Jack and me, and soon the rest of Seale House, the grosser something was, the more Ervy it was.

Slimy cafeteria stroganoff: "Ugh! It makes me want to Erv."

The mold growing in the fridge: "That's just Ervy!"

Dog mess on the sidewalk: "Careful, don't step in the E-r-v!"

A chewed-up three-legged tomcat: "Oh, look at that poor little Erv."

Nessa's new perfume: "Did somebody pass an Erv?"

✦   ✦   ✦

I could feel Noah looking at me in the dark. Jack and I had never explained our inside joke. "But I thought Erv was a word you two made up. Now you're telling me it was someone's name?"

"Yeah, well, I guess it was just our way of getting revenge on a guy we despised."

"Who?"

"Melody's boyfriend. The reason we ran away."

"What happened?"

"It's a long story."

"I've got time."

Through the shadows I could barely see the line of his jaw and cheek. He didn't say anything else, and I appreciated him not pushing me.

"Before we came to Watertown, we lived outside Boston. We stayed in this tiny apartment and didn't have much, but it was okay. I liked my teachers, and so did Jack. We had some nice friends."

A mental image of my brother from back then came into my head, his shaggy brown hair and eyes almost too large for his face. At twelve, his knees were always skinned. He could look so solemn, until he smiled in that mischievous way of his.

"Back then, Melody worked as a waitress. Until one day after she had a huge fight with her boss. When he wasn't looking, she stole money from the cash register and took off. She picked us up from school, dragged us home, and told us to pack in a hurry. We never got to say good-bye to our friends and teachers. Or even get the stuff out of our desks. Then she drove to New York, just one of the many places she took us. Once we finally got to Syracuse, she left Jack and me with Cheryl, her cousin."

"What was that like?"

"Not bad. Cheryl was single and worked as a legal secretary. I remember she lived close to the library and cooked lasagna, and she had a cat named Minkie. She was nice and didn't mind having us around. We hoped we could stay. While she was at work we dusted and vacuumed, and made sure the dishes were always done. It seemed like it was going to work out. But Melody came back for us like an unwanted boomerang. She always came back. Until the last time, when Jack and I were fourteen."

I brushed the hair from my forehead. Talking about my mother always made me angry. "Melody was excited because of this new guy she met. Erv. She'd say stuff like, 'Wait until you meet Erv. He's really handsome. He drives a black Jaguar and has a French accent.' She blathered that way the whole trip up to Gatineau, Quebec."

"Is that the city we could see from the Peace Tower?"

"Yeah. It's where he lived. But before we met Erv, Melody said she wanted us to look nice. At least that was her lie to us. Being stupid kids, we believed her. She started out by buying us some new clothes. Jack and I got the same kind of jeans and T-shirts. Then she took me to the hair salon."

I paused, uncomfortable. "Do you really want to hear all this, Noah? It's kind of boring."

"Sure I do." His tone was kind and showed he knew the story was deeper than I wanted to go. That helped me keep talking.

"Back then my hair was down to the middle of my back. I knew it was kind of scraggly, so at first I didn't mind getting it trimmed. But then my mother told the hair guy to cut it really short, like a boy's. I tried to say something, but Melody gave me this icy stare. She'd knock my head off if I didn't just sit there and shut up. The man asked if I was okay with cutting it short, and I only nodded."

I could still see the long pieces of my hair dropping to the floor and feel the sadness at being so powerless. "Even though I felt like crying, I didn't. Melody sat there watching, nodding and smiling like it was great. 'How cute!' she kept saying. I knew she was lying."

I stared into the darkness and wondered why the sharp edge of that memory still sliced away at me.

"You used to hate your short hair. I remember you couldn't wait for it to grow."

"That's why I wear it long now. Anyway, after we met up with Jack and he saw what she'd done, he pretended my haircut looked okay. But I saw his first reaction. He was just trying to make me feel better."

"Why did Melody cut your hair like that?"

"Because Erv, her new guy, was on parole. He wasn't allowed to have little girls in his house. So she told him she had twin boys and started calling me Josh."

Noah swore. Just then I sensed that he hated her almost as much as I did.

"Thanks," I whispered, for the first time not objecting to the colorful words he used to describe my mother.

"Did this Erv guy figure out you were a girl?"

"No, so I guess one good thing came from getting my hair chopped off. Except I think his parole should've forbidden him from being around all kids, not just girls. He was mean. We'd never seen any of her guy friends have such crazy eyes." I paused, recoiling from the prickly memory. "We were there only a couple of days when he got furious at us for eating the last of the Kix cereal. Erv knocked Jack across the kitchen."

"And, of course, your hag of a mother didn't do anything."

"Nothing. We knew we had to get out. Melody wasn't going to leave him, and we couldn't stay. We got our stuff together and climbed out the bedroom window. Our plan was to go back to Cheryl, her cousin. But we only made it to the border, where we got stopped. The Canadian officers handed us over to the authorities in New York."

"Because you had US passports?"

"Yes. They questioned us for a while. We had no intention of telling them why we were in Canada or that we'd come from Gatineau. We were also afraid to give them Cheryl's name, in case she had Melody's phone number. Since they couldn't find any current info on our mother, a social worker came and took us to Seale House."

I stared into the dark and listened to the quiet settling sounds of the house. "No matter how long my hair is or how much makeup I wear, when I look in the mirror I still see Jocey with her boy haircut. I don't know if I'll ever lose that ugly part of me."

Noah made his way over to me. "You listen to me. You're the most remarkable person I've ever known. Since you've grown up, you're beautiful, yes, but I don't really care about your looks. Never have. It's your head and heart that's always gotten under my skin like nobody else could. Understand?"

I heard the truth in his voice. All the feelings I had for him from so long ago became as fresh as if we were kids again. He was close enough that I could just make out the concern on his features. Noah brushed a strand of hair from my face. I sensed his uncertainty.

"What is it?"

"I want to kiss you."

I let out a surprised breath. "Okay."

He slid his hand beneath my hair to the base of my neck, gently pulling me into him. I closed my eyes and we kissed, fulfilling my secret five-year longing. His mouth was tender and his kisses passionate. Images of a flaring vampire cape and a black-clad ninja came to mind before we finally separated.

"I've been waiting for you to do that since I was twelve."

He chuckled. "Glad you didn't tell me that before I kissed you. That's a lot of pressure."

"No, it was perfect. Do it again."

twenty-four

MONOPOLY

The padding from the quilts wasn't enough to make a comfortable resting place. I slept fitfully. It was a couple of hours after midnight when I roused from a dream. Melody was crying about her lost love Calvert, and I slapped her. She turned and ran into the dark, leaving me with the old woman wearing the silver cross who touched my head and my heart before fading away. I woke up just enough to know how tired I was, my conscious mind barely breaking through the surface. I turned on my side and sank back into a deep sleep.

The next time I dreamed, it was a dream within a dream. Once again I was at Seale House, standing in the girls' bedroom, mesmerized by the walls. As young Jocey I'd just woken up from a deep sleep. At first it seemed I must have still been dreaming, because the wall had changed from plaster to flesh, the slowly undulating side of a giant snake. Spellbound, I reached out and felt its pulsing life force beneath my fingertips. The beat was sluggish, like the thump of a heart big enough to belong to a great blue whale. Twelve-year-old Jocelyn's breath got trapped in her lungs as the wall continued to distort, taking on the appearance of a malignant growth. Crying out in terror, I staggered away.

Jerking awake, I found myself standing in a different room, this time in the small town house. My hand was against the wall, which pulsed beneath my fingertips. Disoriented, I stepped back, my heart racing, my body shivering with fear. I squeezed my eyes shut and reminded myself of what Dr. Candlar always said during our therapy sessions: realistic nightmares were simply my mind's way of dealing with past fear and pain. After I opened my eyes and reached out again, there was nothing but a normal wall.

I heard Noah's angry shout and hurried back downstairs. In the dim morning light he was sitting up and breathing heavily. His eyes were so furious that it reminded me of my last night at Seale House, just before I ran away.

"Noah? Are you okay?"

He shook his head and ground the heels of his palms into his eye sockets as if trying to wake himself. Had we both experienced bad dreams at the same time? We'd had enough stress during the last two days to give each of us nightmares and then some. Once he lowered his hands he seemed more himself, though his expression was still angry. I asked what was wrong.

"I dreamed about Gerard setting that bomb. He was

grinning the whole time, and I wanted to kill him." His voice was enraged. Noah could be sarcastic and angry, but pure hatred was something I'd seldom seen in him.

"I can't blame you." I sat down close by.

He grabbed the sweat-soaked hem of his shirt and yanked it over his head, using it to wipe the dampness from his chest before tossing it aside. In the growing light I could clearly see the muscular outline of his torso and arms, which only emphasized how much he'd changed since we'd last been together. The awkward kid from five years ago was gone, and if I'd been drawn to him during that gangly phase, he was much harder to resist now that he was older.

Noah stretched his arms and back. "It's just that I was finally on my own, getting some stuff I wanted. Even if it didn't look like much. I should've gotten renter's insurance, but who thinks about that until it's too late? Now everything's gone, including my computer and all the tech accessories I bought."

"It's horrible."

"I know it's just stuff, but that's pretty much all I've ever had. I wanted to make a home for myself that was different from Seale House." He looked at me for a while. "It doesn't matter. We're both safe. And at least I still have my laptop."

"It matters, Noah. Of course it does." I moved closer. Reaching out and touching his face the way he had done with mine last night, I leaned in for a kiss.

"I didn't mean to upset you," he apologized against my lips, the last of his words smothered by the kiss. Slow warmth spread through me in response to what his mouth was doing, and my fingers traced the muscles of his chest as he pulled me closer. We parted, and I felt flustered but happy. He seemed better too.

The water in the row house was still turned on, but it was freezing so we didn't shower. We changed clothes, dressing warmly since the sky was even more overcast and the air in the house cool. I put on a black turtleneck that hid the fading finger marks on my throat.

By the time we'd tossed our things back in the bags and put away the quilts, there was enough light to read by. We sat on the floor and laid out the clues, looking at the puzzle pieces, the small key, and the scytale. We reread the verse about Hazel, and then I picked up the key.

"When we first saw this, you said it looks like a post office box key with the number scratched out. What if that clue on the bottom of the scytale, *two six nine*, is the number to a post office box?"

"Hmm . . . maybe."

"I think we should try looking for it."

"Do you know how many small postal outlets there are?"

"Then let's start with the main post office over on Arsenal Street."

"Why there?"

"Because that's what I'd do if I was hiding this clue for you and Jack."

"Okay," he said at last.

We carried everything out into the garage and transferred our stuff to the older-model Toyota that Noah had the key to. Its windshield was grainy and chipped. The teal paint was also rusting away along the bottom of the car, deteriorated by years of driving on winter roads crusted with salt. Apparently it had sat idle for a while, since the engine didn't want to turn over. Noah jump-started it with battery cables from the Jeep, and then we climbed inside.

"Are you sure your friend will be okay with us using her car?"

"Yes. She doesn't need it right now, and we can't ride around in the Jeep because Gerard will be looking for it."

Outside, the sky was a somber gray. The one sure thing about April weather in Watertown was that it always changed. Yesterday's wind had given way to a strange calm, and the clouds hung above us like soggy wool.

Noah said, "Let's grab some breakfast first."

"Yuck! It's not even eight yet."

"I don't think you eat enough."

"Whatever. Were you always so bossy and I just forgot?"

His expression seemed to withdraw from me a little. I added, "Sorry. I didn't mean it like that. I know looking out for me seems the natural thing for you to do. Back then you were only a kid running everything at Seale House and keeping us all going. Especially on those bad days when Hazel was really stoned. You were a whole lot more of a foster parent than she was. It's one of the reasons I loved you so much."

222

As soon as that confession slipped out, I felt nervous and a little uncertain; however, my embarrassment evaporated when Noah reached out and took my hand in his. It was surprising how comforting it felt to have his warm fingers encircle mine.

We pulled into the drive-through of a McDonald's. He ordered an Egg McMuffin, and I agreed to juice and hash browns.

The main post office was still closed, except for the lobby with its wall of boxes. We got out of the Toyota and went inside, where I took the key out of the envelope. It didn't take us long to find box 269.

"Here goes."

I inserted the key and it turned, opening the box. Inside was only one item, a brown envelope. Opening it, I saw a handful of puzzle pieces and a half sheet of paper. We walked to a nearby counter stocked with mailing stuff and a chained pen. I put the puzzle pieces down and opened the paper. Reading through a list of six clues, I laughed.

"It's a logic problem."

"Guess it was inevitable he'd leave us one, since they were his favorite. I'm just glad it's not encrypted."

"Listen to the directions: 'Five players are involved in a sudden-death playoff of Seale House Monopoly. They are: Jack, Jocelyn, Noah, Beth, and Hazel. Each player is represented on the board by a different token: the candlestick, the knife, the revolver, the poison, and the lead pipe.'"

"Wait a minute. Those are the tokens from Clue, not Monopoly."

"So Jack bent the rules; let me finish. 'In the final round each player gets one last roll of the dice to see where they end up. Can you figure out where each will be?'"

I flipped the paper over. "Here's the list of clues." He looked at them too, and we read silently.

1. The five players are: the one with the poison, the one who landed on Oriental Avenue, Jocelyn, the person with the lead pipe, and the player who ended up in Marvin Gardens.

2. The player with the candlestick never landed in Jail or on Oriental Avenue, while the one with the revolver got stuck on the Chance square.

3. Jack and Noah wouldn't touch the poison.

4. Beth preferred the dark and so didn't use the candlestick. She didn't go to Park Place.

5. Noah never visited Oriental Avenue.

6. Jack drew the card that said: *Go directly to Jail. Do not pass GO.*

I said, "Look at that last clue. Is Jack hiding out because he's afraid of getting arrested?"

"I don't know, but that would explain a lot."

"What could've happened? My brother's never done anything to break the law."

"Not that we know of."

"Hey, I'm telling you he wouldn't."

Above the counter was a bulletin board with postal information and other papers. I tore off a sheet, flipped it over, and picked up the pen chained to the counter. To solve it, I needed to draw a graph for the clues.

	Candlestick	Knife	Lead Pipe	Poison	Revolver	Chance	Jail	Marvin Gardens	Oriental Avenue	Park Place
Jack										
Jocelyn										
Noah										
Beth										
Hazel										
Chance										
Jail										
Marvin Gardens										
Oriental Avenue										
Park Place										

I glanced at the jigsaw puzzle pieces. "It looks like there's enough to finish that. Why don't you see if you can fit them together?"

Noah pulled out the ziplock bag from the first envelope and dumped the rest of the pieces on the counter. We both worked in silence for a while, and I became engrossed in the clues as Jack's player went to jail and my character ended up stuck on the Chance square. That was fitting, since so much in my life seemed to have happened through chance.

"Heads up," Noah said as someone approached the door. We watched an older man in a red driving cap enter the lobby and head for his postal box. Relieved it wasn't Gerard, I kept working.

"How's it coming?"

"A minute more." I crossed out boxes on my scribbled grid and marked circles in the correct squares. "There, finished. According to this, Beth ends up on Oriental Avenue with the knife. No surprise with that, is it? And I've got the revolver."

"You would, wouldn't you?" We both remembered what happened the night I ran away. "It looks like I'm on Marvin Gardens. That's clever."

"Why?"

"The man Zachary Saulto works for is Sam Marvin. He's the founder of ISI. Didn't Jack mention his name?"

"Yes, but I didn't make that connection until you pointed it out."

We paused, watching the older man pass by with a

handful of mail. He nodded at us and went out the door. I turned back to the grid.

"You've got the candlestick, but Hazel has the poison, which the third clue says you and Jack both refuse to touch."

"Drugs."

I nodded. "You used to say, 'Why does she poison herself with that weed and powder?'"

Her addiction to marijuana and cocaine did more to turn us kids against drugs than any school program ever could.

"Noah, what about that other clue? 'Tares of hazel, weeds that stink . . .' Do you think Jack meant her tokes?"

"Probably, though what does any of this have to do with finding Jack? Look at these jigsaw pieces. All his clues and we're still not there."

The puzzle was nearly together, the edge pieces finished to form a frame that still had a hole in it. The black-and-white photo showed a small, seedy-looking building with narrow windows and a wooden door. Closer to the top, where the name of a shop might be, there were four missing pieces.

"Have you seen this place before?" I asked.

"Maybe. I can't be sure. There are dozens of rundown stores like that in the older sections of town. We could drive around looking for it, I guess. Except I don't know how long that would take."

"Too long, and we don't have much time left." I turned back to the logic problem. "It just feels like we need to reach the end soon. I know Jack didn't leave us this logic problem as a little bio about ourselves. I think he wants us to find Hazel. Why else did he give us the scytale clue about her? And since the logic problem puts Hazel at Park Place, we need to figure out where that is."

There was a phone book on the next counter over and I grabbed it, thumbing through until I reached the listing for businesses starting with the word "Park." There were several. Scrolling down I put my finger on Park Place Assisted Living Facility and looked up. "How old do you think Hazel is? Wasn't she already in her mid-fifties when Jack and I were there? So she's maybe sixty? This might be where she is."

"Sixty only sounds old. It's not like eighty."

"But the only other Park Place business listed here is a mortgage broker." I scribbled down the addresses for both. "If she's not at the assisted living center, then we'll try the other."

Noah shook his head. "I'm not going to look for her."

Surprised, I stared at him. From his withdrawn expression it was clear he was serious.

"Why?"

"I don't want to, that's all."

"No, that's not all! We can't quit now just because you don't want to see Hazel again. You're the one who said we have to keep going to get away from Gerard."

"Yeah, well, right now I'm more than ready to meet up with him. I'd prefer a straight-on fight to all this running around."

"But Gerard won't fight straight. You already know that."
I gathered up the clues and puzzle pieces, putting them in
the envelope. Then I headed for the door.

"Where are you going?" Noah asked.

"Where else? To that Park Place facility since it's not
that far from here."

He caught my arm, turning me around. "Why are you
always so stubborn?"

"Why are you afraid to face an old woman who can't
hurt you anymore?"

"I'm not."

"Then take me there."

"No."

"Fine!" I shoved through the glass door and stomped
outside. The one thing I knew about Noah was that if he
said he wasn't going to do something, he meant it. There
was no reason to waste time arguing. All the exasperation
I'd known as a kid returned. Fuming, I cursed his stubborn
nature. We were finally getting close, so why did he have
to turn chicken?

I took off walking. Just then there was a painful sting
on my upper arm, distracting me from my furious thoughts.
I slowed and grabbed the sleeve of my black shirt. I jerked
it up and stared at the bite mark on my arm. Small drop-
lets of blood oozed to the surface. The indents also looked
deeper and more bruised than ever. I ran my fingers across
the wound and winced at the thin layer of blood that tinged
my fingertips. Shouldn't the teeth marks be healing by now

instead of getting worse? And why was it starting to hurt again?

Overhead, the gray clouds were thickening. I heard the distant rumble of thunder, felt the pressure in the sodden air. A sense of dread washed through me, like when I was in the elevator of the Peace Tower. It seemed as if all hope was being sucked away into a black tunnel, threatening to take me with it. Maybe Noah was right, wanting to end our search. What good could come from Jack leading us back to the woman I'd hated so much, second only to Melody?

I yanked my sleeve down and forced myself to start walking again as the Toyota drove up beside me. Noah rolled down the window. "Get in the car."

"No."

He swore a string of words. I swung around, hands on hips, and tried to ignore the pain in my arm. I said nothing.

"You are such a royal pain!" he finally ground out.

"And you're not?"

I could see him trying to control his anger. "All right! I'll take you to see Hazel. Just get in the damn car, will you?"

I climbed in and slammed the door as a peal of thunder rolled across the sky. There was a loud pop and the windshield started to crack. We both gaped at the line rapidly working its way from the large chip in the upper corner. It ran through the glass in a downward slant.

"What the hell?" Noah said.

We watched the crack form its own image of lightning.

It forked and then finally ended. Just then the eerie became funny and I started to snicker. Noah slowly turned his head to glare at me and I shrugged. "Don't look at me! I didn't slam the door that hard. Maybe it's all the low pressure."

"Right."

"I hate it when you're sarcastic."

He put the car in gear and drove, still studying the crack. "I guess it was ready to go."

"Yes, it's a chipped mess. I just hope your girlfriend who owns this heap doesn't get upset."

"She's not my girlfriend."

By the time we reached the Park Place Assisted Living Facility, both of us were less irritated. It was the same unspoken truce we'd often reached as kids after a fight.

The single-story building of white brick had a jutting overhang and circular driveway. After parking we walked through the sliding glass doors. I went to the information desk and asked where we might find Hazel Frey. The gray-haired man sitting there searched for the name and then said she was in the Alzheimer's wing. He gave us directions down a hallway decorated with nice watercolors.

So Hazel had Alzheimer's disease. Learning this about anyone else would have made me feel pity, but it was hard to wring out even one drop of compassion for someone who had been so heartless.

We found the room, and the door was open. No one was inside. "She's not here," Noah said.

I stepped in and he followed. The room had cream

wallpaper and a large window looked out on a grassy view. There was a bed, a comfortable chair, a bureau, and a television on a stand. A quilt in shades of blue and green was folded across the foot of the bed, and on the wall were three small paintings that had once hung in Seale House's front room.

"Let's go," Noah said.

"Just a minute, okay?" I glanced at a framed corkboard that had a few papers and a card tacked to it, and then paid closer attention to the shelves. On one were several trinkets that had sat atop the now-ruined little table I'd seen in her upstairs bedroom at Seale House. The other shelf had three framed photographs, which really grabbed my attention. The first was of Hazel as a young woman, the resemblance still there though her smile seemed out of place. Another was of her at about age forty, sitting in a chair holding a baby. The third was of a small child in overalls.

"What are you doing in my room?" a raspy voice hissed from behind us.

We turned. There was a woman in a wheelchair. She still had the same helmet hairdo, but now it was grayer. Her face was drawn, her sagging body more pear-shaped than ever. Yet there was no mistaking those cold eyes as they narrowed in accusation.

The nurse's aide who pushed the wheelchair smiled at us. She had a round, friendly face and a no-nonsense expression in total contrast to her patient's. "Look, Hazel, you have visitors." Her voice was cheerful as she nodded and asked, "How are you doing, Noah?"

Tearing my gaze from Hazel's grouchy expression I turned to him, surprised. Did this woman know him?

Hazel shook her head in protest. "Get out of my room!"

"Now you stop that," the aide warned in a firm voice. "This is your son."

twenty-five
NOAH'S STORY

It was the third weekend in October. The sky was bright blue and cloudless, and the wind carried with it the cool kiss of autumn. It stirred the leaves that littered the forested ground, rustling them as if they were brittle paper. I edged forward, making sure my footsteps couldn't be heard as I breathed in the smell. The dusty aroma of dying leaves was a favorite scent of mine, next to rain and movie popcorn. I scanned the dark tree trunks, looking for Noah and Jack.

On this post-chore Saturday, the three of us were playing a wicked game of hide-and-seek in the trees behind the Seale House property. I was "it" and made sure to check overhead limbs and behind fungus-covered stumps. Peering through the trees, I knew the flash of dark blue just beyond was Noah's jacket. I moved fast, skirted a rotten tree trunk, and crouched down behind a log. He was making his way straight to me; I stayed low and waited. Setting the trap, I snickered at the idea of his surprised face when I popped up and grabbed him.

My thoughts were suddenly distracted by the uncanny realization that someone was moving in close behind me. I started to turn around when a stringlike object flashed past my eyes and traveled downward. A wire tightened around my throat with surprising speed and a startled squawk escaped me. I grabbed at it, too late to get my fingers between the wire and my skin. It grew tighter. My arms flailed in desperation as it cut off my air. I tried to slug the person behind me but couldn't reach him. The pounding of blood in my head filled my ears. I thrust my feet beneath me and pushed with all my strength. It lifted my attacker off the ground, the pain excruciating as the wire cut into my skin. Still, he didn't let go and dizzying blackness engulfed me.

Unable to hold his weight, I sank to my knees. My head buzzed and blood thundered in my ears. I was slipping into unconsciousness when the boy behind me yelped in pain and the wire went slack. Air made it into my windpipe, but not soon enough to keep me from passing out.

In the odd place reached by fainting, I had a brief but very real dream of a black silk cape slowly fluttering down on me like a giant leaf. Awareness returned and I opened my eyes. As Jack leaned over me, talking, my ears still buzzed so that I couldn't understand him. It was like he spoke a foreign language. Above me the stark tree limbs were backed by blue sky, and a single leaf fluttered on a branch. I expected it to break free and drift down, changing into a black cape.

"Noah!" Jack cried, his voice nearer to a sob than I'd ever heard it. "Leave him and get over here!"

Soon Noah was leaning over me too, talking in his beautiful low voice even if the words seemed mostly garbled. I gazed up at the two boys I loved more than anyone and then started to cry. After I lay there for several minutes, my mind was finally able to understand what they were saying and my strength returned. They helped me sit up. As the dizziness passed, I looked around and saw my attacker. Corner Boy's face was a mess; his nose dripped blood. He staggered to his feet and glared at me with hatred. Noah leaped up, slugging him so hard that he buckled.

"Don't," I said in a raspy voice. "You already broke his nose."

Noah came back over. "Not us. You did that."

I started to shake my head then stopped as it pounded even worse. "He was behind me and I couldn't reach him."

"We saw him and started running. I thought we wouldn't get to you in time. Then his nose started bleeding and he let go."

"Maybe you head-butted him and didn't know it," Jack added. Clearly shaken, he held up a homemade garrote fashioned from a thin wire and two sticks. "He tried to kill you, Jocey."

I gazed at Corner Boy's limp form and his shirt streaked with blood.

"Can you stand?" Noah asked me.

"Yeah, I think so."

Somehow we three made it back to Seale House with Corner Boy in tow. Hazel was slicing beets in the kitchen when we came in and Noah explained what happened. Then he picked up the phone and handed it to her. "Call his social worker and get him out of here."

I was surprised by his bold demand and the fact that Hazel didn't get mad at him. She did, however, shake her head. "He has to stay." Hazel turned and coldly studied Conner. "Get down in the cellar. You're staying there for the rest of the weekend. And no food, either."

He gave her a slow, crazy smile. "Goody. I like it down there."

We knew he was lying because of the way his eyes flitted back and forth like a frantic bug scurrying between two dark corners. But he went downstairs and slammed the door behind him. She locked it and turned the light out just as Noah faced off with her.

"It's not enough, Hazel!" His voice was firm, his eyes serious. "Conner is dangerous. He's not like the other kids who are so scared they'll do anything to stay out of the cellar. No punishment will ever be strong enough to make him mind. Especially if that's the only punishment he gets for trying to kill Jocey."

Hazel barely glanced at me. "She can take care of herself."

A note of desperation crept into his voice. "For once, can't you do what's right?"

She folded her arms across her flabby stomach. "Young man, don't you dare talk to me like that! You don't have any idea how much I've sacrificed for you."

Hazel turned and stomped upstairs to her private room.

We watched her go, and Noah stared after her with icy resentment. Jack put a hand on his shoulder. "You're wasting your breath."

"I keep waiting for her to change and start caring about us more than she cares about getting high."

I said, "She never will." I had held on to the same sort of hope for Melody until the incident with Erv forced us to run away.

✦ ✦ ✦

I made it through the glass doors of the care center and outside, where I sucked in great gulps of air. Running across the lawn, I found my way to a bench beneath a tree and sank down. What I'd just learned clicked into place more neatly than any puzzle piece Jack had left so far. For the first time I finally understood so much about the young vampire boy who had intrigued and bewildered me. Everything he had done at Seale House now made sense.

I looked up. Noah was walking across the lawn.

"Why didn't you tell me?" I asked.

He sat down on the bench in a way that said he felt defeated. "Most of the time she doesn't remember who I am. I just didn't count on that nurse saying something."

"That's not what I mean. All the hours we spent together as kids and you never said a word!"

"Why would I tell you Hazel was my mother, when you both hated her? I wasn't stupid."

"Jack and I always just assumed you came to Seale House like the rest of us, but you didn't! Those photographs of the little boy and the baby she was holding—were those you?"

"Yes."

I searched his face to find a resemblance to the pictures I'd seen. It was slight. "A couple of nights ago, why did you lie when I asked how you ended up at Seale House?"

He leaned forward and rested his forearms on his knees, interweaving his fingers. "I didn't lie. I told you my mother was a drug addict who got pregnant from her dealer and never really wanted me."

"But she's so old."

"Yeah, so? She was in her forties when it happened, and too stoned to do anything about it until it was too late. I don't know why I wasn't born damaged or brain-dead."

"How'd she get Seale House?"

"She grew up there. Her mother died when she was little and her father raised her. He was mean. She may have seemed strong-willed, but she was always weak and scared . . . trapped, I guess. She took care of the nasty old guy for years until he died. Using drugs was how she dealt with him."

"So? Who didn't have a hard life? At least she had a home. Besides, when I was telling you about Melody's past, you said you didn't have any sympathy for people who blame their rotten behavior on a bad childhood."

He sat up and looked at me with those fathomless brown eyes. "I'm not making excuses for her, Jocelyn. I'm just explaining."

"How did she end up taking in foster kids?"

"I was about seven. Her inheritance money had gone up in smoke, literally. All she had left was the house. It was such a big place that someone suggested she use it for foster care."

"That was a happy day."

"Wasn't it?"

"All this time I thought you were being a hero. Standing up to her for us and acting so brave. But you were really just her errand boy."

He looked away. "That's not fair, Jocelyn. I was a kid trying to get by, like the rest of you."

I recalled that first night when Noah had come down into the cellar to tell Jack and me where the blankets and flashlight were. Jack and I believed he was just another foster kid who'd learned how to survive in the system. We didn't realize how much more there was to his story.

"I guess you're right. It must've been hard doing that constant balancing act of keeping everyone in line. You took care of her and ran the house too."

"The worst part was seeing how all of you hated her. I was afraid you'd hate me too, if you found out. When I was little, Hazel and I learned the hard way what it was like. The first foster kids beat me up to get back at her. So after we got a new batch of kids, she decided to make it look like I was just another boy in the house. I didn't have my own room, and I called her Hazel the way everyone else did. No one knew I was her son since we didn't look alike. And she'd given me her mother's maiden name, Collier, as a middle name. That's when I became Noah Collier."

"How did that make you feel, having Hazel deny you were her kid?"

"It was a survival tactic, that's all."

"Come on, Noah. I was raised by a mother who didn't want to be bothered, either. Remember?"

He took a while to answer. "I sometimes wondered how it'd be if she just let me be her son. I hoped maybe then she might start to care about me, the way real moms do. But even after all the foster kids went away, she stayed the same."

His unhappy expression reminded me of the times in my own life when I'd secretly hoped Melody would someday love me the way she loved Jack. Those kinds of desperate dreams were always the wish of unwanted kids.

"What happened to Hazel that she ended up like this?"

"A bad stroke a couple of years ago. Then the Alzheimer's, and she really started going downhill. All her past drug use didn't help, either."

"She's the reason you didn't move out of Watertown," I said with sudden understanding. "How can you be loyal to her when she was such a terrible mother?"

"Guess I'm just a sucker that way. After all, I'm still hanging out with you in spite of what you did."

He stood, looking down at me with an expression I couldn't decipher. "So are we done talking about all this crap? We need to figure out why Jack had us come here."

It started to sprinkle, sweetening the smell of the humid air. The last thing I wanted to do was see Hazel again. Why had I been so determined to find her in the first place? There were too many unresolved feelings churning inside me, but I also knew that until I found Jack, most of them needed to be shelved. When I did finally see my brother, he'd have some hard questions to answer about bringing us here.

"Okay," I said at last, standing.

We walked back to the building, and I steeled myself to face the old woman again.

twenty-six

CIPHER

Hazel had moved from the wheelchair to an overstuffed chair in front of the television, where she hunched forward with her fingers clutching the remote control. The sound on the TV was low. Her eyes were riveted as she shot through the channels, a blur of soap operas, game shows, and infomercials.

Noah pulled up the other chair and reached for the remote, which she snatched away. "Hazel," he said in a gentle voice, "how about turning that off so we can talk?"

She shook her head, jiggling that cap of stone-gray hair, eyes still glued to the passing channels. Despite her age and mental deterioration, I still had the strongest urge to smack her. Instead, I said, "Can't you for once in your life try to be nice to Noah?"

Her eyes flicked to me. "You're that bad girl! You locked the door, didn't you?"

I refused to back down, instead staring at her with cold dislike.

"Why don't you let me handle this?" Noah said.

He indicated with a glance that I should start searching the room. I moved out of Hazel's line of sight, and her eyes slid back to the TV screen. Noah tried again. "Hazel, do you remember my friend Jack?"

She didn't answer.

"Did Jack come visit you?"

"Jack in the Box value meal," Hazel said, stopping on an ad for fast food.

"Remember how Jack was really smart? He always got good grades in school and helped me shovel the sidewalk. We made those chocolate chip cookies you liked."

No answer.

While Noah patiently tried to prod her memory, I looked around the room. I started with the small corkboard, which had a few papers and a card tacked on it. None of these were clues, and the birthday card was from her insurance agent. Hazel wasn't exactly one of those nice old ladies who got any sort of attention from people other than the paid care center workers.

I again glanced at the photos and took in the details of Noah as an infant and toddler. It touched me with a strange melancholy. I felt irritated with Jack, since I would have been happy to live my entire life without knowing the truth about Hazel and Noah.

After scanning the knickknacks on the shelves and

dresser, I quietly opened one of the drawers. Searching through Hazel's personal items was unpleasant, but since Noah was making no headway with his questions, I kept going. There was nothing much in the first two drawers. Opening the third, I looked under several pairs of old-lady slacks. In the very back of the drawer I found a narrow black leather box. I opened the lid. Inside, embedded in a foam liner, was a polished steel knife with some red paper wrapped around the handle.

"Thief!" Hazel shouted in such a familiar way that I jumped. Turning, I saw her staring at me with angry eyes. "Get out of there!"

"Calm down, Hazel," Noah said. "I'll take care of it."

She threw the remote at me. I ducked as it whizzed past and smacked into the wall. It clattered to the floor and the back came off, batteries scattering.

Noah grabbed her wrist and shut off the noisy TV. "That's not nice! If you can't be nice, then I'm going to tell the nurses you can't have your medication tonight."

Hazel sank back, sullen. "But she's digging in my drawer and she's going to take my pants."

"No, she's too tall to wear your pants." He looked at me as I closed the leather case and hid it behind my back. "Are you going to wear her pants?" I shook my head and he turned back to Hazel. "There, you see? She's leaving your pants right where they were."

Hazel's face all but folded in with a teary expression. "Now my TV is broken."

Noah went and gathered up the remote and its batteries, putting everything back together. "There," he said, handing it to her. She turned on the television, starting to channel surf even before the picture came on.

He glanced at me and I nodded, slipping around the side of the bed and heading to the door. Noah started to follow when Hazel's hand shot out. Her fingers grabbed his wrist and they looked at each other. "I did it all for you, Noah. I did everything for you." Her voice wasn't feeble or whiny anymore, and her gaze was clear as she stared up at him.

"I know," he said in a quiet voice.

A few seconds later she returned her attention to the TV and began clicking the remote so fast that the images and sound became a garbled blur. We left her room.

Outside, the pavement was soaked from a brief rain burst, though the sun was now peeking out. I felt unsettled, not only because of what I'd learned about Hazel and Noah, but also because of seeing her as such a helpless person. During my time at Seale House she'd been an enemy I'd come to hate, and the passing years had only increased my loathing for her. Now that Hazel was such a pitiful wreck, some of the energy went out of my resentment. I wasn't sure how I felt about that. In a way it was deflating, like in the final *Star Wars* trilogy scene when Darth Vader's mask was removed and he was just this old guy who didn't look even a little dangerous.

Once inside the car, I opened the narrow case. I took

out the knife and unwound three strips of red paper from around the handle.

"Hazel's never owned anything like that," Noah said. "Jack must've put it there."

"I agree. Besides, it has these clues, so we know it's from him. Which means he was in Hazel's room not that long ago."

"Either she was asleep or she doesn't remember seeing him."

"Or she didn't want to tell us. Look at these strips of paper."

Noah and I studied them. The first was covered with printed letters, the second with a series of Roman numerals. The third was blank.

"That one looks like simple substitution cipher," he said.

I examined the groupings of letters. "You're right. There are a lot of *G*s, which are probably either the letter *T* or *E*. I'm guessing the double *Z*s are replacing an *S* or *L*."

I grabbed a pencil, recopying the letters onto my notepad. Then I started substituting letters to solve the code.

EXTROL KXH XOOHZOL FTZZ ZOKH GI HOKGU
GNCLG ZOKLG GNCLG BILG ICN KXYNA MOGU

Taking the blank strip of red paper from me, Noah turned it to the light. "This has some sort of imprint on it that I can't quite read, though I'm sure you'll sort it out." He tossed it back to me.

"What's wrong?"

"Everything. These clues are just a bunch of kid's stuff. And why did he bother coming to Hazel's room to hide that knife?"

"I don't know, but I'm sure he'll tell us when we find him."

"Did you ever stop to think that Jack might be doing all this because he's had some sort of mental breakdown?"

"Don't say that."

"Listen to reason, will you? Nothing he's doing seems normal . . . at least not to me."

"You're upset that he led us to Hazel and I learned the truth."

"No," he said in an annoyed drawl. "Because right now I don't really care what you think."

We were interrupted by his cell phone. He looked at it and then answered. "Hi, Don, what's up?"

After a few seconds talking to his detective friend, he scowled. "Oh, that. Yes, I know. I was going to take care of it . . ." Noah's glower deepened. "But do I have to right now?"

I could hear the indistinct buzz of the detective's voice cutting him off. Noah said, "Yes, sir. Okay, I'll head there in a minute."

Ending the call, he bit back a swear word.

"What's the matter?"

"Sometimes Don can be such a pain! I have to go to the courthouse."

"Why?"

"He ran my name through the system and found out I have an unpaid speeding ticket. It's kind of overdue."

"How much overdue?"

"A lot. He says because of the investigation into what happened at my place, I need to get it cleared up right now."

He started the engine. As we drove, my thoughts returned to our conversation on the bench. "Noah, I'm sorry for what I said back there about you being Hazel's errand boy. Fact is, you probably had the hardest time of us all."

He only gave a curt nod, but it was enough to make me feel relieved I'd set things right. I picked up the knife and turned it over. Examining every centimeter, I found nothing but a high-quality blade with the brand name *Cold Steel* etched into the handle. Putting it back in the case, I picked up the clue with Roman numerals on it and counted how many English numbers they represented.

XX-XV-XVI-XIX-V-VIII-XX-
XIX-XI-XVIII-I-XIII-XXIV

Soon we reached the Jefferson County Courthouse, parked, and got out. We entered the main lobby, and Noah found the appropriate line. I went down a hallway in search of a drinking fountain. On my way back I was surprised to see Zachary Saulto, the guy from ISI who had talked to us at the library. He had the same confident strut as last time. Smiling at me, his Silly Putty face looked even creepier in the fluorescent light. "How are you, Jaclyn?"

"Jocelyn, you mean. What are you doing here?"

"My boss, Sam Marvin, asked me to check in with you. We heard about the fire. Are you okay?"

"Look, you can talk to Noah if you want. But I don't have anything to say." I headed to the lobby and he started walking beside me.

"Hey, we're just trying to look out for Jack's sister. We owe him that. We're concerned and want to make sure you're all right."

"I got that part already. Anything else?"

He smiled again, pretending to be friendly—but he was also blocking my path. "We think it's important to give you a heads-up about one of our past employees. His name is Paul Gerard." Saulto studied my expression, which I tried to keep neutral.

"What about him?"

"Seems he and Jack had a run-in a couple of days before the car crash."

"What do you mean?"

"It's a long story." He moved a step closer and leaned in, as if what he was about to say was confidential. "Basically, Paul Gerard took something that belonged to our company. Jack went to get it back for us."

"Why would he do that?"

"Your brother was very loyal to ISI."

"What was it he went after?"

"I can't discuss that. We have a security policy." He returned to his former stance. "We wouldn't have let Jack go meet with Gerard if we thought there might be a problem."

"Was there a problem?"

Saulto shrugged.

I really disliked the way he was dangling bits of half-information in front of me. "So did Jack get what you sent him for?"

"We're not sure. Because of the car crash, there was no way to find out."

I didn't say anything and he added, "Gerard is an interesting guy. He used to be one of our best security specialists. Then he started stealing from us and went to work for himself."

"If he stole from you, then why didn't ISI involve the police instead of my brother? Wait, let me guess. You didn't want to go public with the fact that you couldn't protect your own assets."

Saulto ignored my sarcasm. "Sometimes it just happens that we hire a bad apple, regardless of all the background security we run. Gerard hasn't tried to contact you, has he?"

I shook my head.

"Just so you know, the guy has always been a sucker for tall, pretty blondes. But then so have I."

"You're not going to start flirting with me, are you?"

"I'm past starting," he grinned, and I wondered if that

phony smile hurt his cheeks. "Tell me something, what do you see in a computer geek like Noah?"

I studied Saulto's shaved pink head. "His hair. I'm totally into guys with hair."

The smile disappeared and I moved around him. Under my breath I added, "And brains."

He hurried to keep pace with me as I entered the main lobby. Noah was just leaving the traffic ticket counter, stuffing a receipt in his wallet. He looked up and his expression darkened. "What are you doing here?" he said to Saulto.

"Sorry to hear about your place. Do you know how the fire started?"

"I don't like being followed by you, Zach. In fact, I just don't like you. So stay out of my way."

They glared at each other until Saulto shrugged and turned back to me. He held out a business card. "Again, if you need anything, just call."

I didn't take it. "There is something I want."

"What's that?"

"The truth. If you guys are so concerned about me, then be honest. Tell me what it was Gerard stole and my brother tried to get back."

"I'm really sorry, I can't."

I looked at Noah. "Let's go."

We turned away and I felt Saulto's eyes on us as we left the courthouse.

twenty-seven

JASON DECEMBER

During the next few minutes, Noah kept an eye on the rearview mirror while he drove. I told him everything Saulto said, and wondered aloud what Paul Gerard had stolen from ISI and how my brother had managed to get it back. Noah and I agreed on one thing: Jack had most definitely gotten it, which was the reason he'd faked his death. It was also the reason Gerard attacked me and later set fire to Noah's house.

The more we talked, the more sober Noah's face grew, and I knew what he must be thinking. Saulto's story explained a lot, it just didn't explain enough. We both felt frustrated at getting closer but still being in the dark.

Remembering the livid sound of Paul Gerard's voice and how he'd choked me, I experienced a new wave of fear. He must be certain that Jack had passed on the stolen item to me, and the fact that we didn't have it made our situation really risky. If he cornered us, there was nothing for Noah or me to bargain with. Zachary Saulto was being a stubborn jerk by not telling us what Gerard had stolen. Noah and I would have to finish this crazy scavenger hunt soon to figure out what was going on.

Noticing I was unconsciously chewing on a fingernail, I dropped my hand to my lap. Worrying was getting me nowhere, so I told myself not to think about Gerard. Finally I tossed Noah a mischievous grin.

"Isn't Saulto the biggest sack of Erv you've ever met?"

He chuckled. "Yeah, he really is."

"I hate it when big-headed guys like that come on to me."

"You mean he was hitting on you?"

I secretly enjoyed his jealous glare. It was great to be more to Noah than just his best friend's sister. "Don't worry. I made it clear he's not my type."

We left the downtown area and I turned back to the clues. On one of the strips I converted the Roman numerals to regular numbers.

20 15 16 19 5 8 20 19 11 18 1 13 24

Noah glanced over at what I was doing. "Since none of them are higher than twenty-six, they must represent letters."

I nodded in agreement. Scribbling an alphabet list, I assigned a number to each letter. I started with 1 for A through 26 for Z:

T O P S E H T S K R A M X

"I must've done something wrong."

When we stopped at a light, Noah looked at the letters. "Maybe they're an anagram. Try switching them around."

"Hang on. I see what it is."

The light turned green and we started moving again. I reversed the letters and wrote out the words. "Okay, got it."

I showed the clue to Noah.

X MARKS THE SPOT

"You're joking."

I stared at the words, equally unsure.

"I know. It doesn't make sense. Jack's favorite phrase from the third Indiana Jones movie was: 'X never, ever marks the spot.' He wrote that more than once in his Jason December notes. Why would he contradict himself with this clue?"

I remembered the many times we'd watched those "Indy" movies. Hazel didn't allow cable or any rentals, but she did own about twenty DVDs that we viewed repeatedly, including the old *Star Wars* trilogy.

Noah shrugged. "I don't know. The joke of the movie was that *X* really did mark the spot, remember?"

After thinking about this for a few more seconds, I decided to move on. Focusing on the other message that we'd decided was a substitution cipher, I started swapping out the letters in the puzzle. This one was harder and I kept scratching out wrong letter choices until it was finally decrypted. I stared down at two sentences,

thinking this new clue was about as bad as being told to
find Hazel.

> Knives and needles
> will lead to death.
> Trust least trust
> most our Angry Beth.

I read it to Noah. "What do you think that means:
'trust least, trust most'?"

"No clue."

"Very funny," I said, and he smiled. "Do you know
where Beth ended up?"

"No, but it's not surprising the puzzle is about her. He
left us a knife, didn't he? And she's in the logic problem, too.
We should've known it would involve Beth. What about
that last clue?"

I picked up the blank strip of paper, tilting it to catch
the light, though I couldn't quite make out the impressions.
With my pencil I rubbed the tip back and forth across my
scrap paper until there was a dark spot, then ran my finger
over the graphite. Just the way I'd done all those years ago
on my thirteenth birthday, I smeared it across the indented
paper until I could read a reverse template of the writing.

> Just what has Jason
> December done?
> Can you find his obit
> in the Evening Sun?

I read this aloud to Noah and tried to squelch my concern about what it might mean. "Do you know what the 'Evening Sun' is?"

"Probably a newspaper, because 'obit' means obituary. But I've never heard of it. Anyway, this is the clue we need to follow. The one about Beth doesn't tell us where to find her. And the other one could mean anything."

"We should check the Internet."

He drove onto a side road and pulled over. Reaching into the backseat he grabbed his laptop, handed it to me, and turned it on. Then he pulled back onto the road as the laptop scanned for wireless service.

"I'll head over by a couple of the larger hotels and see if we can pick up their wireless signal. They don't usually require a password."

About ten minutes later we made the connection and Noah drove into the parking lot of a motel. He turned off the engine and we got on the Internet. "Start with New York newspapers," he suggested.

After some searching we found *The Evening Sun*, which was in Norwich. I said, "There wouldn't be an obituary about Jack in that newspaper. Norwich is down toward the bottom of the state. The car accident happened on his way back home from Albany, after a work assignment."

"Let's check it out anyway. Go into their archive section and search by date."

I did, and typed in March sixteenth, the date of Jack's car crash. We scanned the front page. Scrolling down,

I paused at an article: "Elderly Couple in Fatal Crash." We stared at the picture of a totaled car being towed from a river. Scanning the names and circumstances, none of it was familiar to me—except that their car had gone off into the river the way my brother's had.

"This doesn't really have anything to do with Jack."

I was ready to click on the next page but Noah stopped me. "Yes it does. You know the report about his accident that ISI e-mailed to me? That's the picture they sent of his totaled car."

twenty-eight
THE REQUEST

"You're sure?"

"Positive. I spent a lot of time studying that photo."

"Well, I can tell you one thing, that's not Jack's car. He drives a Civic like me. Only his is a newer model and it's blue."

"Did you see any photos from his accident?"

I shook my head. "I couldn't face them. No one in the family wanted to."

I didn't add that the thought of reviewing the details of my brother's death made me afraid I'd go off the edge. "This is a picture of a car crash from the same day he was supposed to have died, and I feel sure it's tied to ISI."

"Either Jack wanted them to believe he was gone, or they're the ones faking his death."

A small gasp of fear escaped me. "What if they have him somewhere? What if they're hurting him?"

"I don't think so, because he left all these clues for

us. He couldn't do that if he was locked up somewhere. But one thing we do know: something happened on March sixteenth. And it put him in such serious danger that either he or ISI faked his death."

I exited the Internet, turned off the laptop, and put it in the back. I slumped in the seat as Noah started the engine. He said, "Until we figure out the clues, we need to stop guessing."

"I can't help it. And I can't stop worrying."

"Worry isn't productive."

In the past he used to say the same thing to me, though it never seemed helpful. I sighed. "Okay then, what should we do now?"

"That's a hard one. Jack gave us three clues with the knife, but none of them has enough information. The newspaper told us something important, but what do we do with it? As for the other two, we don't know where the *X* is that marks the spot, and we don't know where Beth is, either."

"Beth! Why her? Even though she and I were roommates, it wasn't like we were friends. No one could be friends with her. She was too messed up."

We drove through the outskirts of town, both of us somber, neither wanting to share our thoughts. Several miles later, we ended up on a road lined on either side with birch trees, silver maples, and willows. Cattails grew in marshy spots and wild primrose edged the road, while orange daylilies were just starting to bloom. At any other time I would have enjoyed how pretty it was. Not now.

Eventually we passed through the tiny town of

Alexandria Bay and headed toward the St. Lawrence River. Noah stopped the car at a grassy park and we got out. In the distance there was a vendor selling food items from a cart near the bike path. Its yellow-and-purple-striped awning flapped in the breeze.

"Hungry, Jocey? Let's get something."

We bought drinks and bacon burgers from a woman in a checkered vest. Heading down to the river, we found a picnic bench beneath a maple. We sat on top of the table like we'd done when we were kids, our feet on the bench. In the summer the gray-green river would be filled with boats, but under today's cloudy sky there were just a couple of sailboats.

"You know, I've spent a lot of time trying to forget about my past," Noah said as I bit into my hamburger. "But for the last couple of days, it's been like trying to avoid a bunch of falling meteors."

I nodded, sensing that he wasn't just making small talk. "It's like Jack is forcing us to remember."

"Yeah."

We ate in silence for a while until I finally said, "I think you want to ask me something. I just can't figure out what."

Noah smiled and I caught a brief glimpse of the boy who had meant so much to me. "I guess it's like having a sliver come to the surface. Until you get it out, you know it's going to keep making you nuts." His gaze drifted away to a distant marina, where masts swayed gently along the pier. "I want to know how it happened, when you did what you did. Before you ran away."

I stiffened, staring down at my now-tasteless hamburger but not answering. He looked at me. "I think you owe me that."

"But you already know what happened."

"No, I don't. Jack and I were gone running errands, remember? Hazel sent us to the post office. Then we picked up those things that got left off her grocery order."

"Maybe if you'd been there it wouldn't have turned out the way it did."

I squeezed my eyes shut. Noah said nothing and I waited, silently hoping he'd withdraw his request.

✦ ✦ ✦

I ran across the snowy ground, my feet tingling between numbness and pain. The flakes had quit falling and the night sky was clear, cutting the world in half: glittering white on the ground, star-strewn black overhead. The frozen air burned my nose and throat, pluming ahead of me as I exhaled. Tears became icicles on my cheeks. Despite the bitter sting of freezing weather, it was the pain throbbing inside me that hurt the worst. I kept replaying the look of betrayal in Noah's teary eyes as he slowly raised his head from his arms and stared at me with hatred. "If I ever see you again, I'll kill you."

✦ ✦ ✦

I finally opened my eyes. "What's the point? It's just going to make you hate me all over again."

Noah crumpled up the wrapper from his hamburger. Then he reached out, taking my hand. He held it in his, studying my chewed-up nails. He slid his fingers between mine. "I could never hate you."

"Back then, you said you'd kill me if you ever saw me again. I thought about that when you were choking me."

"Jocey, I was just a really scared kid. But from this end of the telescope it's okay. I survived, and so did you."

"Conner didn't," I whispered.

twenty-nine

CONFESSION

I was washing dishes and singing along with the Beatles, holding all the wavering notes of "Ticket to Ride." We were only allowed to listen to Watertown's oldie station, and to make sure of this, Hazel had used Superglue on the dial.

"Your singing is so bad," Beth said, though her tone was mild. Her long, wavy red hair was pulled back with an elastic band, and her eyebrows were so pale you could hardly see them.

I grinned. "Aw, come on! You know I'm gonna make it big someday as a rock star. Especially with this body." She just shook her head and I continued to sing.

Her criticism didn't bother me, since I'd always known my singing voice was more flat than not, and I took her comment as a positive sign because she'd actually spoken. I'd known Beth for a year now. We shared a bedroom, and I had carried on so many one-sided conversations with her I had lost count. Recently, though, she'd started saying a few things to me, and she didn't seem so angry.

Outside the house the backyard snow was already a foot deep in the bitter-cold world that was Watertown during winter. Just beyond the kitchen window new flakes were falling, whirling mist fairies that both enchanted and dismayed. It was hard for me to believe there was already so much snow on the ground when it wasn't even December yet. And despite the roaring furnace that was in the cellar, the house always felt cold, especially on the second floor. I already had a wistful longing for the days of summer and early fall when we were free from the confines of Seale House.

I took the plate Beth handed me and dried it. I wished I'd been able to go with Jack and Noah on their errands. More and more, I wondered how much longer life in this house could go on without something bad happening. Only this morning Georgie had tried to set the curtains on fire again, and I'd watched them self-extinguish before chewing him out. Two nights ago I woke up from another dream, finding myself standing by the bedroom wall. It undulated and pulsed beneath my palms like a living organism. I had a fearful vision of it seeping out toward me, engulfing me like the alien blob in the movie. Oddly enough, all this upsetting stuff seemed to run parallel with Hazel's growing agitation and Corner Boy's increasingly warped behavior.

Since Conner had announced to everyone that he liked it down in the cellar, the lie became his twisted truth. Soon he was spending every free minute down there. If Hazel tried to make him come up, he'd purposely break something or hit one of the little kids to get sent back down. At night he would sneak away, creeping down the stairs to the strange nest he'd made for himself from rags and old blankets. Sometimes Hazel would forget he was there and he'd miss the bus. We didn't bother to point this out since he was such a problem at school. It was a relief for us to have a break from him too, but coming home was another challenge. All of us were careful about what we said and did, determined not to do anything that might upset him or get us sent into his lair.

Noah had several talks with Hazel about Conner. Nothing changed. Once she had been such a stickler about enforcing Seale House's rules, but now she seemed to have lost her determination. We wondered if it was because of her drug use. Either the marijuana and occasional snorts of cocaine weren't giving her the escape she craved or there was a problem with her supplier. We didn't know, and it wasn't a topic we could bring up without getting in serious trouble. But she didn't seem to care as much about what we did unless it crossed her directly, and then she'd fly off the handle.

And she refused to deal with Conner. So far as she was concerned, if he wanted to live in the cellar that was fine.

The radio moved on from the Beatles song to a Beach Boys surfing number that seemed out of place in November. I paused to look out the window. Twilight had become a soft shade of violet and flakes began to decorate the black trees with lace. Beth had finished washing the knives and I was drying them. I wiped off the butcher knife and put it back in the block, then reached for the long carving blade when I heard a frightened cry. It was Dixon, rounding the corner and running to me. He wore blue-and-yellow pajamas, and his thin socks slipped on the floor. I put the knife on the table and looked at his frightened face.

"What is it, buddy?"

He grabbed my waist and clung to me in a desperate grip as

Hazel stormed into the room. She took hold of his thin little arm. "Don't you dare run away from me, you brat!"

Dixon struggled to keep his hold on me, but when she jerked his arm he let go and cried out in pain. "How many times have I told you kids not to run in the house? Now you've broken that lamp, and I've had it!"

She dragged him to the cellar door. He started to sob, a wet stain darkening his crotch. It made Hazel even more furious. I dropped the dish towel and lunged for him, grabbing his other arm. "Hazel—no, please! He can't go down there!"

A cloud of rage turned her ugly face red. "How dare you!"

I'd never seen her so out of control, and I desperately wished Noah and Jack would get home. Her voice turned threatening as she commanded, "Let . . . go . . . of . . . him!"

Dixon was hysterical now, both from fear and from the pain of being in a human tug-of-war. I shook my head. "Conner is down there. Make him come up before you send Dixon down."

"Maybe," she said, "Dixon will learn to mind and not pee his pants. And maybe you'll learn to keep your mouth shut when you go down there with him."

Using her free hand to open the cellar door, she dragged Dixon toward the gaping darkness. She and I were about the same height, and were equally matched in our battle over Dixon, but I was afraid we might pull his arms out of their sockets, so I let go. I heard Corner Boy scurrying up the stairs, his muffled snicker crazed and cold-blooded as he waited just out of sight. Dixon squealed like a terrified animal knowing he was going to be eaten alive, and his arms flailed as he tried to escape. I looked at Hazel's unfeeling eyes. She *was as inhuman as a snake. A calm understanding came over me. I absolutely could not let her do this. Lunging forward, I slugged her in the stomach. Hard.*

A little woof of air escaped Hazel as she doubled over. Dixon leaped away and I rammed her, shoving her back into the cellar, where she hit the steps with a thump and tumbled backward. She had just managed to find her voice and began screeching when I slammed the door closed. I locked it with shaking hands. Dixon clung to me, sobbing. Beth scowled and strode forward.

"You can't do that!"

I snatched the carving knife from the table and pointed it at her. Unable to find my voice, I gave it a little shake. Knives were the one language Beth understood. Her usually intimidating anger now seemed pale next to my own livid feelings. She didn't come any closer but she did say, "You're going to get in big trouble!"

Hazel must have gotten her feet under her, because she started pounding on the door and screaming at me to unlock it.

"Let her out," Beth ordered, frantic.

I shook my head as other children came to see what was happening. They looked at me with wide eyes, and then at the door shuddering beneath Hazel's hammering fists. "Dixon," I finally managed, putting my hand on his curly head. "Go get me the phone."

His sobs ebbed as he scurried over to the counter and brought back the handset. Punching in 911, I waited until the operator answered. Then I told her there was an emergency and gave our address. Disconnecting, I glanced around the room. The children were still staring at the cellar door as if it were more fascinating than a movie, while Beth furiously shook her head and Georgie stuck his thumb in his mouth. I tossed the phone on the table but kept the knife in my hand as I turned to face the door. Hazel was still shouting and banging on it, this time with such force that it seemed she might actually break it down. If she did, then I knew I'd definitely need the knife.

Dixon came and stood beside me, staring at the closed door as if it were some cursed portal that might at any moment swing wide and swallow us all. Beth said in a frightened, half-pleading voice, "She'll kill you if you don't let her out. Open the door!"

"Not until the police get here."

Suddenly we heard a startled squawk as Hazel's voice was cut off. I thought about Corner Boy's homemade garrote and wondered if he'd made another one during his days in the cellar. Soon there came some noisy thumping and thrashing that supported my theory.

Dixon stood with his hands in fists at his sides, his thin little body stiff. " 'The air was littered, an hour or so,' " he whispered, " 'with bits of gingham and calico.' "

Beth took a step forward. "Let her out, Jocey."

More thrashing sounds drifted up to us from the cellar steps and the door shuddered under a big impact. There was a high-pitched squeal that could have come from either Conner or Hazel.

" 'The gingham dog and the calico cat,' " Dixon breathlessly recited, " 'wallowed this way and tumbled that . . .' "

"What she doing?" little Georgie said around the thumb in his mouth.

" . . . 'employing every tooth and claw,' " Dixon droned, " 'in the awfullest way you ever saw.' "

Screaming and hammering sounds came from behind the door,

followed by thumping that had to be the two of them tumbling down-stairs. All of us stood rigid and silent, breathing hard and straining to listen. My heart knocked as if I'd run a race, and I felt a greasy clenching inside my stomach. No one spoke except Dixon, whose voice had dropped to a raspy murmur.

" 'Next morning where the two had sat . . .' "

"Shut up!" Beth hissed.

" 'They found no trace of dog or cat.' "

"I told you to shut up!" she cried, reaching for him. I stepped between them, holding the knife with both hands, prepared to use it.

Dixon seemed not to see us at all. Instead, his eyes were riveted on the door as he recited the words from his beloved book. " 'The truth about the cat and pup . . .' "

"Come away, Dixon."

" '. . . is this: they ate each other up!' "

"I know, I know," I said. He slipped his cold little fingers in mine and we waited.

We waited for a sound from the cellar, waited for the police to come, waited for Jack and Noah to return. Two of those things happened at once. First we heard the doorbell, which Juliann scurried away to answer, and then we heard a fist slowly pounding on the cellar door. The police officers came into the kitchen. One of them asked me for the knife, which I handed over. The other answered the pounding on the cellar door, unlocking and slowly opening it.

Hazel stumbled out.

thirty
LIES

Hazel sat in one of the dining room chairs and blood oozed from the scratches on her face. There were bite marks on her arms and some of her hair had been pulled out. To my dismay, her pathetic appearance seemed to fuel the older officer's sympathy. He had a round face with gray hair flat as cardboard, and he talked to her calmly. The younger policeman was down in the cellar, searching for Conner.

During my time at Seale House, I'd learned several things about Hazel. I knew she was a cold-hearted woman who could not be persuaded to any form of compassion. I also knew she was harsh, demanding, without conscience, and completely uncaring about children or their needs. And she was a drug addict. But the one thing I hadn't learned was what a skilled liar she was. For the first time I was able to understand why the social workers who visited were so accepting of her.

I was at the far end of the kitchen where I could still see and hear her, my back in the corner the same way Conner so often sat. I listened to her weave a story about the troubled boy and how she'd gone down in the cellar to convince him to come up. As she tried to reason with him, he'd attacked her and they'd fallen down the stairs. It was dark, so she couldn't see what happened to him, and then the door accidentally locked. This, she insisted, must have been the hand of God meant to keep the other children safe.

I was ready to jump up and call her a liar when the officer came up from the cellar. He whispered something to his partner, who turned to look at Hazel with sympathy. Then he expressed his sadness at having to inform her that the boy was dead. It appeared his neck had been broken in the fall. Hazel burst into tears. She covered her face with her hands and sobbed.

A deep sense of guilt welled up inside me. Although I'd hated and feared Conner, I hadn't meant for him to die. I'd only wanted to save Dixon, and for Hazel to stop being cruel and to understand what it felt like being locked in the cellar. I watched as the older officer started writing in his notebook and the younger one stepped away from Hazel to use the phone. Unobserved, she lifted her face and looked at me with tearless eyes and a silent, vicious snarl.

Shaking, I stood and edged over to the policemen. "She's lying. She doesn't care if Conner is dead, except that she'll lose the money she gets paid for him. She locked him in the cellar all the time. She's locked every one of us down there, too, when she got mad."

The older officer turned to Hazel, who looked up with a teary expression. "Jocelyn is just distraught right now. She gets so confused, trying to deal with the abuse she lived with before coming here."

I looked at her with hatred, even though I knew it would only help the officers believe her story. "She does drugs! Go check her room and you'll find marijuana and probably cocaine."

"Calm down, young lady," the policeman said. "Ms. Frey has run this foster home for a long time and she's got a very good reputation. I know, because I'm the one who found that boy Conner sleeping beneath an underpass. He fought me like a wildcat. I know what she's been up against in taking him on." He eyed her bites and scratches with sympathy.

Hazel gave him a watery smile and pulled up a saintly expression that looked as alien on her as if she'd sprouted antennae and fangs. I felt sick with dread, but this was how it was in the world of foster care. Because we were troubled kids with troubled pasts, nobody would believe us.

The younger policeman hung up the phone. "The coroner's office is sending someone."

I stared at his gun and saw the holster flap was unsnapped. A crazy idea niggled at the back of my mind. Just then there was some yelling from the front room that sounded like Beth, followed by sobbing from several small children. The officer turned in that direction and I acted quickly. I grabbed his gun and stepped back. He swore as I pointed it at him.

The older man turned in my direction and held his hands out in a calming gesture. "Give me that gun, missy."

"I will, but first you go up to her bedroom. Look in the drawer of her trinket table. You'll find drugs. Then you'll know I'm telling the truth!"

The squalling in the front room increased, and a few seconds later Noah and Jack came hurrying around the corner. "Jocey!" Jack said in a startled voice, coming to a stop. "What are you doing?"

"Hazel was going to send Dixon down in the cellar! I shoved her down there instead, and she got in a fight with Conner. She killed him."

"No, no!" Hazel pleaded with the officers. "The boy fell down the steps and broke his neck. I would never hurt one of my children."

"Give me the gun, young lady," the older police officer said.

"Not until you look where I told you to!" Panic thrummed away inside me like a trapped moth beating itself against a jar. Despite that, I held the gun steady in both hands. The cold metal seemed to send courage through my body to keep me standing.

"We'll go check it out," the older cop promised. "First give us the gun, or you'll be in a whole lot of trouble."

"I already am."

"Listen, I give you my word we'll go look. But I can't just leave you here with the gun, can I?"

Realizing this was true, I gave a slight nod and relaxed a little until the younger officer lunged. He grabbed the gun. Shocked, I panicked and pulled back. It went off with a loud blast that hurt my ears. Dropping it and staggering back, I watched in dread as his angry expression changed to one of shock. He grabbed his arm just below the shoulder, and blood oozed between his fingers where the bullet had grazed him. His partner snatched the gun from the floor.

What happened after that was mostly a blur until I eventually found myself sitting in the front room along with the other children. We'd been herded there by the social workers the police had called. In my shaken daze it seemed odd that we were finally allowed to sit in Hazel's special room, where before we'd only come to dust or vacuum. Through the lace draperies covering the windows, we could see that it had grown dark outside. The snow on the ground reflected an eerie glow. It seemed as if the flakes were frozen in freefall, but then I noticed it was only the pattern of the lace backed against the night-time windows.

I sat on the brocade chaise, Dixon on one side and Jack on the other. I looked at the kids in the room. Juliann and Georgie were sharing the rocker, hugging each other. They looked at me with blame in their eyes. Beth sat by herself on the loveseat. Her closed switch-blade rested in her hand, her thumb stroking it like a talisman, and she continually murmured something to herself. I strained to listen, finally understanding what she kept repeating: "I won't go back home . . . I won't!"

All around the room I met eyes that were frightened, upset, accusing. Noah's expression was hidden from me as he sat on the floor, knees up, his face buried in his arms. Everyone else was glaring at me. "Why are they so mad?" I asked Jack in a miserable whisper.

"Why do you think, Jocey? Most of these kids came from really bad places. They don't want to go back, or into a worse foster home than this."

"But Hazel is a monster."

"What's gonna happen to me?" little Evie wailed. She'd only been with us a couple of months.

"They'll make you go back to your grandpa's house," Beth said in a cruel hiss.

Evie started to cry. I half expected Noah to intervene, like always, but he didn't even lift his head.

All conversation was cut off when a policeman and the coroner pushed a gurney past us. A black bag lay on top. Acid rose in my throat, and I looked away until they'd gone through the front door.

One truth about Seale House, I knew, was that the only two times children used the front door was the first time they came here, and the last when they left. Stunned into silence, we sat listening to the tick of the clock on the mantel and the distant murmur of voices in the other room. Soon Hazel was led past in handcuffs. She looked right through us with dazed eyes, as if we didn't exist. We overheard one of the social workers in the kitchen making anxious calls.

"They must've found her stash after all," Jack said.

More seconds ticked by and Juliann whispered, "Maybe they'll hire a new mom for here."

Beth shook her head. "Nope. They'll shut down Seale House for sure now." Her voice was emotionless and so unlike her. She'd always run boiling hot, but someone had turned off the steam and now she'd melted into a little puddle of nothing. "Then they'll send us back to where we came from. Or a worse place, with bigger kids and a meaner mom. At least here we had each other. At least here we knew what to expect."

I had never heard so many words from Beth, though for the first time I actually wished she'd shut up.

Georgie hopped down from the rocking chair and came over to me. His white-blond hair and the purple shadows under his eyes made him look like a wraith. "I hate you, Jocey!" He threw his whole body into the accusation.

As he stalked back to the rocking chair, Dixon slipped his hand in mine. I hardly noticed. A few seconds later I stood and moved over to where Noah sat. Hunkering down on the floor beside him I said, "Don't you understand, Noah? I had to stop her."

He slowly raised his head and I was startled by the glaze

275

of hatred and betrayal. "Get out! If I ever see you again, I'll kill you."

Tears stung my eyes, which had been so dry only seconds ago, and I recoiled from him. At that moment the lightbulbs in two lamps on either side of the room exploded, glass shards hitting against the shades. Darkness settled on the room, and Dixon let out a terrified wail as Evie started bawling.

Jumping up, I ran through the house, a sob escaping me. I reached the back porch, pulled on my boots and coat, and hurried outside and across the yard, my feet sinking into the snow. Avoiding the cops out front, I slipped through the fence and onto the street, glancing back at the glowing lights from the windows. My eyes moved up to a sky gone black since the snow clouds had moved on. Stars stood out like bright chips of broken glass that soon blurred through my tears. Heartbroken, I ran.

✦　✦　✦

Noah and I sat together on the picnic bench, looking out at the river. It had turned choppy. The sky was more overcast now, the wind blowing. The boats had left the water and the vendor had packed up and gone. I shivered.

"After we left the gallery, Dixon said he didn't blame me," I murmured in a low voice. "He was taken care of by a nice family and then adopted by his new mother."

"Are you cold?" Noah moved closer and slid his arm around my shoulders.

"It hurts so much to remember that night. I wish you hadn't asked me to tell you."

"We were all just a bunch of frightened kids, more scared of facing the unknown than of continuing to live with what was bad. After you left, and I cooled off, I felt rotten about how I reacted. And I wondered what happened to you. I worried about you, in fact, and thought about both you and Jack all the time. It wasn't until I connected with your brother that I found out where you went that night."

Jack had grabbed our stuff and left Seale House soon after I did. He followed my tracks in the snow and once he found me, we stayed together during that long night. Early in the morning we caught a bus to Syracuse, where our mother's cousin lived. Melody was there, since she'd broken up with Erv a month before.

"Our mother took us to Bennington, Vermont, where she got a job as a restaurant hostess. She bought us some new clothes and enrolled us in school. We were with her about a year when she dragged us back through New York again and abandoned us for good."

"At least you ended up with the Habertons."

I nodded. "And during those years after leaving Watertown, I really tried to forget everything. But now I want to know. What happened to you, Noah, after that horrible night?"

"At first I stayed at Seale House."

"How could you do that? You were a minor. I mean, who watched over you when Hazel went to jail?"

"She didn't go to jail. They didn't press drug charges

277

against her. Something about wrongful search and seizure. And the coroner ruled Conner's death an accident. Of course they didn't let her keep foster kids after that, so she put Seale House up for sale. It sold fast, and we made good money. To make everything up to me, she let me buy a new computer with all the accessories and programs I needed. She even paid for Internet access."

This was surprising, and he saw it in my face. "Hard to believe, I know, though it kind of saved me. I became a computer hermit and tried not to miss all the kids who used to be part of my life. Mostly you and Jack, of course. A while later Hazel had that stroke. Don Iverson really stepped in then. Remember I told you he helped me become an emancipated minor, so I could live on my own? That was when she went in the nursing home."

"I'm sorry about everything, Noah. I still feel terrible for you and all the kids."

"It wasn't your fault. It was Hazel's. You have to know that by now."

"But still . . ."

He turned to face me and his hands moved to my arms. "Hey, Jocelyn, let's make a truce, okay? Let's agree that what we did when we were kids doesn't matter anymore. The only thing that matters is what we do from now on. And where we go from here."

A smile wavered on my lips as I tried to shove away all the sadness, grief, and guilt. He pulled me close to him, kissing me long and tenderly as the cool wind swirled around us. A sense of calm threaded its way through me, and I relaxed. At last Noah released me, and we smiled at each other until he let go of my arms and his expression grew puzzled.

He raised his left hand, gaping at his crimson palm. I sucked in a startled breath as he grabbed my arm. The sleeve of my shirt was soaked with blood.

thirty-one

RECOGNITION

"What the hell is going on?" Noah said in a low voice as he pushed up my shirt sleeve.

I shook my head, unable to speak. We both stared down at the bloody bite mark on my arm. He pulled a white handkerchief from his pocket and wiped the wound. "Why does it look so much worse than yesterday?"

"Maybe it's infected."

"We need to get you to a doctor."

"No. A doctor would call my foster parents. I don't want them to know I came here instead of going camping."

"But you can explain. They'd want you to have it looked at."

"Let's give it one more day." I pushed my sleeve down, trying to keep calm. "This will sound crazy . . ."

"Tell me."

"In some weird way I feel like there's this connection

between me and Seale House. Maybe it's because of what happened."

"You mean Conner?"

"Yes, of course. I caused his death. It doesn't matter that it was an accident. It never would have happened if I hadn't locked Hazel in the cellar. You said we should let go of the past, but I don't know if the past will let go of me."

I recalled my first run-in with Conner, and how he'd bitten me in this exact same spot on my arm. Noah's worried face showed he had the same thought.

The darker clouds were moving in, and it started to rain. We headed to the car and drove away from the park, each of us quiet. Noah eventually pulled up at an ATM and we both got some cash. Then he drove to a drugstore, went inside, and returned with a sack of first-aid supplies. We decided to stop at McDonald's, since we knew their public restroom would be clean. Noah hauled my small suitcase inside.

He locked the door while I stripped off my blood-soaked turtleneck and tossed it in the trash. I rinsed the wound in the sink the best I could, and Noah opened the bottle of peroxide he'd just bought. He dumped it over the swollen bite mark, which smarted some, and we watched it foam.

He patted it dry with a paper towel. To his credit he tried to be a gentleman and keep his eyes on my arm. I knew this wasn't easy, since I was wearing a low-cut lavender sports bra. "Go ahead and look if you want," I finally said. "After all, the last time we were together I was flat as an ironing board."

"Jocey . . ."

"What? It's not every guy I let see me in my underwear."

"I guess I'm just privileged then."

He coated the wound with a heavy dose of antibacterial gel and covered it with gauze. "Hold this in place." He tore off a piece of surgical tape.

After Noah finished bandaging my arm, I grabbed a blue shirt from my bag. As I pulled it on he said, "You do have a great body."

I slid my arms around his neck. "Thanks," I murmured, kissing him and enjoying the way he kissed me back.

Deciding the restroom of a McDonald's wasn't the best place to make out, we left. The afternoon light was fading fast because of the thick clouds, and at that moment I longed for the warmth of sunlight and the cheer of blue skies.

Back on Arsenal Street, he said, "Let's go to the library."

"Why?"

"I can pick up wireless there, and I want to do an Internet search for Beth. I don't know if there's a chance I can find her, but it's worth a shot."

Soon we were inside the library at the secluded table where we'd solved Jack's earlier clue leading us to Dixon. While Noah worked on his laptop, I checked my e-mail and then pulled up the English assignment on my netbook. Finishing the essay was the last thing I was interested in, but I'd promised Ms. Chen I'd get it done before spring break was over.

My foster parents had always been proud of the good grades I got, and I hoped this essay didn't drop my overall English score below a ninety because there was no way it was going to stand up to my usual work. I borrowed more facts about Mary Shelley from Wikipedia, stuffed them in, faked a couple of internal citations because Ms. Chen didn't like us to use Wiki sources, and then pounded out the last two paragraphs. Quickly proofing it one last time, I e-mailed it to my English teacher and then sat back with relief.

A couple of minutes later Noah closed his laptop. He didn't need to tell me that he'd found nothing on Beth. We left the library. Outside, twilight had draped its shadowy shawl across Watertown. We stopped at a drive-through taco place. By the time we finished eating and made it back to the small town house, I was tired and discouraged.

Noah pulled the Toyota into the garage and closed the door. He grabbed his flashlight out from under the front seat. "Stay here a minute while I look around."

I slugged him on the arm, though not hard. He looked at me in surprise and I said, "Hey, Captain Solo, I'm a big girl now and can handle myself outside the Millennium Falcon."

He laughed and we left the car, going inside. We checked through the empty rooms, both upstairs and down, before hauling our stuff into the front room. I grabbed a change of clothes and headed to the bathroom. Washing with cold water by the small light of an LED and drying off with a T-shirt wasn't fun, but it did feel good to at least put on clean clothes. I pulled on a comfortable pair of drawstring pants, socks, and a sweater because the house was growing cool.

In the front room, I stuffed everything back into my bag, including the two tan envelopes with their pieces of clues. Then I gathered the worn quilts from the linen cupboard and started to spread them out. One of them reminded me of the quilts at Seale House. I laughed in disbelief and turned to Noah, who was changing the batteries in his flashlight.

"I just got it! Hazel used to live here, didn't she? That Toyota we've been driving around is hers, not some old girlfriend's."

"You're the one who jumped to the wrong conclusion. I've been taking care of Hazel's stuff, and this is where we moved after Seale House and before I got my own place. I couldn't wait to get out of here. After she had her stroke, Don helped me put it up for sale."

"So who bought Seale House, anyway?"

"A husband and wife. They paid a lot for it, since Hazel let them keep most of the furniture. They turned it into a bed-and-breakfast. It wasn't very successful, though, and eventually they tried to resell it. The place was on the market for about a year when the fire happened."

I imagined bed-and-breakfast visitors trying to settle in for a stay at Seale House, only to have the walls go weird or have someone bite them while they slept. Even if that didn't happen, there still must have been the sad feeling that lingered in the house because unhappy children had lived there, and one died in the cellar. I wasn't surprised the couple couldn't make a go of it.

A slow exhaustion seeped its way through me, and I grabbed a couple of sweaters out of my bag and fashioned a pillow. Noah pulled his quilts next to mine and lay on his side facing me. "If that arm of yours isn't better in the morning, we're going to the emergency room."

I turned my head to look at him. "It's not hurting right now, so let's not worry about it."

"Okay," he murmured, leaning in for a kiss. The warmth and sweetness of his mouth on mine slowly overpowered me. I drifted away to a place of happiness, my thoughts becoming a blur and my worries fading. In one tiny corner of my mind, I admitted that for the first time I understood why everyone made such a big deal about kissing.

Yesterday's experience had been really great, but this was edging on fantastic. In fact, I'd never been kissed like that. Either the other guys I'd been with just weren't very good at it, or my intense attraction to Noah was coloring my judgment. Finally, when things were getting really steamy between us, I reluctantly pulled away and said against his mouth, "I'm not ready to go all the way."

"Yeah, well, I think it would be good to have a real bed for that."

This made me laugh. I looked at Noah through the

shadows; I'd always loved his voice and his eyes. Now I loved his lips too. Light-hearted, I began falling down the deep well of love. I hoped with all my heart that nothing happened to ruin it.

We kissed a little more, and by the time we finished I was more relaxed than I had been in days. I lay in his arms and said, "Noah?"

"Yes?"

"I want this to last."

He reached up and stroked my hair. "It will, Jocey."

We stayed like that for a long time, and I was on the verge of falling asleep when an old thought surfaced to pester me. "Noah?"

"Hmm?" he said drowsily.

"There was this article I read a while ago about twins. How they can almost share each other's thoughts. Think there's anything to that?"

His breathing was so slow that I wondered if he'd fallen asleep until he spoke. "I don't know. Most people would say that's not very logical. But I used to watch the way you and Jack acted with each other. Sometimes it was like you shared the same brain. He'd start a sentence and you'd finish it."

"Yeah." I exhaled, my eyes too tired to stay open. "I miss him so much. Except that now I'm with you, it doesn't hurt as bad."

I turned in his arms and Noah pulled me close, his breath gently stirring my hair.

We both dozed off and slept for several hours. A while

later I woke. Noah wasn't beside me. I lay still, my ears straining at the muffled night sounds. I could hear rain falling outside and knew the cloud cover had finally released its heavy load. Pressing the stem on my watch, I saw it was a little past three. Maybe he'd just gone to the bathroom. I longed for the warmth of his arms around me and turned on my side, my hand sliding under my makeshift pillow.

There was a sharp sting on my thumb. I gasped and pulled out my hand. In the dim light I saw blood oozing from a cut. I sat up and tossed back the sweaters that my head had been resting on. Something dark glinted there. Hesitant, I reached down and touched the cold metal. It was the knife that had been part of Jack's clue. Fear swept through me, since the last time I had seen it was when I placed the black leather box inside my bag. How, then, had it gotten out of the container and ended up under my sweaters?

Memories surfaced of other times: the darkness of night at Seale House, when a kitchen knife—and even Beth's switchblade—had shown up under my pillow as if by magic. It was so long ago since those eerie incidents, I'd half convinced myself they'd only been bad dreams. Yet now I knew they must have happened, just as surely as I held this heavy steel blade in my palm.

"Noah?" I whispered, peering through the shadows. Where was he? Still holding the knife, I stood and walked down the hall to the bathroom. The door was open and he wasn't there. I checked the other empty rooms downstairs and was just heading to the kitchen when I heard a low tone of music. Recognizing it as Noah's cell phone, I hurried back to the front room.

The notes grew louder as I approached his duffel bag and saw the phone lying beside it. Sensing that I had to answer and find out who was calling at this early hour, I flipped it open and put it to my ear. I didn't speak, but only listened. I heard a voice I once believed I'd never hear again.

"Jocelyn," Jack said. "Get out of there now!"

Before I could say a word, the phone went dead.

thirty-two

FIGHT

I dropped the phone, grabbed my backpack, and shoved my feet into my shoes. I reached the front door and fumbled with the dead bolt, the knife still in my hand. Finally getting the lock unlatched, I jerked the door open and saw a steady downpour of rain.

Fingers on my shoulder startled me. I cried out and spun around to see Noah standing there, his face hidden in shadow. I pulled away, trying to go through the door when he grabbed my arm. "What are you doing?"

His voice was so withdrawn and distant that I wondered if I really knew him at all. Had he put the knife under my pillow?

"Let go!"

"Come back here and calm down."

That's when I recognized the Noah I knew, and relief flooded me. I started tugging at him. "We have to get out of here!"

"Why?"

"Come on!" A terrified sob crept into my voice. "Get your stuff and come now!"

I headed through the door, the cold rain a shock as it hit me. The sound of Jack's warning echoed in my ears, and I ran.

Noah called my name. Glancing over my shoulder, I was relieved to see he was following me, carrying his leather laptop bag. He sprinted forward, catching up with me.

"What's the matter? Why are you so freaked?"

A loud blast filled the air and we instinctively ducked. Turning back to look at the house, we saw fire. The windows on the upper floor exploded. Noah and I ran to the road, where it was safer. Flames shot skyward and hissed in the rain.

His face grew livid. "What's going on?"

I had no chance to answer. Running through the shadows, coming straight at us, was the dark outline of someone dressed all in black with a hooded face. Crying out a warning, I pointed and Noah turned as the man leaped through the air. His foot slammed into Noah's chest, causing him to drop his laptop case. Noah staggered backward and spun away, running across the driveway. The man chased him. Noah turned; his foot shot out, striking his opponent hard on the shoulder. The man faltered, took a step back, and Noah attacked. They started to exchange blows.

I stared at them with disbelief. It seemed as if I were inside the weirdest dream of all—the black ninja from our childhood had come here for a fight. The attacker lunged at Noah but was repelled by a sharp blow. They threw punches and kicked each other with skilled precision. It became an uncanny war dance, with Noah blocking the ninja's blows and delivering kicks and strikes of his own. At one point he blocked a hit and caught hold of the guy's hand, bending it back so sharply that it brought him to his knees.

The ninja didn't stay down long, rebounding in a nearly unearthly way and giving Noah several hard hits. They jabbed and kicked each other. The attacker sidestepped a roundhouse and punched back. Noah flew through the air. His foot glanced off the guy's chin. Their movements became a blur in the curtain of rain, and I stood in trembling fascination and watched the vicious thrusts of fists and feet. I heard no sound from either because of the rain.

Several neighbors were outside now, their shouting voices muted by the crackling flames and hiss of rain. In the distance we heard sirens. Turning back to the fight, I wiped the rain from my eyes and missed seeing the move that felled Noah. The ninja had the advantage. He stood above, his hands on Noah's head, getting a grip to snap his neck.

I was still carrying the knife. Noah stared up at me as his hands uselessly dug into the arms of his assailant. His eyes focused on the knife and I knew he was telling me to throw it. And yet I was too far away, my aim so weak it might hit Noah, or not hit anything at all. I froze with dread, only able to watch helplessly as he gazed at the dagger.

Despite the cold rain, the steel blade seemed to grow hot in my hand. I opened my palm, glancing down and then up again at the ninja readying himself to snap Noah's neck. I opened my mouth to scream, but then the attacker reeled backward, releasing Noah. Blinking through the rain, I saw the knife's hilt sticking out of the ninja's shoulder. Stunned, I looked back down at my palm. The blade was no longer there, and yet I knew I hadn't thrown it! Noah twisted around, striking hard, and the other guy faltered. The sound of sirens grew closer as the ninja cast another blow. Noah staggered back and the man in black sprinted away, the knife still in his shoulder. He disappeared into the shadows.

Rushing to Noah, I put my hands on his shoulders. "Are you all right?"

He was gasping for air but his gaze met my eyes and he nodded. Then he stood, snatched up his laptop case, and limped back to the house. The roof was near collapsing, but the flames were dying in the rain. Reaching the garage, Noah forced the door up and disappeared inside. I heard a car engine turn over. When he backed his Jeep Cherokee out onto the driveway, I climbed in.

We drove away, turning onto another street as a police car came around the corner, sirens blaring. It was followed by a fire truck. Neither of us said anything for several minutes, but I kept shivering. "Are you hurt?" I finally managed.

"Nothing permanent."

Nighttime shadows slid in and out of the car as we drove, and the wiper blades hypnotically sluiced rainwater from the windshield. "Where were you, Noah? I woke up and you were gone."

"I thought I heard something and went to investigate. I don't suppose you have a reasonable explanation for why you were heading out the front door without me?"

"Oh. Not reasonable, no."

"What then?"

"You're angry."

"No kidding!"

I took a deep breath. "I woke up and you were gone. At least, I couldn't find you. I was scared, because I found the knife under my pillow. It cut my thumb." It had stopped bleeding, but I held it up and showed it to him. "I wondered if maybe you put it there."

"Why would I do that?"

"I don't know. Why did that bomb go off, and why did the black ninja show up tonight and try to kill you?"

"It wasn't the black ninja, Jocelyn. It was Paul Gerard."

"How do you know?"

"I sparred with him once at my dojo, remember? He has some signature moves I've never seen anyone else use."

I sighed with relief. "I thought . . . I don't know what I thought. Sometimes I can't seem to separate the dreams of childhood from what's going on now." Pausing, I took in a slow breath. "While you were gone, Jack called on your cell phone and told me to get out of the house."

"What?"

Neither of us said anything for several seconds until he asked, "You're sure it was Jack?"

I only looked at him and he nodded with a sober expression. "Okay. So how did he know about the bomb?"

"I don't know. I'm still reeling from the fact that I heard his voice and know for sure he's alive."

Noah studied me. "Why call? Why not just show up and help us? I could have died tonight, and then Gerard would have nabbed you."

Discouraged, I shook my head. The rain had slowed and the wipers were squeaking. Noah turned them down. "I don't suppose you stuck my cell phone in your bag, so we could find out where Jack was calling from?"

"I didn't think of that. Sorry."

"It's official then. I've lost everything I've ever owned except for my laptop, this car, and the ibuprofen in the glove box. Which I need, by the way."

I handed him three tablets, along with a bottle of water from the backseat. "I'm so sorry, Noah. I should have tried to find you. But after I found the knife under my pillow and then got that call from Jack, I was scared. I grabbed my backpack because the clues were in there."

My small suitcase full of clothes had been left behind, along with my netbook. I inwardly cringed at such an expensive loss, not to mention all the files that I'd been too busy to back up. At least I'd already e-mailed the English essay.

"Okay, I understand. But we can't go on like this, you

know. We're following bread crumbs that just lead in a circle."

"And now we've lost the knife," I added, shivering again.

Noah switched on the heat and turned the vents in my direction. "Yeah, well, if you hadn't thrown that knife, I'd be having an unpleasant visit with the coroner right now."

"But I didn't throw it."

He gave me a doubtful look, and I shrugged. "At least I don't remember doing it."

"Maybe that's because you were scared. Hell, I was scared! I knew he was going to snap my neck and there was nothing I could do. Then I saw that knife in your hand and thought, 'Throw it, Jocey, or I'm dead.' The next thing I knew, his grip was broken."

"You were amazing, by the way. I didn't know you could fight like that."

"But it wasn't enough against Gerard."

"He had the advantage of surprise. And he's a lot older."

Thinking of how dangerous our enemy really was, and how close Noah had come to dying, more waves of cold fear swept over me. We drove along a road following the Black River and Noah asked, "So where do we go from here?"

I shook my head. "I don't have any idea. Though I do feel if Jack can't come to us, we've got to go to him. But how do we do that? The clues wrapped around the knife don't tell us enough. Maybe there's nothing left for us to figure out."

Noah steered the car into the empty parking lot of a closed drugstore and stopped beneath a pole light. "Where's that box the knife was in?"

"In my backpack."

I dug around and pulled it out, handing it to him. He opened it, picked up the strips of red paper that were still inside, and tossed them in my lap. Grabbing the black foam lining where the knife had been embedded, he tugged until it came out. Then he smiled with triumph and dumped the box upside down. Four jigsaw puzzle pieces fell into his open palm.

thirty-three
THE ASSIGNMENT

Beneath the harsh glare of the parking lot light, Noah and I finished the puzzle together. With the last four pieces in place, it showed a black-and-white photo of a small shop with a sign above the door that read: TATTOO ORIENT.

"Oriental Avenue," I murmured. "That's where Beth ended up in the Monopoly logic problem. And the clue for her said, 'Knives and needles lead to death. Trust least, trust most our Angry Beth.' I didn't think about needles being from a tattoo parlor."

"Me either."

"This looks kind of familiar," I said, peering at it. "Do you know where it is?"

"No, but we can find it on the Internet. That is, if my laptop is okay after I dropped it."

We got Noah's laptop out of its case and it booted up just fine. We drove down a deserted street, trying to pick up a wireless signal. Finally we found one. After a quick search we pulled up a simplistic website for Tattoo Orient. The address was only a few blocks from Seale House. We looked at each other.

"Maybe that's why it seemed familiar."

"Yeah," he agreed.

The rain had stopped but the air was heavy with humidity, and a hazy mist was starting to drift in from the river. We drove across Watertown to an area not far from Keyes Avenue, the Seale House street. The tattoo shop sat between a hair salon and a consignment boutique.

Noah said, "I know this place, but it's been remodeled. Borke's Shoe Repair used to be here, remember?"

Stopping the Jeep in front, we read the sign on the door. "It doesn't open until nine."

I pressed the stem on my watch. "That's hours from now."

He leaned back against the headrest and closed his eyes. "We'll just have to wait."

He was right, though it was uncomfortable to sit in our wet clothes as time slowly ticked by. Noah left the car running for a while, the vents blowing hot air on us to help dry our clothes. In time I shut my eyes and tried to ignore the low thud in my temples. At last the adrenaline seeped from my body and I dozed in and out, often jerking awake. As the sky became a translucent gray in the east, I heard something and opened my achy eyes to see a police car pulling even with us.

"Noah, wake up."

He roused, slowly sitting up. "Just great!" he said, his voice thick from sleep. Two officers got out of their car and came over to us. Noah rolled down the window and one of the policemen looked inside and asked to see his license and registration.

"Is there a problem with parking on this street?" Noah asked as he handed over the items.

The policeman studied the papers and then said, "Please get out of the car."

"Why?"

"You and your passenger will have to come with us. Detective Iverson has been looking for you."

A sinking feeling washed through me as I grabbed my backpack. Locking the Jeep and leaving it parked in front of the tattoo parlor, we did as they asked and climbed in the backseat of the squad car. As we sped away I glanced at Noah and murmured, "Terrific."

"I can't really blame Don. Two houses I'm connected with got blown up in less than forty-eight hours."

Gazing at the foggy haze, I grew more anxious with each mile that separated us from Tattoo Orient. Being taken off course when we were so close was just plain rotten. And I wasn't exactly crazy about going to the police station.

Once we got there, I was made to wait by myself in an empty interrogation room, where I picked at my nails and wondered if someone was going to come in and talk to me. My mind plodded along in a confused cycle. The memory of hearing Jack's voice on the cell phone filled me with relief and joy. Now I had proof he hadn't died in that car accident. And yet the truth also brought with it more confusion and unanswered questions than ever. Only Jack could tie up the loose ends.

I also couldn't help thinking about Paul Gerard in his black mask. The mental image of the bomb that nasty creep had set, which could have killed us, made me furious, as did the memory of his surprise attack against Noah. It also made me afraid, especially for Jack. Did my brother know how closely this dangerous guy was trailing us, and would he be safe from Gerard's uncanny ability to track his prey?

The minutes crept by for more than an hour, and finally I rested my head on my arms and dozed off. Eventually I woke and stretched. My need to visit the restroom sent me to the door, where I tested the knob and found it was unlocked. Opening it, I peered out but saw no one. The officer who had been sitting outside the door when I came in was no longer in his chair and the hall was empty. I guessed he must have gotten bored and left. I couldn't blame him.

"Okay," I said to myself, slinging my backpack across one shoulder. If they were going to forget about me, then they could track me down.

I found the restroom and afterward stood in the hall for a few minutes, trying to decide how much trouble I'd get in if I didn't go back to the interrogation room. Deciding it was worth the risk, I walked past the room where I'd been and kept on going. I passed a closed door and was nearing one that was half open when I heard Noah's voice. I stopped by the wall and listened. Someone was talking to him.

"Maybe you've missed something obvious," a man said. He sounded familiar, but I didn't think it was Detective Iverson.

Noah's voice was cross. "Don't be dense, Saulto."

"I'm just trying to help. What if you've left something out?"

"I haven't. And I'm not going over this whole thing again."

"We're not asking you to."

Now that Noah had said the name, I recognized Zachary Saulto's voice. But why was someone from ISI talking to Noah instead of the detective?

"Do you realize how close Gerard came to getting his hands on her last night?" another man with a deeper voice asked.

"But he didn't," Noah retorted. "Do I need to remind you that he found her in the first place because he was following Saulto? And I'm still trying to figure out why you decided to steal her car. Was it to give her no choice but to come to me?"

My car!

"Calm down," the man said. "You know we're looking out for you both. If it wasn't for some fast talking on my part to that detective, you'd still be getting grilled."

"I know. Okay, Sam?"

My mind worked over the name, and then I remembered. Sam Marvin ran ISI. He was Zachary Saulto's boss.

"Do you? We're in a tight spot right now, Noah. It's not looking good."

"But you're not helping. For one thing, why just drop off her car in my driveway? Were you trying to spook her?"

"In a way, yes." It was Saulto who answered this time. "We wanted to put some pressure on to get her moving."

"She doesn't need any more of your head games." Noah sounded angry. "There's enough of that going on with Gerard and everything else. Where is she now?"

"Asleep in the room two doors down," Saulto said.

"Why don't you talk to Detective Iverson again? See if he'll let Jocelyn and me get out of here so we can finish what we started."

"I don't know," Sam Marvin answered. "You've had four days. We still don't have the goods, and it's getting too dangerous. Hell, Noah, this can't go on! You almost got blown up last night. If it's too much for you to handle, then I'll have to step in."

"Do I need to remind you that you're the one who called me? You waited until she'd already come to my house and then you panicked. You begged me to hire on with you again for one last assignment. So why don't you back off and let me do what I'm supposed to?"

A sick wave of heartache passed through me, and I quietly crossed to the far side of the hallway. Moving fast,

I slipped past the door. My mouth felt dry, my face flushed. *Assignment,* he'd said. *One last assignment.* I reached the elevator and slammed the button, praying it would open before they came out in the hallway and saw me. As the doors finally parted I slipped inside and punched the first-floor button, counting the seconds until the doors closed and the elevator started moving. I let out the breath I'd been holding.

My mind became a spinning kaleidoscope as I recalled coming into the kitchen when he was talking on the phone. He'd been irritated and growled, "I said I'd take care of it!" Now, I knew, he must have been talking to Sam Marvin. And the "it" he was supposed to take care of was me.

Everything made sense now. After that first night Noah had seemed anxious to get rid of me. He'd even left money so I'd go away. But then the second time, when we met at the pizza place, he went out of his way to befriend me. He practically demanded I come back to his house and stay. For the first time it was all so clear.

Noah hadn't stuck with me through this because he cared about Jack or me. Sam Marvin was paying him. And all the stuff that had happened between us must've been a lie too. I'd been so stupid to trust anyone other than Jack. Right then I became gawky old Jocey again, the girl no one could want or love, whose life was a joke and whose heart wasn't worth anything.

The doors opened. I left the elevator and walked with calm determination past the front desk. The officer there didn't seem to see anything out of the ordinary, for which I was grateful. I made it through the front doors, down the steps, and out onto the sidewalk. A hazy mist still lay over Watertown like a ghostly bridal veil. I hurried away, moving quickly until the police station seemed to be nothing but a distant mirage in the morning fog.

I'm not sure how many blocks I walked, lost in the haze, until I finally found a taxi. Climbing in the backseat, I shut the door and gave the address of Tattoo Orient. Then I sat there as Noah's harsh words, *one last assignment,* circled through my head. I tried to shove the pain away, but it battered me like stinging grains of sand in a dry storm.

After the taxi pulled up in front of the tattoo shop, I paid the driver with the twenty I'd gotten from the ATM. He drove away, and I walked past Noah's black Jeep Cherokee. Once again I experienced the sick rush of crushed hope. Looking away, I pushed open the door of the parlor and stepped inside, an overhead bell ringing.

"Be with you in a minute," a gruff voice called through black draperies behind the counter.

The walls were covered with dozens of tattoo designs, and a glass display case was full of specialty knives and daggers. Most had decorative handles and hilts, but some were more practical. One, in a black leather box, was just like the knife Jack had left me.

I could hear the sound of two voices and peered through the slit in the draperies. All I could see was the back of a heavyset guy with a buzzed head and tattooed arms and neck. Beside him were the legs of a young woman lying in a chair. She seemed to be getting something etched on her ankle, and the wincing sounds made it seem that a bony ankle was a painful place to get needled.

Soon the tattooed guy put his instrument aside. He turned around and came through the draperies, looking at me. Staring seemed rude, but I couldn't help myself as I realized it wasn't a guy.

"Hello, Beth," I managed. She was quite a bit heavier than she'd been when we were kids. Her once-long red hair had been buzzed to a quarter inch, her ears and pale eyebrows heavy with multiple piercings. She wore a loose tank top that showed a body thoroughly tattooed with every writhing design imaginable.

She smiled at me and said, "It's good to see you again, Jocelyn."

thirty-four

"X"

If anyone had ever told me that Angry Beth would some-day hug me with flabby tattooed arms and rattle on a mile a minute, I wouldn't have believed it. And yet that's exactly what she did. I stood there watching her yammer away like we were old friends who'd just seen each other a few days ago. It was amazing.

"By the way, Jocey, I've been thinking that I should've told you something the last time we were together. You were one of the best friends I ever had. When we shared that room at Seale House, you always took the time to talk to me. Even if I was hurting too much to answer. In the beginning I couldn't tell you how much that meant to me, and later I kind of forgot. You know how it is, right?"

"Excuse me," the leggy girl from the back room called. "Are you going to finish this or what?"

"Just a minute!" Beth bellowed through the curtain.

Turning back to me she raised her eyebrows and shook her head as if we shared some secret. "Don't you think she'd know better than to annoy someone using a needle on her?"

"Yeah, no kidding." I started to laugh, though not because it was funny. In fact, Beth still seemed sort of scary.

She lowered her voice. "I get sick of these little sluts that want a butterfly on their ankle or a flower on their navel. Know what I mean? It really bugs me."

"I can understand that."

"I've gotta get back to the ink. Will you come by later so we can talk?"

"Okay." I couldn't figure out why on earth Jack had sent me here or how I might bring up the subject.

Beth moved behind the counter. "By the way, I'm not sure how long I was supposed to hold on to this." She picked up a plain envelope with my name printed on the outside. "Do you want it?"

I nodded and took it, murmuring my thanks as she turned away. Over her shoulder she said, "I'll be done in about an hour. Why don't you come back then?"

Leaving the shop, I stepped out onto the sidewalk, thinking of Jack's clue about Beth: *trust least, trust most.* In the past I had trusted her least of any girl at Seale House. Yet with her transformation of a buzzed head, a pierced and tattooed body, and maybe some serious group therapy, it looked like she was now someone Jack felt I could trust.

Opening the envelope, I reached inside and pulled out

a small ink drawing of an elaborate medieval cross that formed a two-inch square. Beneath it, in Jack's blocky writing, were the words: X MARKS THE SPOT. That's when a long-buried memory seemed to rise up out of the opal-colored mist surrounding me.

✦   ✦   ✦

"We're going to get in trouble," I whispered. "You know we're not allowed in Hazel's room."

Jack slowly opened the door. "Don't be a coward. Come on."

"Where's Noah?"

"He doesn't have to be in on everything we do, does he?"

The two of us crept into Hazel's dimly lit upstairs parlor, and I glanced around the room, which I'd never been in before. My heart was beating fast but I followed Jack, believing—as always—that wherever he went, I must go. He led me to the small, round trinket table topped with an embroidered lace doily and several knickknacks. Lifting up the doily, he grabbed the side and opened a hidden drawer. On top lay a filigree crucifix.

"X marks the spot," he said, lifting it out and pushing aside a couple of papers. Beneath lay neatly arranged packages of marijuana and small packets of what I guessed to be cocaine. There was also some drug paraphernalia.

"Oh no," I breathed, holding my hands up in protest and backing away. "Jack, if she knows we've seen this, she'll kill us!"

"The old dragon isn't going to know." He put everything back in its place and shut the drawer. "Listen to me, Jocey. How many times have I told you that you can't beat your opponents until you know what their weaknesses are?"

"I don't want to beat her," I whispered, hurrying to the door. "I just don't want to get sent to the cellar."

I cracked the door and peeked out. Stepping into the hallway with Jack behind me, we shut the door and I sighed with relief. Then I slapped him on the arm. "Next time, leave me out of your stupid schemes, will you?"

✦　✦　✦

Hurrying through the fog, my backpack bumping against my shoulder blades, I clutched the paper in my hand. Five years ago the reason I'd been able to tell those two police officers where Hazel kept her drugs was because Jack had shown it to me a few weeks earlier. This knowledge had eventually caused Seale House's foster program to come tumbling down.

I thought about my second visit to Hazel's parlor a few days ago, when I had unexpectedly found myself transported there. Someone or something, I now knew, had taken me there for a reason. I was supposed to open the drawer of the small, water-stained trinket table that was still sitting in her upstairs room. But because that girl had shown up swinging her chain, I never got the chance.

As much as I wanted not to, I headed in the direction of Seale House and started running. I sensed that this was what Jack had wanted all along. I ran headlong toward him, hoping he would be there—desperate to reach the one person who cared about me.

Jack, where are you? My shoes slapped the concrete and made a muffled echo in the fog. *Jack, my dragon slayer . . .*

Wasn't he the only one who had never betrayed me? This truth was clear, bitterly revealed in the overheard conversation between Noah and Sam Marvin.

Oh, Jack, Jack . . . where are you when I need you most? Jack be nimble, Jack be quick, Jack jump over this nasty trick . . . flapjack . . . jumping jack . . . Jack Sprat . . .

On I ran, my chest heaving. *Jack and Jocelyn went up to Seale to fetch a pail of evil . . .*

A car coming from the other direction seemed to vaporize from the mist, passing me and vanishing as its engine droned away into the distance. *Carjack . . . hijack . . . jack of all trades . . . Jack of Spades . . . you don't know Jack . . .*

I turned a corner and ran back toward the house that I had spent the last five years running away from. *This is the rat that ate the malt that lay in the house that Jack built . . .*

Then I got a cramp, a sharp pain in my side, and I slowed my pace, gasping for air.

The Jack of Hearts, he stole some tarts, all on a summer's eve . . .

Forced to walk now, I held my side, hoping the ache would go away. Finally, in the distance, Seale House rose up, a half-burned behemoth in the mist. I hurried across the street and up the steps. Pushing the door open, I moved into the gloom.

Instead of diminishing, the pain in my side grew worse, and I nearly doubled over. Right now was not the time for an appendicitis attack. Making myself go deeper inside the house, I reached the stairs and started to climb. Another intense spasm of pain cut through me and I had to pause.

Pulling my shirt up and untying my drawstring pants, I jerked down the fabric and looked at the spot low on the right side of my abdomen. At first I was relieved to see nothing there. Then, as I watched in horrified fascination, dark lines began to emerge from beneath the flesh.

Gasping in pain and fear, I couldn't pull my eyes away from the swirling ink marks rising up from beneath my skin like some ancient rune. More details and lines appeared, and it seemed like a hot needle moved with lightning speed and burned the ink into my flesh. Staggering back against the banister I nearly fell, but I gripped it and steadied myself.

"What's happening?" I screamed.

Seale House was silent. No sound echoed back to me, as if the walls had swallowed my words. I gaped down at the black-ink image, mesmerized as it continued to evolve into scrolls and lines. Eventually it created an exact replica of the tattoo drawing of a medieval cross that I held in my hand. I threw the paper away with loathing, knowing it would not be so easy to get rid of the design burning itself into my flesh.

"What are you doing to me?" I sobbed, staring at the now-complete image.

At that moment it seemed as if Jack's voice echoed an explanation from across a cavernous distance.

"X *marks the spot.*"

thirty-five

JACK

Somehow I made it up the stairs and along the dim hall-way leading to Hazel's sitting room. My side was still aching but the intense burning had lessened a little now that the image was complete. I couldn't look at it, not if I was going to hang on to my sanity.

The floor creaked and moaned, far more warped now than it ever had been. I needed all my courage just to walk through Seale House. It still reeked of smoke and soggy wood, also taking on what smelled like the fetid stench of death. I had a fleeting vision of this place as a massive cadaver where nothing human could survive. I passed the door to the girls' room and remembered Evie talking to her doll, Juliann and Laura putting a jigsaw puzzle together, and Beth polishing her knife. It was the place where I'd spent so much time dreaming of the day when Jack, Noah, and I might leave this house together.

I finally reached the door to Hazel's room. Pushing it open and cringing at the squeal of rusted hinges, I stood at the threshold and peered in. Because of the fog outside the windows, the light was even grayer and gloomier than the last time I was here. My eyes searched the shadows. I desperately hoped to find my brother but didn't see him anywhere. A heavy feeling pulled me down, as if my soul were stuck in cement shoes destined for the murky bottom of the river.

I walked deeper into the room. My feet sloshed through a puddle left on the floor when the rain had come in through a hole in the roof. Sure now that Jack wasn't here, and not knowing what else to do, I put my hand on my aching side and went to the small trinket table. It was ruined, but I was still able to get the drawer open. I peered inside. It was empty.

All the misery of coming back into Seale House, and for nothing! I jerked out the drawer and threw it across the room. It hit the wall with a loud bang and flipped upside down. That's when I saw something taped to the bottom. I hurried over and pulled off a cream-colored envelope with my name written on the front.

"Why, Jack?" I whispered.

Why another clue leading nowhere? And in the meantime, why set me up to fall in love with Noah all over again, only to have him stab me in the heart like I was the vampire and he was Van Helsing?

I shrugged out of my backpack and tossed it on a dry

spot on the floor. Opening the envelope, I pulled out several pages written in my brother's familiar print. I walked over to the streaked window and turned the paper to catch the light.

Hello, Jocelyn,

If you pick up this letter the first time I bring you to Hazel's room, then some of this won't make sense. However, I'm hoping you'll start with the clue in the cellar and follow the route I've laid out for you.

"That's so like you, isn't it?" I said aloud, smiling sadly in spite of everything.

Before I get to the main reason for this letter, I need to let you know what happened at ISI. It all started when my boss, Sam Marvin, came to me. He said there was a man named Paul Gerard who used to work for the company, and he stole something from them. Since I was the only employee Gerard hadn't met, Sam asked me to get it back. He said he couldn't tell me what it was, but he made it clear that in the wrong hands it could ruin his company.

I agreed to help because I didn't want Noah to get hurt. If ISI crashed, it might ruin everything for the one guy who always looked out for me.

I couldn't let that happen, so I took the info Sam gave me and went to find Paul Gerard.

I won't write the details here, but things ended up bad. Though I got the stolen file from Gerard, he soon figured out what I'd done and followed. He attacked me, and I barely escaped. I was hurt, and it left me really shook up. Sam Marvin never should have sent me after that file, because I could've been killed.

Once I finally got to a safe place, I decided to check out what Gerard had taken and why it was so important. After opening the file, I was upset to learn that back doors had been coded into many of ISI's security programs. What Gerard stole was the master list of the passwords to enter all those hidden back doors, which I'm guessing he could sell for a lot of money. Sam was right about one thing: in the wrong hands it could wipe out their company. It could maybe even cause some arrests, because it's illegal.

I still wanted to protect Noah, but I wasn't sure about giving the passwords back to ISI. I needed time to think things over, so I hid the list. Then I drove up to Canada and toured Parliament and the Peace Tower. That's where I first got the idea for leaving the clues.

You've probably been asking yourself why I've led you on such a strange treasure hunt. First,

I wanted you to revisit the cellar. You were always so afraid of it, and especially afraid of facing the memory of Conner and what you did. Do you know, the last time we were talking about Seale House I brought him up but you had forgotten him... or at least blocked him out? I think it's important for you to let that go. After all, you were just a girl trying to be the grown-up and do what was needed. I don't think anyone can blame you for that.

Second, I sent you to the Peace Tower because I wanted you to look down at Gatineau, Quebec, from a great height and realize that even though Melody was so abusive to you there, she and Erv and that whole place are insignificant. Although we were there only a few days, what Melody did left a scar on you. But viewing that city, and her, from a distance, can you see how small and worthless she was? So were those bratty girls at school in Watertown, and the same with Hazel and her cruelty. All of them are like pebbles on the shore. If you hold them close to your eye, they seem gigantic. But if you put them where they belong, you can have a better perspective on what they really were.

Third, I sent you to the Seventh Book in the Memorial Chamber because it represents those who lost their lives in times of peace, and in some ways that signifies me.

I looked up and clutched the paper. What did Jack mean by that? I continued reading.

It also seemed important for you to find the other people who haunted your past. You know how you are, Jocelyn, how you don't let go of anything. That's why I wanted you to meet up with Dixon, to see for yourself that he's all right, and the same thing with Beth. I also wanted you to see Hazel and recognize how powerless she's become, and how pathetic she always was.

Now, for the main reason I left the clues. I did it because most of all I wanted you to spend time with Noah. I knew if I left these tricky puzzles, neither of you would be able to resist figuring them out.

"Yeah, right. He was happy to do it if he was being paid."

There's something you don't know about him, Jocey. One time when we were chatting, he confessed something to me. He told me that ever since we were kids, he has secretly been in love with you.

Shocked, I stared down at the letter. How could that be? Noah had acted so cross when I'd first shown up. Of course, as a boy he'd always put up walls. I'd never been sure what he was thinking.

Several times now Noah has asked me to let him talk to you, but when I brought it up you were always so stubborn. I know how upset you felt about our last night at Seale House and what Noah said to you, but that was five years ago. He's not angry anymore, and though he's not a guy who would ever send you flowers or write a poem—which you wouldn't like anyway—there's a lot more inside him than what you can see on the surface.

And I know you care about him too. Maybe you were just a twelve-year-old kid back then, but your feelings for Noah never went away. I heard it in your voice every time I'd tell you about him. That's when I started to think that if you're going to have a future, then I need to stop running interference. It's time for you to heal and let go of the pain.

While I was hiding the clues, I also decided that I didn't want to keep working for ISI because they couldn't be trusted. So I checked the state news online and read an article about this bad accident in Norwich. I downloaded a photo of the totaled car, wrote up a fake accident report, substituted my name, and sent it to Sam Marvin. I knew it was time to sever my ties with them and disappear. I know how much this must have hurt you, and I am sorry.

Jocey, I know you've always believed I was the strong one, but I'm not. I've stuffed down so much anger and hatred, while you've been the one who is kind and good. I'm only bringing you down—hurting you when I don't mean to, which is why you're better off without me.

Before I leave, I want you to know that I've always been aware of your heartache. When you weep on your pillow, your tears dampen my face. Even before I faked my death and you suffered because of that, I have known your pain. In too many ways I've held your anger and hatred for you, while you've carried the grief for both of us. It's time for you to let me go.

—Jack

I raised my teary eyes from the letter and then slumped down on the floor, a sob escaping from me. "But I have nothing by myself," I whispered. The ache in my side worsened.

Slowly folding the letter and slipping it back in the envelope, I brushed away my tears. Another strong spasm made me grimace, but I felt afraid to look at the medieval mark. Why had Jack left so many things unexplained?

At the sound of approaching footsteps, I stood and clutched my side. Might Jack be coming to me after all?

I faced the door as it banged open, and squinted at the outline of a man walking across the threshold. Gray light from the windows illuminated him enough for me to recognize him and see the gun pointed in my face. It was Paul Gerard.

thirty-six

THE ENEMY

In the dim shadows, Gerard's handsome features and olive complexion took on a sinister look. He smiled. "Good to see you again." His calm tone of voice made it sound more like a pick-up line than a threat.

"How's your shoulder?" I asked.

"Healing. How's your throat?"

"All better."

"You know, I have to admit I admire your bag of tricks. I think you're the smartest bitch I've ever been up against. Not the prettiest, but the smartest."

"Well, if I have to choose . . ."

He grabbed me by the hair, shoving the gun beneath my jaw and cutting my comment off midsentence. The psychotic glint in his eyes reminded me of Conner, and I knew I couldn't talk myself out of this trouble.

"Let go." My voice was strangely calm.

He smiled with that phony confidence I'd seen at the gallery. "Sure. First tell me where it is."

"Afraid I can't do that."

"Where's your gratitude, Jocelyn? You owe me. If I hadn't shot that kid, he would've stabbed you."

His cocky confession made me angry. Why was he taking credit for killing Georgie in the same way a Boy Scout would talk about doing a good deed?

"So where is it?"

I spoke slowly, like he was stupid. "I. Don't. Know."

His face darkened with rage, and he started spewing vile names at me, telling in graphic detail what he was going to do to me. The pitch of his voice rose as his fingers twisted my hair and jerked my head back until my neck was throbbing with pain. I understood why Jack had been so frightened of him. Afraid to look at his Conner eyes, my own slid away to the walls with their peeling wallpaper and chipped plaster. They had begun to pulsate, and beneath Gerard's shrill threats I heard the low thrum of the slow-beating heart that had haunted my Seale House nightmares.

Shoving the gun harder against my throat, he threatened in the foulest language to blow my head off. I tried to keep my voice even. "Then you'll never find the password list, will you?"

He threw me to the ground and kicked me. I curled up to try and protect myself. The pain in my side was intense now, and I worried that his blow had ruptured my appendix. In a fearful haze, I wondered if the ink oozing up through my skin was merely an omen of some infection underneath. He stomped down on my wrist and I stared at his shiny shoe, thinking that Noah would never wear something so dorky.

"I don't need to kill you." He put his weight on my wrist until I was gasping in pain. "I'll just shoot you in the hand, for starters. How about that?"

Looking up at him, and how he towered over me, I also saw the wall behind him begin to warp and writhe. "Don't," I pleaded.

"Too late." He squatted down and put the gun against my palm.

Squeezing my eyes shut, I braced my body against the blast that would bring more pain and disfigurement than I could imagine. But then a hostile curse escaped Gerard, and he staggered back, freeing my wrist. My eyes flew open as his gun thudded to the floor. He swore and shook his hand. I grabbed the gun but released it immediately—it was hot!

He stumbled back against the wall, which was swelling and undulating. With a shout of alarm, he tried to step away but couldn't. The wall held him like a fly on a web, and when he struggled to pull free it surged around him like *The Blob*. He panicked as it began to suck him in. The wall slurped at him like it was starving and he was the morsel it had been waiting for.

Gerard started screaming and I did too. Jumping to my

feet, I lurched away from him and through the door. His cries of terror followed me down the hallway, where the walls shuddered with waves and spasms. The water stains twisted in fantastic and eerie designs. Horrified, I bolted into the room where I'd once stayed with the other girls. There was only a bench and beat-up dresser in here now. Tattered curtains framed two windows, and a spotted mirror hung lopsided between them.

Dark stains began to emerge from the walls in the same way the X on my abdomen had done. My heart was beating so fast that it seemed ready to tear itself in half, and yet I couldn't pull my gaze away. Glass from the panes of a window suddenly exploded, raining all around me as I screamed and crouched down, covering my head.

"Stop it!" I sobbed. I plugged my ears against the low, pulsing heartbeat interwoven with Gerard's distant cries.

Those next few minutes became incoherent for me until the walls finally stopped their sickening pulsations. When I looked up the room was the way it had been, except for glass shards covering the floor. And Noah was there. He knelt beside me and said something, maybe asking if I was okay. Just like that autumn afternoon years ago, when Conner had nearly killed me, I couldn't make out his words because of the buzzing in my ears.

Two other men hurried into the room, one of them Zachary Saulto. I closed my eyes, gasping at the renewed pain in my side, clutching at it with hands that became claws.

"What's wrong with her, Sam?" Noah asked from what sounded like a great distance.

Beyond the ringing in my ears I heard the man say, "Show her the picture."

Noah held up the crumpled drawing of the medieval cross with Jack's writing underneath. "I found this on the stairs, Jocey. Is it from Jack?"

I nodded, my voice catching as I said, "But he's not here."

The man knelt down in front of me. He was in his forties and had long features and washed-out gray eyes. He wore a red tie with a dark business suit, and when he looked at me I had a strange feeling of familiarity.

"Jocelyn, I'm Sam Marvin, Jack's boss. I want to help you. Do you know what he meant by this paper? Is it important?"

I ignored him and turned to Noah. "I know why you stayed with me. You're still working for ISI. How could you betray me? I thought we were in this together, for Jack."

"We are."

I shook my head. "How much did they offer to pay you for going through all this with me?"

"Not enough."

As I looked away he caught my chin and turned it back to force eye contact. "There's not enough money in the world to make me go through all this crazy stuff. I only agreed to it because I care about you."

I just stared at him, wanting to ignore the intensity in

his eyes but finding it hard. He lowered his voice so only I could hear. "I was just trying to keep you safe, Jocey."

"You should have told me."

"If I did, you would've left."

There was another wave of pain in my side, and I remembered Paul Gerard's hard kick. Turning my head, I looked through the open door and out into the hallway. Had Seale House killed my attacker? "Where's Gerard?" I asked.

"Gone. We saw him run out of the house and get in his car. He was holding his arm like it was broken, and he looked scared—his eyes all wild. He peeled out fast. Did you fight him, Jocey, and break his arm somehow?"

I shook my head. I wanted to tell him the truth but was afraid to explain what the house had done.

"Jocelyn," Sam Marvin said with a sincere gaze. "It's very important that we talk to Jack."

An unexpected surge of anger filled me. "He doesn't trust you anymore!"

Another window in the room exploded and we all ducked for cover. There was a sting in my arm. When I looked down, I saw Zachary Saulto push in the syringe of a small hypodermic. I jerked away as Noah lunged at him, his fist smashing into Saulto's face. Sam Marvin began shouting and pried Noah off the guy, who now had a bleeding lip.

I grimaced in pain, hunched over, and grabbed my side. Noah hurried back to me. "What's wrong, Jocey?"

"It hurts." I rocked back and forth.

"Did Gerard do this to you?"

I shook my head, another spasm worse than the first now washing through me. Sam Marvin crouched down again. "Listen to me. Jack hid something for us, and you're the only one who can get it. Tell us what you need—"

Noah said, "She needs a hospital. I'm calling an ambulance."

"No!" I protested. "No hospital."

I couldn't go on in such agony. Untying the drawstring on my pants, I peeled down the fabric just low enough for them to see the medieval cross atop the place where my appendix might be. "*X* marks the spot," I whispered in a ghastly voice that didn't sound like me at all.

They stared at it until Zachary Saulto said, "It's hidden there . . . I can't believe it."

Sam Marvin nodded. "Where else would be safer? Can we get it out?"

"Yes. There's a scalpel in the first-aid kit in the car." Saulto hurried through the door.

Outraged, Noah turned on Marvin. "You're crazy! We're not cutting her open!"

"It'll only be a surface incision."

"Get her to a hospital if you want, but you're not doing it here!"

Marvin scowled and shook his head. "You really don't know what we're dealing with, Noah. Jack put our data beneath that mark, and now he wants it taken out."

"Jack? Are you nuts?"

"Trust me, he did."

"I don't believe he'd do that to her."

I reached for Noah's arm as another spasm shook me and I gasped. "Let them get it out. It's all right."

He studied me for several seconds, our eyes locking. "Okay," he said, sitting beside me.

Saulto entered with a first-aid kit and a laptop. He came toward me.

"Wait! Not him." Saulto scowled at me, his sore lip making him look pouty. "I don't want that guy touching me. Noah, you do it."

He looked grim. "Are you sure, Jocey? I mean, really sure?"

I nodded and Saulto shoved the kit into Noah's hands. He opened it, unsheathed a scalpel, and grabbed some gauze. I squeezed my eyes shut and held my breath. Truthfully, I hardly felt the incision because of the biting spasms. When whatever Jack had hidden inside me slipped out, the pain stopped. Panting as if from a terrible ordeal, my body coated with sweat, I opened my eyes. Noah dabbed the incision in the middle of the tattoo.

He held up a tiny sealed packet taken from beneath my skin. Marvin used his handkerchief to take it from Noah, wiped off the blood, and opened it. He removed an IC chip. Inserting it into a flash memory stick, he handed it to Saulto, who walked over to his laptop, which was sitting on the old dresser. He plugged the flash drive into the computer's USB port, fingered the touch pad, and studied the screen. "Okay, we've got it!"

A wave of dizziness washed through me. I started sinking down into a slow-moving haze—the injection Saulto had put in my arm was affecting me. I was on the edge of slipping into unconsciousness when Marvin crouched down and looked into my face. He smiled with relief.

"Terrific job, Jack. We owe you a lot."

thirty-seven
MEMORIES

The road twisted away from us like a white-gray ribbon, the moon a lopsided orb. It had been a year since we left Seale House and Watertown. We were with our mother. During that time Jack and I had begun to rebuild a life in Vermont, but now it was all left behind in a moment of panic. We didn't even go back to our small apartment to get the few possessions we owned.

The road seemed to disappear into the hills as we rattled along at breakneck speed. Melody muttered to herself in partial sentences while she drove, blurting out bits and pieces of regret, anger, and heartache. Sometimes she laughed with vengeful derision, other times she wept for Calvert, her first love—the only man she ever really loved.

My brother and I, who at fourteen had already seen far too much of the world, sat close to each other. Jack was slumped against the passenger door, his head resting on the window. His breathing was shallow and his forehead red. There was a bloody, swollen spot on his brow.

As the old pickup shuddered, I desperately wished he would wake up. Peering through the cracked windshield, recently broken by the impact from Jack's head, I stared at the red rust that corroded the hood and seemed to be inching closer. Sitting between sleeping Jack and ranting Melody, a chill went up my spine. It was now clear that the red on the hood wasn't rust alone, but also blood. The dented hood was stained from the violent impact that had killed Melody's beloved Calvert and the woman he was with.

I trembled at the memory of what had happened only an hour before. Jack and I were waiting for our mother in the parking lot of the restaurant where she worked. When she came out, she was shaking and sobbing. As she started the truck, Jack tried to talk to her, to find out what was wrong. He was still trying to calm her when the man she identified as Calvert and a woman with long dark hair exited the place. They strolled along with their arms around each other.

Melody revved the engine, released the brake, and stepped on the accelerator. They looked up and screamed. She screamed, too, ramming the pickup into them and smashing their bodies against the brick wall of the restaurant. I braced myself for the impact, but Jack's focus was on trying to stop our mother. His head smashed into the windshield and cracked the glass.

During the next hour, Melody drove our pickup in a one-car chase scene through the night, safely out of Vermont and across the state line to New York. My pleas for her to turn the truck around and get Jack to the hospital back in Bennington were useless. She heard nothing but her own twisted thoughts. She talked about how Calvert never should have abandoned her at a truck stop all those years ago, making the rest of her life a wreck. Both their lives would have been wonderful and perfect if he'd stayed with her. It was all his fault that she was forced to do what she did. After hearing so many retellings of the story of Calvert's desertion, I couldn't believe she had actually found him again and taken his life in revenge.

In the distance we finally saw lights against the velvety black landscape, a necklace of shimmering jewels. I took Jack's limp hand in mine and told him to hang on. We would get him to a hospital soon.

We sped our way into town, reached a small hospital, and found the emergency entrance. Melody leaped out of the pickup and screamed for help. Anxious attendants came and felt for Jack's pulse. They transferred his unconscious body onto a gurney and hurried inside. I followed them into the hospital, staring at the closed doors they took him through, tensing every time a technician raced past.

After a while a doctor came up to me. He had kind eyes and his nametag said Dr. Brent Haberton. Motioning to a nurse, he asked her to take me to the waiting room. I followed the woman there but didn't go in, because Melody was there, sitting in a chair and crying. I couldn't tolerate being near my mother. Instead, I walked down a hallway and found a small, deserted chapel with darkened windows. I sat there for a long time, rocking back and forth, begging for Jack's life. The door opened, and I turned to see Melody come inside.

"Jack is dead," she said, weeping.

I stared at her. I didn't believe it. "No," I whispered in a low, dreadful croak.

"First Calvert and now Jack," she sobbed. "I've lost the only two people I ever really loved."

How could she speak those two names in the same breath?

331

I stared at her with cold disgust. She grabbed my arm and said, "The police are here. I saw them at the desk. We've got to get out before they try and talk to us!"

I jerked free and slapped her so hard across the face that my palm hurt. She staggered back, surprised out of her tears. At fourteen I was taller than her, though until now she was never afraid of me. But the look on my face must have been terrible because she edged away.

"You killed Jack," I hissed, spitting words as if they were stones breaking my teeth. "He's dead because of you! I'm going to tell the police what you did to him. And if you stay here or ever try to see me again, I'll tell them what you did to Calvert and that lady."

Melody gaped at me. She forgot her tears for Jack, even forgot her tears for the stupid boyfriend who had dumped her. She turned and rushed away, leaving me alone in the gloomy chapel. I sank down on the bench. There was nothing left in me, only a tattered soul with no seed of hope and no reason to live. I longed to be with Jack, and I loathed myself for grabbing the dashboard and saving my life. We had always been two parts of a whole. I didn't know how I could survive without him.

The door to the chapel opened. I turned around, ready to lunge at Melody if she was back. Instead, an old woman walked up to me. She had papery skin and a halo of wispy hair. A cross rested atop her purple blouse next to a name tag that said VOLUNTEER, and she looked at me with sorrowful green eyes that seemed to understand. She asked if she could sit beside me, but I didn't answer. She sat down anyway. Then she told me about losing her son to cancer here in this hospital. She said many things in a gentle voice. I hardly heard them.

After a while she stopped talking and we sat together in silence.

As always, my thoughts cried out to Jack. I begged him to tell me that he was still alive, that this cruelest of all hoaxes wasn't real.

"You know," the lady said at last, "one thing I've learned is that you'll always have him with you."

I turned to look at her and she reached out with her slender old-woman fingers, touching my temple. "You'll always have him here," she said, and then moved her fingers to my heart. "And here."

After a while she left me alone with my grief, and I sat unmoving inside the gloomy chapel. Her last few words kept repeating themselves in my mind. As I raised my eyes to the dark window, I saw Jack's dim reflection. Standing, I turned around, hardly able to believe he was there after all. There wasn't a mark on his forehead, no misery in his eyes, and he smiled at me.

"Don't cry, Jocey," I heard him say inside my head. His lips didn't move and his smile never wavered. "She's right, you know. I'll always be with you, in your mind and in your heart."

✦ ✦ ✦

I drifted up from the depths of slowly returning consciousness. I heard Noah's voice. His mellow tone had always drawn me in, and I let my mind travel in that direction.

"I just don't see how this can be true. I talked to Jack all the time."

"But only on the computer, right?" Sam Marvin said. "You never got together in person, did you?"

"No." His tone held an awkward uncertainty.

"But you weren't living that far away from each other. Didn't you want to see him?"

"Sure. We even made plans. At first I asked to visit him and Jocelyn, and meet their foster family. Jack said she didn't want to. So he and I planned for him to come here, but then stuff just kept happening."

"Like what, exactly?"

"Car trouble. An unexpected family trip . . . and then he got strep throat." Noah's voice turned sour. "But Jack e-mailed me photos of himself."

"Probably age-enhanced. She was very skilled with digital photo editing. And Jack really wanted to have your friendship. He did whatever it took to keep your online communication going."

"You're not making any sense! Are you talking about Jocelyn or Jack?"

"Both, because they're the same person."

"That's absurd!"

"Let me explain. Jack died in a car accident the year after he and Jocelyn left Watertown. They were both just fourteen. Unable to deal with that terrible loss, Jocelyn erased the memory of his death and then internalized his personality within herself. It's similar to multiple personality disorder. Being twins, and as close as she and Jack were, it was easy for her to embrace his identity. That way she could keep him alive.

"So you see, when Jack worked for us, it might have been in Jocelyn's body, but she has no memory of the things he was doing. It's almost like she gave some of her brain to him, which she doesn't know anything about. Likewise, when Jocelyn was involved with her own activities, Jack's personality wasn't present. His part of the mind was always aware of what she was doing. In a lot of ways it's like two separate beings sharing one body. He was the programmer, she was the graphic artist. Though she's the one who created them, of course. It's hard to grasp what a truly brilliant mind she has."

"How did you find this out?"

Sam Marvin hesitated. "The private investigating firm I use for background checks is very thorough. They were able to lay hands on a copy of her therapy file."

"You had no right to do that."

"Hang on—Jack knew."

"What?"

"He was starting to distrust his therapist and wanted to know what Dr. Candlar was writing in his file. In fact, he okayed our getting it. Especially since I assured him he had an important future with our company."

"But what about Jocelyn, Sam? Look at what's happening to her."

They were silent for several seconds, and I drifted back down into darkness, terrified to hear more.

✦ ✦ ✦

I stood outside a tattoo shop, trying to summon the courage to go through the door. When I finally stepped inside, Beth was there. She was tattooed and pierced in ways fantastic and bizarre, her red hair buzzed as short as a man's. At first, as I pretended to look at the display case, she just stared. She couldn't believe it was me.

Eventually I bought one of the knives, which softened her up.

I chose a design from her books, asking her to tattoo an X over the small recent scar on my lower abdomen. Beth was delighted to use her needles on me. It created a bond that hadn't existed when we were kids. I lay in the reclining chair while she talked in a soothing way that was a total contrast to her tough appearance. We chatted away and I never felt a thing, which impressed her all the more. Before I left the shop, I asked her to hold on to the original X pattern, promising to come back for it.

thirty-eight
FREAK

"You can't blame us," Sam Marvin was saying the next time I woke up. "Do you have any idea what would've happened if Paul Gerard sold that list of passwords to the buyer who wanted them? Once he stole it from us, he also destroyed our other copies. We had no way to protect our clients."

"Spy on them, don't you mean?" Noah sounded irritated. "Listen, I don't care about your problems. What bothers me is that you were willing to put her in danger."

"It didn't seem that big a deal. We assumed Jack was handling his run-in with Gerard okay. The next thing we knew, he sent us a phony death report and disappeared. Jocelyn had no idea about any of it, either. She truly believed Jack had died. We didn't want to lose the data she stole back from Gerard but couldn't figure out where she'd hidden it. Then she drove up here to Watertown earlier this week. We were sure she was going to the place where she'd stashed it. Instead, she started following you."

"Following me? Trying to find Jack, because to her he's real?"

"Right."

I lay still, listening to the conversation. Inside me was a tight knot of grief for Jack. The pain was as fresh as the day it happened, all the horror of what Melody had done to him weighing heavily on me. And yet there was a difference between accepting this loss now and accepting it back then. I had become stronger—more able to withstand the heartbreak that would have destroyed me when I was fourteen. Something in me—maybe spurred on by the danger from ISI—must have known that this was the time to let go.

For weeks now, I realized, Jack had been tearing himself away from me. I thought about school. The counselor had called me into her office because my English teacher, Ms. Chen, had noticed that all my poems were about death, loss, and grief. She showed them to the counselor.

"My brother died, so why shouldn't I be sad?" was all I would say. After that I refused to talk about it, explaining I had my own therapist outside of school.

Everyone, including my foster parents and friends, seemed concerned because of how depressed I acted. But they were all clueless about what was really happening inside me. In some twisted mental way, I had come to believe that Jack's death had taken place mere weeks ago—not years in the past.

Slowly opening my eyes, I blinked to clear my vision. I sat up and my head throbbed.

Noah came and knelt on the floor beside me, trying to hide his unease. "How are you feeling?"

Sam Marvin said, "Zach, get her a drink of water, will you?"

Zachary Saulto was focused on his laptop. He glanced at me with a closed expression before heading down the hall. I heard him turn on the faucet in the bathroom.

"Are you okay, Jocey?" Noah asked.

"Apparently not." I felt humiliated by the truth of what I really was. *Oh, Jack!* I sobbed inside. The loss of my brother was a pain I physically felt.

Saulto came back. He squatted down and held out a glass of water. "Here you go, Jaclyn."

"Jocelyn," I corrected.

"Jocelyn . . . Jaclyn . . . Jack. It's all the same thing, isn't it?"

The glass shattered in his hand. Startled, he dropped it and stood, cursing and holding a cut finger.

"That's enough, Zach," Sam Marvin said. He turned to me. "Please stay calm, Jocelyn. I know this is all very confusing. If you could just let me talk to Jack for a minute, I really want to ask what's going on with him."

There was a loud crack and the mirror exploded, raining glass onto the floor with a tinkling sound.

He looked at me with a firm expression. "You've got to stop."

After a silence that lasted several seconds, Noah said, "What's going on?"

"Don't you know? You're the one who used to live with her. She has telekinetic abilities."

I shook my head. "That's a lie."

"It's time you accept the truth, Jocelyn. Who do you think kept stopping the fires at Seale House when you were kids? Or blew up those lightbulbs in the lamps the night you left? And what do you think saved you from Gerard this morning?"

Could he be right? The rational part of my mind pushed the thought away.

Noah glared at Sam Marvin. "Wait a minute! Even if that's true, how could you possibly know all that stuff?"

Sam didn't answer.

"Was that in her therapy file, too?"

"Only some of it. You forget that I've had a number of conversations with the Jack side of her that she doesn't even remember. He told me how her telekinesis didn't develop until she was at Seale House, and it's always been unpredictable. Of course, at first I didn't believe it and asked for proof." Sam gave Noah a wry smile. "That was a mistake."

"Why?"

"Her therapy file was open on my desk. It burst into flames and was destroyed before I could douse it with my cup of coffee."

Sam turned to me. Despite his casual manner, I could see he was weighing my reaction. "Once you re-created

Jack's personality inside you, he learned to funnel off your psychic energy. He also used it to block your awareness of him. That's why you haven't had any memories of it, or even seen it happen again until he recently decided to go into hiding."

I shook my head. "But what about Seale House?" Rolling up my sleeve, I showed him the bite mark on my arm. "Look at this! It happened when I was in the cellar."

"Probably just a form of stigmata. Fear and guilt will sometimes cause a person to self-mutilate. With your mental abilities it could easily happen. Accept the truth, Jocelyn. There are no ghosts in this house, only the ones you brought with you." His voice softened. "Just look inside yourself and you'll know what I'm talking about."

I couldn't deny the logic of his reasoning, and once I accepted his account, everything else fell into place. Jack's cell phone call, the scary ride in the Peace Tower elevator, and even the emerging tattoo previously hidden from my eyes, all had an explanation: *they were entirely in my head.* And what was in my head could change the real world too.

"Do you know what a rare and special talent you have? The things you and Jack can do are hugely impressive. Look at how you dealt with Gerard. Until you took him on, we'd lost hope of ever getting the file back. With your abilities, you could be unstoppable. And like I told your brother the last time we spoke, no more meager internship wages. Instead, we're willing to pay you a good deal of money to come work for us full time after you graduate."

"Doing what, exactly? Industrial espionage?"

Noah stood, rigid with anger. "Sure. I get it now, Sam. You're using her, aren't you? That's what this whole thing is about."

Sam folded his arms. He studied Noah with annoyance and shook his head.

I looked at the lean man in his expensive suit and said, "Of course it is. They've never been interested in Jack as a programmer . . . or me as a person. What they want is to use my abilities. If they think it's okay to write back doors into their clients' security programs, they won't mind having me steal important documents and programs, either."

Sam's face reddened. "It's not like that! Don't you see? We're on your side, Jocelyn, and we can make you rich. You'll never have to be a poor foster kid again. In fact, we'll give you a huge bonus just to sign with us."

Clenching my fists, I looked away from him and at Zachary Saulto, who stood by the dresser. His bloody finger was wrapped in a handkerchief as he obsessively reviewed the data on his laptop.

I spoke to Sam Marvin, even though my eyes stayed on the computer. "Jack didn't want the deal you were offering. He didn't want to give you the passwords to those back doors either, because what you're doing is wrong."

Glaring at the flash drive sticking out of Saulto's laptop port, I watched a thin ribbon of smoke start to rise from it. Saulto didn't notice until his screen went blank. Letting out a dismayed cry, he reached for the flash drive and then jerked his hand back, swearing and shaking his singed fingers. Sam Marvin yelled and rushed over to the laptop.

I jumped up and ran out of the room and down the hall, ignoring their panicked shouts, stopping in Hazel's room only long enough to get my backpack. My eyes avoided the wall that had grabbed Paul Gerard.

Racing down the stairs and across the entryway, I pushed through the front doors and out into the hazy morning. I fled down the steps, determined to never again return to Seale House.

There was the sound of someone running behind me, and Noah called my name. Slowing just enough for him to catch up with me, I kept walking.

"I'm sorry," he said, matching my stride. "I didn't mean to hurt you, Jocey. I was only trying to watch out for you."

I pulled in a jagged breath. "None of that matters now." Seeing the sadness in his face, I whispered, "I'm sorry too."

It was then that another hidden memory surfaced. I saw myself sitting at the computer in the middle of the night, chatting with Noah online and loving it. "I never meant to lie."

He reached out and caught my hand, halting my stride. "Stop for a minute, will you?"

I stood beside him on the sidewalk, watching the subtle movement of the fog. "I wouldn't blame you for hating me."

"I don't hate you. Mostly I just feel rotten about Jack dying all those years ago and the hell you've lived through."

The pain of losing my brother still hammered at me, but I pushed it down. Tears stung my eyes and I blinked, forcing them back. "All the times we wrote to each other, and you believed I was Jack . . ."

"It gave me the only real friendship I've ever had. Now that I know it was you, so much more of what we've had together these past few days makes sense."

Flooded with humiliation at the elaborate delusions I'd created and the insane quest I'd led us on, I could hardly look at him. "Until a few minutes ago, I never even remembered doing any of it. Guess I really am . . ."

Noah looked at me with a puzzled expression.

"A freak."

He was unable to hide how overwhelmed he felt. "Is that so bad?"

I started crying and he pulled me into his arms. "It'll be okay, Jocey."

"How can it? I'm crazy, aren't I?"

His mouth grazed my temple and he sighed. "It looks that way."

I loved him all the more because he didn't lie to me.

Pulling back, I brushed the dampness from my face and whispered, "Take care of yourself, Noah."

His hands slid down my arms and then he released me. I turned and ran into the fog, not looking back.

thirty-nine
SUNSET

After I drove away from Watertown in my fire-damaged car, I didn't go home to the Habertons. Even though it meant I wouldn't graduate from high school, there was simply no way I could go back to the house where the make-believe Jack and I had lived.

I sent my foster parents a letter thanking them and saying how grateful I was for their kindness. I also apologized for going away so unexpectedly and said I'd never forget them.

During the weeks that followed I lived on my own, moving around and surviving on the cash I had emptied from my bank account. I crossed the border into Canada. At first I went to Toronto, but the city was too large and noisy, and I had a couple of jumpy moments when I felt afraid Paul Gerard was following me. Even though I no longer had the chip and knew his experience at Seale House had probably scared him off, I couldn't forget his psycho eyes. I told myself it was just nerves, but since there was no way to be sure he wasn't still looking for me, I kept moving.

Deciding to travel east, I next visited New Brunswick and Nova Scotia, two places in Canada I'd always wanted to see. During my days there I kept to myself and took the time I needed to really grieve for my brother's death— something I'd never done. I also researched multiple personalities. Several of the online articles I read said that when personalities merge back together it's a good thing and shows progress for the patient. Psychologists called it integration. It didn't *feel* good, though. Despite having gained some of Jack's memories, it still felt like there was a big hole inside me. And whenever I showered or changed my clothes, there was the tattooed *X*, a permanent reminder of the way my brother had marked my life.

As for Sam Marvin's claim that I had telekinetic abilities, I still wondered seriously if it wasn't all tied to Seale House. Now that I was away from that malevolent place, it seemed my powers were gone.

Each day I busied myself with reading, traveling, and just pretending to be an ordinary tourist. At night it was a lot harder, being so alone. Thoughts of Noah often filled my mind, and I could still envision him standing on the foggy sidewalk in Watertown as I left. Although I longed to see him again, I knew there was no going back. For one thing, I was the catalyst that had left his life in ruins;

because of me his home and all his possessions had been destroyed. Even worse, he'd lost his best friend. I didn't see how I could ever face him again.

May faded to June and I traveled to Prince Edward Island, the place I'd most wanted to visit as a girl reading all those L. M. Montgomery books. The island had been my number one pick when Jack, Noah, and I had chosen our top places to live, and once I got there I wasn't disappointed. It was even more beautiful than I'd imagined.

In the small city of Charlottetown, I found a job at a used bookstore and rented a room at a local boarding house. I soon settled into a peaceful routine of working, rereading all the Montgomery books that had made the island famous, and taking long walks. I looked forward to turning eighteen and finally being a legal adult, free from the fear of being put in another foster care program.

The first of July, in the early morning hours of my eighteenth birthday, I had a dream about Jack. We were kids again, celebrating our birthdays by playing a wacky game of kickball at a nearby park. He was pretending to run in slow motion and I was laughing at how goofy he looked. After I awoke, the happiness of that memory lingered, slowly replaced by a sense of calm. It was as if the heavy stone that had been crushing my heart for such a long time was starting to lift.

That evening I sat on a pier by the bay and watched the Canada Day fireworks light up the sky. I smiled to myself and remembered the time we were eight in Toronto. Jack told me it didn't matter if there weren't any birthday presents. We got fireworks instead, and that was better.

The next morning my boss at the bookstore asked me to pick up a package for her from the post office. While I was there I decided to check and see if there was any mail for me at general delivery. An older gentleman handed me the package, and then also gave me a letter.

"You need to check for your mail more often, young lady," he said with a friendly smile. "That letter has been sitting here a while, and after two weeks items get returned to the sender."

He tapped the blank spot on the envelope—no return address. "Except ones like this get thrown out."

I mumbled a polite reply, took the mail, and turned away. Leaving the post office, I hurried over to a shaded bench and sat down, putting the package on my lap. My fingers fumbled with the envelope. I tore it open and looked inside, but there wasn't a letter. Instead, pieces of a puzzle fell into my palm. It was a photo that had been cut up.

My first thought was of Jack and the Jason December clues, though I quickly told myself not to be stupid. I started putting the pieces together and soon saw it was a photo of Noah. He was holding a full-size sheet of paper with a cell phone number written across it. I stared at his solemn face and was taken aback by how his eyes seemed to study me.

For several minutes I just sat there, touching the cut-up pieces and trying to make them fit closer together. Then I dug out the new cell phone I'd recently purchased and punched in Noah's number. He answered on the third ring. Hearing the low sound of his voice after all this time made my heart race even faster. I just sat there, unable to say a word.

He waited, neither of us speaking. Finally he asked, "Jocey, is that you?"

I closed my eyes.

"Don't hang up," Noah said.

I didn't.

"Will you please talk to me?"

I took a deep breath and slowly exhaled. "Hi, Noah."

It was his turn to be hesitant. I could hear his uncertainty, even though he tried to hide it. "So yesterday you turned eighteen. Happy birthday."

"Thanks."

More awkwardness.

"Where have you been, Jocey?"

"Lots of places."

I picked up the two segments of the puzzle that composed his face, wondering why he'd cut himself in half that way.

"Did you get the e-mails I sent you?" he asked.

"E-mails?"

"Yes. I wrote to you at Jack's account, hoping you'd check it. I left messages on the forums too. There's some news I figured you'd like to know."

"I'm not doing much Internet stuff right now. Just kind of taking a break for a while."

"Sure."

"What's the news?"

"A lot's happened since you've been gone. For one thing, ISI went under. Last month they filed bankruptcy. And Paul Gerard is on his way to prison. I told Detective Iverson everything, and the police found his gun where he dropped it in Hazel's room. His prints were all over it. They made a match to the bullet that killed Georgie."

"Good. Georgie didn't deserve to die like that." I paused, listening to the silence on the other end. "Thanks for telling me."

"I've been trying to find you for two months. If you didn't read my e-mails, then I'm guessing you must've gotten the photo I mailed to Prince Edward Island. It was the other way I tried to reach you."

✦ ✦ ✦

"Someday I'm going to California," Noah said. "I'll live on the beach and never shovel snow again. What about you, Jack?"

"China," my brother answered without hesitation, holding up his newly purchased chopsticks. "I want to see the Great Wall and learn to speak Chinese."

Both boys looked at me and I closed the most recent L. M. Montgomery book I'd been reading. I spread my hands across the cover and said, "Prince Edward Island."

Noah laughed and shook his head. "You're going someplace because of a book?"

Despite his teasing words, I could tell he understood.

✦ ✦ ✦

"Can I come see you?" Noah asked. "I could be there by this evening."

I scooped the puzzle pieces into my hand and made a fist. It was hard to believe he actually wanted to see me again. "Okay. Meet me by the Harbor Lighthouse at sunset. I'll be waiting on the trail."

I disconnected before either of us could say anything else.

✦   ✦   ✦

It was just before sunset when I reached the path leading down to the square-shaped lighthouse at the edge of the bay. The sun spread its golden tresses across the water, and the indigo sky was streaked with luminous clouds.

Rounding a bend in the path I came to a halt, my eyes on the distant silhouette of a guy backed by the light reflecting off the bay. He pushed away from the tree he was leaning against and I immediately recognized him by the way he moved. It was Noah.

He came closer. The setting sun embossed one side of his face and head with bronze but left the other half in shadow. We met midway on the trail, and I looked into those warm brown eyes I'd missed so much. Noah started to reach for me but stopped himself. Instead, he slid the fingers of one hand into the pocket of his jeans.

"Have you been waiting long?"

"A while, yes."

I wanted to apologize, but instead I asked, "How have you been, Noah?"

There was more awkward politeness as I studied every cherished feature of his face.

"I've moved into another place. It's a small apartment."

"That doesn't answer my question."

He shrugged. "You're right. The truth is I've been miserable without you. Will you come back to Watertown with me?"

I looked away, gazing at the harbor that shimmered like silk in the growing twilight. He stepped closer and I felt his hands on my waist, his breath against my temple. "If you don't want to be in New York, I understand. We can go anywhere you want, even California. Or we can stay here for a while. The thing is, I can be a programmer from anyplace."

A breeze wafted across the harbor, ruffling the water. "What do you say?"

I couldn't answer.

He reached up, gently brushing back the strands of hair that had blown across my cheek. His voice was tender when he spoke. "What's wrong, Jocey?"

"Why do you want to be with me, Noah? I'm crazy."

"Aren't we all?"

"I'm dangerous."

"Not to me."

"I'm a nutcase."

Noah pulled me to him. He kissed me long and slowly and so tenderly that all my anxious fears began to drift away. Then he moved back just enough to ask, "Do you love me?"

"You know I do."

"That's all I need to hear."

He kissed me again, and afterward his arms encircled me and held me close. My hand was on his chest, the steady beat of his heart beneath my fingers, and I breathed in the scent of him. We stood that way for a long time until I grew relaxed within his embrace. Noah finally let go and stepped back. He looked at me with those amazing eyes of his.

"You'll be with me, Jocey, won't you?"

I nodded.

"Let's go, then."

Noah held out his hand and I took it, letting his fingers slide between mine. He led me away from the lighthouse and back along the path, guiding me home.

Somewhere, I knew Jack was smiling.

Acknowledgments

From raw manuscript to finished novel, there are many people who influenced this book and deserve my deepest thanks.

Rachel: my daughter, friend, and the best writing confidant I could ever have brainstorming sessions with. Deserét and Pamela: how fortunate am I to have two friends with super proofreading skills, insight, and honesty? Jessica Regel, the perfect agent for this work because you not only believed it had potential but—equally important—recognized the changes it needed. And, of course, Margaret Miller, my savvy editor, for being outside the box enough to accept this book and then help reshape it throughout this entire exciting process. Also thank you to Caroline Abbey, Danielle Delaney, Regina Roff, Alexei Esikoff, and everyone else at Bloomsbury.

Two other people hugely influenced my life, and therefore my writing. My sister Linda: you rode the freakish roller coaster of childhood with me but didn't let go of my hand. And, most of all, to Kelly: the man who—when I finally stepped off that ride—was standing there waiting for me. I'm here because of you.